A life-altering experience drives Naya Rollins to the mountains of Vermont. Two months after moving into her new home, she discovers its former inhabitants linger on.

Michael Bradbury had not seen his childhood friend, Naya, for two years. Bumping into her brother Luke and getting invited to visit her in her new home gives him the chance to come clean about his feelings for her. What he isn't prepared for is coming up close and personal with the paranormal.

Charcuterie Board With a Side of Ghosts
Copyright © 2024 Jo Tannah
ISBN: 978-1-4874-4209-5
Cover art by Martine Jardin

Published by eXtasy Books Inc

Look for us online at:
www.eXtasybooks.com

Charcuterie Board With a Side of Ghosts

By

Jo Tannah

DEDICATION

This story would never have seen the light of day if it were not for three beautiful people. KP, who thought naughty and charcuterie go hand in hand; C, who encouraged me nonstop to write about the paranormal activities, and my daughter, for teaching me the basics of preparing a charcuterie board and for suggesting I make this a paranormal horror just because. When great minds think together, beautiful stories come to life.

CHAPTER ONE

Naya Rollins floated in the black void of a dreamless sleep one moment, and the next, she opened her eyes fully alert. Something had woken her up. She wondered what was going on as she looked around her dark bedroom. Nothing moved in the dim light of the nightlight, and all was quiet. She pushed her hand under her pillow and pulled out the phone she'd shoved there. Staring blearily into the activated home screen, her eyes took a moment to focus, only to see it was four-thirty in the morning. It was no longer unusual to wake up at that particular time. Not since she'd moved into the new house.

Moving slowly and silently, she slipped her feet into the slippers by the side of her bed and stood up. The dog snores told her that Jenny, her Pocket Bully, hadn't heard her. She really didn't want to deal with her pet's early morning rowdiness. She took a moment to listen to the silence yet detected nothing unusual nor heard any sounds that would alert her or her dog of an intruder.

By the time Naya exited the toilet, she was too wide awake to attempt to go back to sleep. Jenny was sitting up in her bed, her tail wagging a mile a minute, clearly ready to start her day. Jenny's wide-eyed stare made her laugh. When she opened the bedroom door and signaled Jenny out, the dog excitedly took to her feet and exited the room.

Naya stumbled out of the bedroom with cobwebs still in her eyes, following the trail of night lights plugged in at four-foot intervals along the corridor. She stopped at the top of the

1

staircase, where she'd placed a huge Chinese camphor wood chest. A friend had found it for her, and it only took one whiff to fall in love with the scent. The aroma cleansed her lungs whenever she breathed it in. Jenny scrambled past her, and she hurried to follow the dog down to the first level of the house.

After letting Jenny out the back door, she turned and headed toward her coffee station. She stopped in her tracks mid-yawn when she stepped into the kitchen. Something didn't feel right.

Not for the first time since she'd first set eyes on the house could she swear something had moved just out of the corner of her eye. There was no explanation, no proof something moved. Just that nagging feeling that something wasn't quite right. As she looked around, nothing seemed out of place. It couldn't have been her friend, Carol Sweetman, who had surprised her by arriving two hours earlier and announcing she was staying for the weekend. But judging by the quiet, Carol was still asleep.

She flicked on the light switches one by one, the brightness momentarily blinding her before her vision cleared. Everything seemed to be in its usual place. She must have stood there for a full minute before she gave up, but the curious feeling that someone or something had been inside continued to bother her.

A sip of strong, black coffee later, she heard Jenny's pitiful whining and scratching on the door to get inside. Naya had never liked the idea of a doggy door, and the thought of having one while living alone in the mountains only made her paranoid. As the dog passed her, she looked out into the back garden. A light mist had settled over the grounds, and a strange sort of chill in the air that had nothing to do with the winter weather made her shiver. The perimeter lights lit up the surroundings. She saw nothing out there, yet she couldn't get herself to step back inside the house and close the door. A feeling swept over her, telling her to look beyond the obvious. She continued to stand there, staring and running her hands over the tops of her arms.

What's going on?

No answers came.

After one last glance into the darkness beyond where the gardens ended, Naya turned around and went back inside the house. Picking up her cup, she moved to the living room and sat in one of her comfy chairs, pulling up her feet and wrapping one arm around her knees. She stared at the unlit fireplace, thinking about how different her current lifestyle was.

It hadn't taken her long to get used to the peace and quiet in the Vermont mountains. It was a welcome change from the hustle, bustle, and toxic competition among influencers in Los Angeles. Looking down at her feet, clad in warm fluffy slippers, she wondered, not for the first time, what had driven her to move to Los Angeles at barely twenty years old. She didn't have to live there to be a successful influencer or businesswoman. However, one thing that hadn't changed over the years was her need to know what was going on in the world. It was time to listen to the news.

Bad news first thing in the morning was not something she cared to suffer through, but it had become a ritual for her. Every single channel she logged into played the same miserable broadcast as the others. She gave up and looked through the streaming service before moving on. She tuned into an online video-sharing social media platform, where she watched a Korean lady going about her daily household chores with soothing background music. The site had an abundance of relaxing videos and always showed great recipes that she enjoyed trying out. Her granny's recipes were great, but she liked to experiment. She was successful most times, but there were other times when she followed everything to the letter, and the food still ended up as inedible goo.

The show was halfway through the thirty-minute presentation when she heard Jenny make a weird sound. She looked up to search for her, expecting to see her curled up and asleep. It surprised her to find Jenny sitting on her haunches, staring out the glass doors. Naya glanced through the window and saw that other than the illumination from the perimeter lights, it was still dark outside.

Every so often, the dog would tilt her head, first to the right, then to the left.

She didn't know how long she watched Jenny's odd behavior, but she found it cute. A smile graced her lips as she turned her attention back to finish the Korean show. She checked on Jenny every so often, but the dog never moved from her vigil. She was simply too adorable.

Three years before, one of Naya's influencer friends had an American Bully who had a litter of puppies. Naya had gone to her friend's house one day to discuss the possibility of a video collaboration and left with the six-week-old puppy in her arms. Jenny had climbed onto her lap, gave her one lick on the chin, and successfully maneuvered her way into Naya's heart. The mini-documentary of how she'd met the puppies had become one of the most viewed collaborations she'd ever gotten involved with.

She glanced out the window to see dawn spread across the horizon. Smiling at Jenny's antics, Naya took a picture and immediately uploaded it to her *Instagram* account. As the file finished loading, she sipped on her coffee, only to discover it had gone ice cold. Putting her phone down on the ottoman, she stood up and made a fresh cup of coffee before settling on the sofa. Another program came up, one about homestead gardening. When that show ended, she got up and walked over to the bank of refrigerators. Opening one, she considered what she could do about breakfast. The incessant pinging of notifications in the background didn't sway her from her task.

Preparing food had become a passion, and she was hungry.

It still blew her mind how many followers had set their notifications on for her posts. Thankfully, she'd been on social media long enough and had learned to tune out the incessant noise. With her grilled cheese done and plated, she set it on the kitchen island, arranging it so she could take a picture to post on her socials. After posting it, she ate her breakfast in peace. For once, Jenny was not hanging around her legs, begging for scraps of bread. Done with breakfast, Naya stood up to pour herself her third cup of coffee, placing her empty plate in the sink along the way.

Her breath hitched when her stomach acids churned. "I really should limit my coffee intake." She grimaced as she rubbed a hand over her stomach. She took another gulp and rolled her eyes in appreciation. "I'll never give you up, baby."

She walked over to where Jenny was still sitting and patted her head. It was a quiet morning, but sometime between cooking and eating breakfast, the temperature had fallen, and she could feel the cold seep into her bones. A heaviness in the air made her think a storm might be building.

Her new home was the opposite in terms of weather. The mountains of Vermont were cold, but the air quality was gloriously fresh and unpolluted. LA, on the other hand, was totally different. She had needed a one-eighty, and the town of Amber Ville fit the bill perfectly.

Her phone dinged, signaling an emergency notification. She frowned as she read the weather report that boded ill news of a storm hitting them by seven that evening. She wasn't too concerned, though. She'd ensured that her home could endure storm damage. It had clearly done so for over two hundred years, so there was no reason it couldn't do so for another fifty or more.

The stone house, built in the late seventeen hundreds, sat on a fifty-acre plot of farmland that had included a large barn and two cottages. The house and barn had both undergone renovations, but the two cottages had proven to be beyond repair, and with the Historical Society's permission, had been demolished. Salvaged materials from those two structures had been fully utilized in various parts of the main house. With the modern improvements she'd had incorporated into the house, she was sure she'd not suffer.

The only problem she could foresee was the possibility of a power outage. If it had just been her and Jenny, a blackout wouldn't bother her, but her mother and brother were coming to visit for the week and weren't used to outages. There was also Carol. After some thought, she decided a trip downtown was necessary, if only to add toiletry supplies. Or maybe she could pick up ingredients to prepare something special. Maybe a charcuterie board. Her family would love that, especially with a good bottle of wine.

She was still mulling over her plans when the continuous pinging rose to irritating levels. Really? She'd known her postings of Jenny were popular with her *Instagram* account, but it seemed the notifications had been going on forever. She could mute it, but then how would she know if something important came up? The thought gave her pause. To mute or to unmute. Relying on emails was another option, but reading through a flooded inbox could overwhelm anyone.

Intrigued over what her followers were hyped over, she opened her account and checked on her notifications. A glance at the number of likes and comments made her blink twice. There were over two million views and likes and twenty thousand comments. Even as she watched, the numbers continued to rise. One comment made her frown, and she scanned through more comments. All of them were asking the same question.

Who took your picture?

She laughed at her followers' overactive imaginations. They tended to ship her with men she'd never even met before. But then one comment made her stop and read it again.

Naya? You never told us you had a twin sister?

"Girl, what sister are you blabbing about?"

Her curiosity piqued, she opened the image she'd posted earlier and zoomed in and out, amused by how Jenny's ears were cutely curled at their tips. She tapped on the image to get it back to normal size and was about to close the app when it finally hit her. Her breath froze, and her heart began to pound painfully against her ribcage. Blame it on how early it was or her need for more sleep, but it took her mind longer than necessary to process what her fans were going crazy about. She tapped the image with a trembling hand, zooming in and out and sliding right then left to examine it closer.

Jenny sat with her head tilted off to the left, staring out the glass doors. What her AmBull was looking at chilled her down to her marrow. No wonder Jenny hadn't made a sound or caused a commotion. No wonder her followers were all excited. Seated on the garden set, about to sip from a cup that she had no doubt held coffee, was none other than a duplicate of herself. Right down to her fluffy pink rabbit-ear slippers. The peculiarity of the image hit her a second time, and her vision blurred.

Why hadn't anybody thought to ask what she was doing out there, seemingly unaffected, surrounded by inches of snow?

Naya's finger hovered over the delete option. What if someone had hacked her account? But the timestamp was clear, as was the location, and her two-factor authentication security protocol remained inactive. Her mind raced over the possibilities and how to handle the situation. Should she delete it? Speculations would run wild, and a hidden lover would be at the top of a short list. The only way to handle it was to lie. She didn't think twice and typed out a comment, which she immediately pinned.

LOL pic taken by my CCTV. It's also damned cooold! Sorry to disappoint, but I got no lover, bitches!

Naya chewed on her lower lip as she monitored her fans' reactions. Five earth-shattering minutes later, the comments slowed down. LOLs and laughing emojis flooded the comment section. Relieved that her lie had worked, she dropped her head into her hands and took deep breaths to calm her nerves. When her heart rate slowed, she stood up and started cleaning the remains of her breakfast.

Soon after the renovations had begun, she'd begun experiencing strange, unexplained events. Odd things that she had tried to disregard until they became harder and harder to ignore. It had all started with soft thuds that gradually changed to banging noises. All that had changed two months prior when she'd completed her move and started staying in the house full-time.

Nothing unusual happened the first two nights, but beginning the third night, loud bangs would wake her from a deep sleep. Like clockwork, the noises generally started between three and three-thirty in the morning. Occasionally, the noises would start earlier, but more often, they began later. Gradually, though, the noises were accompanied by the appearance of strange shadowy creatures. Sometimes in her room, most times in the corridor outside the bedrooms. It had happened enough times that she could now identify two entities that kept coming back. One man and one woman. There were others, but they were too fleeting for her to form a concrete impression. Curiously, she'd never once felt alarmed. Surprised, yes. Curious, for sure. But scared? No. Not even nearly.

The month before, she'd asked for help from the sheriff, Amos Ferrise, to rule out squatters. He'd sent two cops to investigate right away. They searched every room and potential hiding place but found no evidence of stray animals or squatters. However, the deputies recommended she install perimeter lights and security cameras in and around the house to keep on the safe side. They even recommended a nearby company that would watch over her property and immediately notify the sheriff's office if there was an emergency. So that was that.

Naya readily agreed with the need to protect herself, so she hadn't hesitated to have the additional safety precautions put in. However, she was not ready to accept whatever was going on inside her house, especially not after seeing her doppelgänger.

After staring at the mute icon for what seemed like an eternity, she finally mustered the courage to click it. For now, muting the notifications was the best way to keep the distractions at bay. She had enough on her plate, and the last thing she needed was a constant reminder of the oddities that seemed to be multiplying by the day. It was a temporary solution, but it would give her the peace she needed to focus on the tasks at hand. Foremost on her mind was how to ask the sheriff to explain her double to her.

"He'll probably dismiss me as one of those baffling California influencers."

Jenny looked up at the sound of Naya's voice. Her tail wagged, and she let out a soft whine. Naya stood up to prepare Jenny's breakfast, but not until after a rigorous round of belly scratching.

"Your mama's not weird. Also, I'm not *from* LA. I only lived there for a while."

With a last pat on Jenny's shoulder, Naya stood and went up to her room. A long hot shower really sounded good. The day was already turning out to be a challenge, and she really needed to relax. There was a lot to do before her mother arrived. She threw the pajamas in the laundry basket, belatedly thinking about having to deal with her laundry that same weekend.

She was skipping down the stairs, busy dealing with the

buttons on the cuffs of her blouse, when she heard a creak. She looked up at the stairwell and frowned at the sound of scurrying on the floorboards coming from overhead. It sounded like an animal had managed to get in her attic, but with the incoming storm, no one would be available to deal with it.

As she reached the bottom of the steps, her mind was occupied with thoughts of how to best handle the creatures. She was wrapping a wool scarf around her neck when suddenly, an odd sensation washed over her. Her hair stood on end, and she quelled the urge to run. Jenny stood at the bottom of the stairs, facing the living room and staring at somewhere in front of her.

Naya slowly traced Jenny's line of sight, and what she saw made her blood run cold. A middle-aged man dressed in outdated, heavy gray overalls was crouched before the roaring fireplace she couldn't remember lighting. Her breath caught in her throat, and breathing became an impossible task. The man shifted to gaze up at her. A gentle smile curled his lips, and it was all she could do to not smile back. He lowered his head as if to say hello, then vanished into a whirling gray mist that briefly floated above the floor before dissipating entirely. She blinked rapidly and sat on the nearest chair when she could finally take a breath of air. Checking around her, she saw that everything was as it had been before, except for the fire. Other than her and Jenny, the room was empty.

Jumping to her feet, she shrugged the strap of her bag over her shoulder and turned her back on the room. "Fuck this shit. I'm out of here."

CHAPTER TWO

Naya pumped the brakes as she slowly drove down the road, her knuckles blanching as she gripped the steering wheel. It was an instinctive action, one she knew she didn't need to do, but she couldn't help herself. It gave her a sense of control over the fear of the car sliding over the ice-covered road. Visibility through the windshield was practically non-existent. Large snowflakes the size of golf balls fell from the sky in a steady stream.

She reconsidered going out to get some last-minute groceries for the eighth time since she'd left her house because of the number of snowflakes hitting the windshield and the wipers groaning under the strain. Already, what normally took her half an hour to drive had stretched to over an hour.

Didn't her weather app warn her of an incoming storm?

"I really should pay more serious attention to those notifications," she muttered at the angry sky.

Although her pantries were full enough, as she was the type who never allowed a shelf to go half empty, she wanted to make something without dealing with the oven or the stove. Of course, the extra heat would raise the temperature in the house, but she just couldn't think of slaving over it. Not now. Moving between states, dealing with the strange things happening in her new home, and everything else in her life mentally exhausted her.

"I really should control these urges of mine," she mumbled. She leaned over the steering wheel and assessed the sky again. "I can make it."

If things had worked out differently, she would be lounging on her sofa with Jenny curled up next to her and enjoying a hot cup of cinnamon chamomile tea while listening to calm music. Not driving in a snowstorm that came out of nowhere because she'd been too unnerved to stay in her house. These days, she wasn't much into socializing or pushing herself to seek out acquaintances for the sake of networking, not like she had before. Not since —

She shook her head. No. She was not going there. Not now. Not ever.

Her attention bounced back and forth between the road in front of her and the GPS on her phone. According to the system, she was still a few hundred meters from her target. Visibility through the windshield was almost nil, so she couldn't tell if she was still on the road or the sidewalk. She reached out and tapped on the screen, zooming in for a clearer image, relieved to see she was still on the road. She only needed to move the car a few more meters further, and she'd be able to park. Wishing herself luck, she lightly pressed the accelerator and sighed in relief when the car moved a little faster.

Suddenly, the sky brightened and the snow stopped. Naya leaned over to peer overhead again and saw the clouds had parted like the Red Sea, revealing semi-clear skies and the blurred shape of the sun.

Her jaw dropped. "Incredible."

Taking advantage of the unexpected respite from a potential accident, she quickly maneuvered her car next to the now highly visible curb. As she did so, people started to walk out of establishments, most likely taking advantage of the weather just as she was.

Amber Ville, Vermont, was not exactly the kind of place she'd envisioned herself moving to at twenty-four. However, with her life map unexpectedly obliterated, the small town turned out to be the perfect place to find herself and feel safe once more. With fewer than ten thousand people, it was a drastic change from what she had been used to in LA.

Despite the small population, the one strip mall boasted incredible selections that one would only expect to find in big cities with hundreds of thousands of people. There was also the farmer's market that didn't have to advertise organically grown fruits and vegetables. The town was already uniquely famous for its choice of green agriculture and cattle farming.

Different.

That, in a nutshell, was exactly why she'd bought a historical landmark house for less than two grand.

She had stumbled onto the property listing, and when she had gone to look at the place, the real estate agent, Rachel McPherson, began telling her about the town's green initiative. She didn't have to think twice. To the older woman's surprise, Naya had paid the full amount in cash and closed the deal within the hour.

Documentation, on the other hand, took longer than expected. Six months, to be precise.

Historical society representatives had been especially concerned about Naya's proposed kitchen renovations. Ultimately, she had gotten her way by not going against structural restrictions and keeping her preferred design within the specified limits.

She had completed her master's in interior design during her rounds of physical therapy and procured her license as a certified interior designer. The credential had kept her expenses to the minimum, which allowed her to channel her money to the materials and equipment necessary to get the house of her dreams.

Gutting and refurbishing costs came in at a little under three hundred thousand. Still, it was an amount she had been comfortable and well prepared to spend, especially because of certain provisions that otherwise would not even be part of a regular heritage house. The house had already boasted a wet pantry, a dry pantry, a cold room, and an ice cellar, of all things. She had been lucky the cellars only needed minor upgrades. It was the main floor where most of her renovations occurred. She had taken down dividing walls to create a more open layout, which required complete rewiring that took up a large part of the budget. That, and her bank of refrigerators, which had given her team a lot of headaches, but in the end, that, too, had been finally rectified.

Naya's ideal layout for a house had always made her mother want to cry out in exasperation, for her dream was all about an open floor plan with thirty percent of the area dedicated to the kitchen. It never failed to confuse her poor mother. Well, Naya got what she wanted. Her mother had despaired but had gotten over that quickly. She was now on her way to visit because she wanted to see what Naya had done to her home and to personally test out the kitchen for herself.

Her stomach grumbled, reminding her that she'd only had a cup of coffee and a cheese melt before she'd left the house . . . and about Carol, who had still been sleeping. Thinking about Carol and how she'd complained about not having the time to pamper herself, Naya sent a quick message to her new friend, Lexi Alexander, whom she'd met the first week she'd moved to Amber Ville. Lexi owned the one spa in town that Naya had walked into in desperate need of a manicure. An hour later, she'd had perfect-looking nails.

The phone vibrating in her hand brought her out of her musings, and when she checked, Carol's appointment was set. That done, she got out of her car in the semi-familiar downtown area and did a slow turn on her heels.

She easily spotted a diner she hadn't tested out yet. It was easy to notice, as it had a huge hand-painted sign that spelled out *DINER* in all caps. She'd never be caught entering one if she'd still been in LA, but here, she couldn't care less. And truly, she didn't see how anyone would recognize her, not in this neck of the woods.

Keeping her influencer name had been a tough decision, but she had not worried about that. For one, she looked different now. She'd lost too much weight and had gone through several plastic surgeries to fix the damage from her fall. Although she had started her influencer hobby again, she maintained a constant veil of mystery by never fully showing her face to her followers. That earlier post of her outside only showed her side profile. The undamaged side.

Her assistant had said the half-glimpse was like a silent promise. Plus, she had to admit, it gave her an air of mystery. Her marketing side acknowledged it as a story waiting to unfold, a secret poised on the edge of revelation which would fan her followers' anticipation. Their reactions, whenever they caught a half-glimpse of her face, was one of eager expectation. Her relationship with her fans was enough that they even wrote threads of their understanding that when she chose to step forward, the world would not be the same.

Still, she hesitated. They most likely expected she looked the same way she'd always had. Little did they know.

Although she was still technically an influencer, her new address and lifestyle change had affected how she dealt with that aspect of her life. In LA, she had been all over social media. Dancer, actress, singer, makeup guru, and businesswoman. For some weird reason that she still couldn't quite understand, she'd managed to rack up millions of followers and successfully made money from it all. With a lot of help and consultation with the right financial advisers, she became one of the world's most influential and successful influencers. Her company had grown rapidly as well.

That was then.

Presently, she had a food and house designer blog where

she shared the hundreds of simple, tested, and approved recipes she'd learned from her grandmother, Irene, and mother, Kelly. The interior design part of her blog was still in its infancy but was gaining attention, especially after she'd posted the reel of how she'd designed her coffee station.

Two years of extensive physical and psychological therapy had involved a lot of pain and frustration, and creating delicious foods had become her source of respite and happiness.

These days, she didn't have to spend sleepless nights thinking up content. Her company was highly popular and kept her financially stable. Her comeback on social media had been met with skepticism, especially when her presentations no longer involved complicated productions. Fortunately, seconds or under-a-minute clips were the in thing, and her short photo presentations and videos of easy step-by-step cooking instructions for her favorite recipes had been accepted by a wider audience. She posted her more detailed blogs on her website, where she wrote down her thoughts and reactions to her creations.

To her delight and surprise, her more than fifteen million followers on *Instagram* had crossed over with her to *TikTok*, which now boasted over thirty million followers. She still couldn't quite wrap her mind around those figures. Especially as compared to her previous releases, blogging about her dog, interior designing, and food preparation should have been considered boring. Of course, according to her analysts, she'd lost several million through her journey, but she'd easily gained more. The loss hadn't worried her. Shifting from dancing and cutesy unboxing videos and such had been good when she'd been in her teens, but not when she was now an adult who'd had a trauma the whole world of the internet had witnessed in real-time.

Thankfully, the many business opportunities that had opened for her then still ran smoothly and continued to give her passive income. The day-to-day running of her business was easily handled online thanks to her great team, including her parents, brother, and personal assistant, who were loyal to her. Her brother especially . . . Dearest Luke.

She'd called him a dweeb when they'd been younger, even been mean to him because she could be and she'd been a self-entitled brat of an older sister. But he'd been her source of strength after the attempt on her life and had helped her through the toughest times. It hadn't been her mother who'd kept the monsters out of nightmares, it had been Luke who would come in and take her in his arms until she settled down to sleep. It had also been Luke who had suggested she consider an influencer makeover when she'd thought about quitting. With his help, and their mother's, she made the journey from a teeny bopper influencer into a mature blogger who no longer had to film get-ready-with-me makeup uploads. These days, designing a coffee station for a particular holiday was racking up the views.

Going back to her analogy of a life map demolished, that had been her life.

Smashed to a million shards and pieces.

But not ended . . . Never ended.

She loved life too much to let a simple distraction like an ex-fiancé attacking her and leaving her for dead at the bottom of a ravine destroy her.

Naya snapped her attention back to the present and stepped into the diner, making a beeline for one of the three empty tables at the far end of the surprisingly expansive room. As soon as she took off her parka and gloves and sat on the chair, a server approached her with a menu.

"I'll be back with you in a sec," the young woman said before leaving her to read the menu.

Nodding her thanks, she took out her phone and checked

her emails. There were several from her assistant reminding her of some online meetings. One schedule caught her attention. The meeting was set for ten that evening. She typed out a message, telling her assistant about the incoming storm, and asked her to cancel all online meetings until further notice.

Naya looked around and saw no one minding her. Then she turned her attention to the menu, squinting at the tiny print blurring in across the page. She placed two fingers over the menu and pinched them together before spreading them apart. Only after repeating the action three or four times did she realize why the print did not magnify.

"Ah, damn." At least with her phone, she had the option to use extra-large font or magnify, but she couldn't very well zoom in on a printed menu.

That was another change brought about by the accident. It had taken the rescuers more than three days to find her, and exposure to the elements had managed to ruin her vision for some reason. A medical diagnosis had been spouted, but she had never been good at understanding those things and no longer cared. Her eyesight had been affected, and she now had to use reading glasses. She dug into her bag in search of the pair, and when she couldn't find them, she upended the contents on the table. The loud clattering noise effectively silenced the low conversations from the other tables, and she dipped her head to apologize to the one nearest hers, occupied by an elderly couple.

The kindly old woman, who bore a striking resemblance to Estelle Getty, smiled endearingly at her. "Lose something, dear?"

Heat rising to her cheeks, Naya managed to smile back. "I seem to keep forgetting my reading glasses."

"Oh, that shouldn't be a problem. Julia will help you out. She'll soon be with you. Have a nice day."

"Good to know. Thank you." With rising self-consciousness, Naya slowly and quietly replaced the scattered items into her bag. No server arrived, so she picked up the menu again and narrowed her eyes to try to make out the words.

"Need help?"

Naya jumped in her seat and blinked up at the young woman from earlier. Now that the girl was standing nearer, Naya could see that she must have been all of sixteen, from how thin she was and the braces.

Naya made a face. "Do you mind if I ask you about what's good? In my mad rush to get to town before the full storm hit, I forgot my glasses back home."

"Sure, what do you have in mind?"

"You don't happen to have a spinach, feta, and egg white wrap, do you?" Her mother always told her it never hurt to ask.

The young server giggled. "In fact, we do. It's a house specialty and one of our daily best sellers."

Naya stared at her server, unable to hide her surprise. "Oh, my God! You're such an angel. Can I have black iced americano with one pump of sugar to go with it?"

"You sure can."

Naya couldn't believe her luck. She might not miss the city, but she couldn't deny her love for some specific offerings. Amber Ville's surprises kept on coming.

"This is a diner, why do you serve café . . . never mind. I'll take it if you have it."

"No worries. My mom was a barista in DC before the lockdown. When that happened, she came back here to help Grandad. She missed the food and tested out a change on the menu."

"Well, you mentioned it's a daily best seller. I take it that means her intuition was spot on?"

"It sure was." The server turned to go but snapped her

fingers and turned back around. "By the way, I'm Julia, your server for the day."

"I'm Naya. And thank you so much for the help. You're a sweetheart."

Julia's answer was a wide grin and a happy skip. Naya shook her head. The girl was such a breath of fresh air, and so very different from the sophisticated teens she'd gotten used to in LA. When Julia returned with her order, Naya thanked her again, snapped a picture of the plate, wrote an amusing narrative of how she got to enjoy the meal in the middle of the boondocks, posted it, and then dug into her wrap.

"God, this is so good," she muttered between bites. It was perfect.

As she savored her breakfast, she thought about how she could help to get more business into the diner through her platforms. She really should learn how to make these wraps at home. For one thing, it would be much cheaper. Then again, if she came to the diner for breakfast, it would make part of her life easier and get her out of the house for a while. She could come to town early in the morning, have something to eat, and swing by the grocery. Really, it would be a simple change to her routine.

She continued to think about the business side of the diner and felt they were doing quite well but had some room for improvement. Something that wouldn't ruin the ambiance of the place. Well, maybe she would brainstorm ideas when she couldn't find the chance to go downtown. Otherwise, she decided to relax and enjoy the diner's home-cooked meals that rivaled big city and big-name cafes.

Feeling somewhat better now that she had food in her stomach, she trudged through the ankle-deep snow that had settled on the sidewalk. The storm signal issued while she'd been enjoying her food said the heavy snowfall earlier was just a taste of what was to come. She stopped in her tracks and stared down at the notification again. Her sigh created a billow of fog in front of her.

"Great. Mom and Luke are coming over, *and* a storm is about to hit town."

The latest notification reminded her that she wanted to make sure she had enough food and other stuff to last several days. Like toilet paper . . .

Her phone vibrated again just as she stepped into the grocery. She winced when she looked at the display but answered anyway. "Hey. Carol."

"Hey you, where have you been?" Carol groused. "I've been calling and calling to give you a message, but you never picked up. It was your dad. He said he couldn't get a hold of you. He also mentioned your mom's on the way here. To Vermont. Amber Ville, Vermont. Did I mention Vermont? Why didn't you say anything earlier? Speaking of which, why didn't you wake me up?"

A wave of discomfort swept through Naya, but she pushed it away and laughed at Carol's dizzying tirade. "Sorry, I completely forgot to mention Mom was coming over. We planned the visit to coincide with her vacation."

"What do you need more stuff for? Knowing you, you've already got everything here."

None of your business. "Look, I needed to grab some stuff. There's a big storm coming, and I must make sure we're fully stocked. Just in case. Do you need anything?"

"There's a storm coming? When? Never mind, I'll check the weather updates myself." Carol sounded impatient, making Naya frown. "The reason I'm calling is that I woke up to the dog on my bed and the phone ringing. Found myself alone in this creepy old house you now call your home. So, I made myself a cup of espresso — barista grade, mind you — and helped myself to a chocolate croissant and strawberry jam. Why you had to go to town to have breakfast is beyond me."

Naya closed her eyes and breathed a prayer of thanks that Carol hadn't mentioned getting woken by anything weird. "Well, so you know, other than Mom, Luke's coming over, too."

Carol's sharp inhale and choking noises made Naya stifle her laughter. She'd known about Carol's huge crush on her brother, but he had always been too deep into his studies to notice the older woman who'd gawked like a teenager whenever he stepped within her line of vision.

Carol cleared her throat loudly. "Luke's coming?"

"He definitely is . . ." Naya added a bit of sing-song in her voice. Just to dig the tease in a little deeper.

"I hate you so much." Carol dragged out her words.

Her friend's clear frustration and embarrassment sent Naya into a fit of giggles, effectively making her forget about her earlier discomfort. When she finally controlled herself, she grabbed a cart and walked to the first aisle.

"I'll hurry. I don't want to linger here longer than necessary. Oh, before I forget. I booked that appointment you asked for at the local salon for shampoo, blow dry, and a mani-pedi for ten thirty this morning. It's now nine, so you have enough time to get off your ass and drive down here. The storm's dropping late afternoon, so you should be fine."

"Oh, my God. I love you. And I don't care. I need to be presentable. Send me the info stat while I take a shower. Don't worry, I can find my way."

Carol was still talking a mile a minute about what clothes to wear, but when Naya rounded a corner, Carol's incessant chatter died.

"Carol? Hello? Hey, Carol? Are you still there?"

The line was dead, and Naya wondered what could have caused the dip in the signal. She looked around and saw the culprit. The store's metal shelves groaning under the weight of the stock on them must have killed the connection. She shrugged, pocketed her phone, and went in search of the items on her mental list.

With her mother and Luke coming and Carol unexpectedly dropping in on her after almost two years of absence, a little housewarming party in the making was in the works. Storm or no storm. Yes, it would only be the four of them, but it was still something that scratched at Naya's need to play hostess, and she did love the role.

Her mother wasn't much of an eater but loved to snack. Luke loved his beer, which meant he also needed something to snack on. Carol loved food, period. Creating a charcuterie spread meant she wouldn't have to slave over a stove to keep them entertained.

She stood next to one of the refrigerated shelves, peering at the selections. She was still mulling over the number of deli meats she would need for the charcuterie she had in mind when her phone vibrated again. Thinking it was Carol, she answered immediately.

"Hey, big sis."

"Luke. Hi. Wait." Naya shifted the phone to her other ear and reached for a carton of milk. "Are you and Mom here already? I thought your plane wasn't going to land until after one?"

"Still in Chicago in pre-departure, don't worry. And before you say anything, you're not picking us up. I already booked a rental."

"Oh. Okay, that's great. So, why'd you call? Did anything happen? Did Dad change his mind? Is he coming with?"

"Dad's most definitely not coming. You know him and flying, he absolutely hates it. I'm calling to ask if you'd mind a couple of friends coming over with us?"

Naya's spine chilled. She didn't know why she suddenly felt defensive, but she hated socializing these days. The thought of having to deal with people she might not know was triggering her anxiety.

"Do I know any of them?"

Luke chuckled. "Yes. It's Rachel and Michael Bradbury. You do remember Michael, right?"

Naya's eyes bulged. Michael was coming? Big Michael? "Michael? Of course, I remember Michael. How dare you suggest I wouldn't, but I haven't seen him in ages."

The thought of seeing Michael made Naya's heart pound painfully in her chest. Forget about Michael? Was Luke serious? Her brother knew exactly how she felt about Michael. Well, before the incident, but still.

"Michael's taken over the firm. Matthew retired and handed him the reins. I think Matthew took off with Margo on some cruise for a month."

"Oh, I remember. Mom told me all about it, but why is Michael taking a break from work? As far as I can remember, he's not one to take a break. Even in high school, he went to class even when sick."

"Well, it so happens that it's doctor's orders." Luke's voice took on a grim note. "He'd contracted COVID six months back, and it hit him hard. Rachel didn't tell us at the time, but she finally told me that she thought they'd lose him. Said he was in ICU for about two weeks. It was a close call."

"Oh, wow. Wait. How did I not know any of this?"

"Rachel asked me not to tell you. Said you didn't need to get worried."

"Excuse me? What the hell? This is Michael we're talking about here." Naya's voice rose an octave.

"I think Rach heard you." Luke chuckled. "She's hiding her face with her hands."

"He's not still sick, is he? Is he even well enough to travel?" Naya gnawed on her lower lip.

"Well, it mainly affected his lungs, and he'd been pushing himself to the point of exhaustion. He actually collapsed at work. Rach used her little-sister charms and blasted the hell out of him, then took him to the hospital. They admitted him for about a week and then ordered him to take a long vacation. He's been on one for a month and is ready to move out of the country if he had to stay one more day at their house."

Naya grinned. She could visualize the rigid Mrs. Bradbury hovering over Michael. "Margo is quite the character."

"She's a terror." Luke agreed. "But Margo was correct to all but physically tie Michael to the bed, and even Rach had to agree with her. Between the two of them, they got Michael to recover. Anyway, I spoke to Rach about going to your place, and it so happens they have a place there, too. She said they had business ventures in Amber Ville. So, what do you think? Think you can play hostess to two more guests? Rach said it'll be like a reunion."

"Well, yeah. These are Michael and Rachel we're talking about here. Of course, I'm looking forward to seeing them. It's been a while. It *will* be a reunion. Only . . ."

"Only?" Luke prompted.

"Carol dropped in unexpectedly."

"Carol?"

"Yeah. She's staying over the weekend."

"I sense some tension going on. Care to tell me about it, sis?"

Naya huffed. "I hadn't heard anything from Carol since the incident. It's been almost two years, Luke."

"Did she contact you before she showed up there?"

"No. That's the thing. She came in around two this morning. I haven't been sleeping well lately, so I was already up. I brought her in and was finally able to get some sleep." Naya scratched her forehead.

"Uh-huh. I remember she was the demanding type."

"Yeah. She requested that I get her an appointment for a mani-pedi in town."

"And did you? Get her one?"

"Yes, I did, actually."

"Naya." Luke didn't tone down the disappointment in his voice.

Naya squeezed her eyes. "I'm tired, and there's a storm coming, and I'm anxious you arrive safely. And I didn't want to look like a bitch, you know?"

"Look—" Luke was interrupted by a disembodied voice announcing some airline notification. "Oh, that's us. Listen, we're going to talk about this when we get there. In the meantime, you need to relax. Also, don't bother with wine. Rach said she's bringing in a crate."

"Of wine?"

"Yep."

"Okay, no wine. I'll see you all later. Stay safe."

"We will. Remember, stay calm. See you later."

The call ended, and Naya was left looking down at the phone in her hand. She was glad Luke was coming. Between them, he was the logical one when it came to interpersonal relationships.

Naya dropped her phone into her bag and consciously pushed the topic of Carol to the back of her mind. She looked around and thought about what to buy. The logistics of housing five guests were vastly different from having just three. The more she thought it over, the more she realized that should there be a medical emergency, she had nothing in her house they could use. Her mother's disapproving look should she find that out came to mind, so she hurried to fix the situation. She could start by getting something that could help Michael.

She craned her neck to check the overhead signs for medical equipment. With a storm coming in and the way the cold settled in the mountains, it was best to be prepared with everything. She spotted a sign and pushed her cart in that direction.

She rounded the corner to a display of different medical equipment. Behind it was a sign that pointed to medical supplies.

"Bingo."

Naya hurried over to a uniformed store employee. "Excuse me, do you happen to carry medical equipment like a nebulizer or an oxygen tank?"

Half an hour later, she left a happily grinning employee. In her cart was an adorable nebulizer in the shape of a beagle. The store employee explained that it encouraged therapy compliance with children. Naya didn't bother to explain that it was for an adult man but took it anyway. Not buying it would be a mistake, especially as Michael was usually a surly patient. Maybe a dog-shaped nebulizer would woof him to submit to his fate. Incredibly, the store had an oxygen concentrator, so she bought that as well. The employee had shown her the required attachments, which she'd added to her stockpile. She took everything—her mom would know what to do and what went where. Should Michael need emergency care, they wouldn't have to rely on an ambulance that might not make it in time at the height of the storm. After a brief pause, she returned to the employee to add a pre-filled medical supplies box that listed over-the-counter oral and topical antibiotics, among other things.

Next on her list was the food. Which was what had brought her into the store in the first place.

Naya looked at the shelves, her thoughts awhirl with plans on logistics and food. The situation had changed into a family and friends gathering. Knowing them the way she did, they were most likely expecting to indulge in drinks and chips but no actual food. For herself, she wasn't really into drinking, although she enjoyed just being with them when they did. And they understood and accepted her little quirks, not drinking being one of them, but truly appreciated her talent in the kitchen. Speaking of which, she quickly maneuvered her steadily overfilling cart into another aisle.

"Damnit. I hope they have Spanish Serrano ham and maybe some of the spicy marinated mozzarella Michael loves so much."

The thought of looming over a hot stove was tempting, especially as she wanted to impress Michael, but she was in too much of a panic mode to successfully cook anything. She wasn't in the mood to buy food from the local deli, either. The more she thought about it, the idea of a charcuterie board was truly the best option, since it was always a crowd-pleaser and was super easy to make. There was also that nicely sized board she could use to arrange the different cheeses and meats. It seemed the perfect time to use it, as it was practically a part of the house.

Luckily, the store sold an impressive assortment of deli meats and cheeses at affordable prices. Why spend over a hundred dollars when she could get what she needed for under or just a little over fifty? A sudden inspiration hit her. She could create a live presentation. The content would be unexpected and could attract many viewers.

Motivated by the burst of inspiration, Naya headed to the refrigerated area, where she knew she could find a great selection of meats and cheeses at unbeatable prices.

Once done with her choices, she went over to the shelves where she'd spotted a wide assortment of locally produced organically grown nuts and berries. If she'd still been in LA, she'd have made do with wildly priced packaged nuts stamped and labeled *organic* to jack up the price, but here, she was given a scooper and directed to a weighing scale. She probably bought more than needed and would most likely store the rest in the dry pantry.

Next, she went to the fruit stand and found some muscat

grapes. They were huge compared to other varieties and super firm, which she preferred. No stringy bits of fiber that could get stuck between teeth, as commonly occurred with regular grapes. The skin of muscat grapes was typically sour and a bit astringent, but it blended so well with cheese. Its flesh was more delicious than any other she'd ever tasted.

Happy with her choices, she made another turn around the stocks and placed more into her cart. Breads and crackers were next. She had some back at the house, but with additional mouths to feed, she wanted to have more rather than less. And the items kept well, especially during winter.

After paying for her purchases, Naya exited the store and placed her paper bags in the back of her car. After the sixth bag, she realized she might just be tipping the edge of a food hoarder, but who cared? She certainly didn't. Besides, she could while away her days creating great and delicious food that she could film and upload as content and enjoy snacking on. Maybe she could gift her neighbors, whom she still had to meet.

CHAPTER THREE

N aya surveyed the ingredients laid out on the island. Carol's car was not in the driveway, which meant the woman was off to her appointment. As a nurse, Carol didn't have much chance to indulge in a mani-pedi. She worked hard, and Naya often wondered if her friend was simply too tired to take some personal time. Maybe that explained her astringent personality, but it didn't explain her absence and lack of communication for the past two years.

She jumped when deafening thunder boomed overhead. A loud rumble followed it, closely followed by another and then another, each getting louder and closer than the ones before. The sound worried her, but on checking the clock, she saw that only two hours had passed since she'd spoken to Luke. It was possible that her mother and Luke, as well as Rachel and Michael, had already landed at the domestic airport. Still, a delay was not out of the picture, given the approaching storm. Thankfully, the airport was only half an hour away, and should the storm prevent their progress, they would be closer to rescue. She hoped it wouldn't end that way, but there was always the off chance.

She sent a quick message to Luke, asking how they were doing. Before she could place her phone on the island, she got a response saying it was her mom answering for Luke, who was stowing their bags into the rental.

Naya quickly sent another message.

Drive safe.

A few moments later, the sound of a new message pinged.

We will. Don't worry. We're going to miss the storm. And yes, it's coming in, but the advisory said it'll hit later tonight. We have more than enough time to get there. Do you have enough fuel for the generator?

Yes, I do. Plus, I got candles. Don't worry about anything. I had everything ready before I moved in . . . per the realtor's advice.

She didn't bother telling her mother about her last-minute purchases.

Alright, sweetheart, we're off. This storm's going to make traveling slow so we'll see you in about an hour. Hopefully sooner.

Naya checked on her generators again, just to make sure, and found she hadn't been wrong. The tanks appeared to be full, based on the gauge reading. Should the electricity go off, they would have no problem. The candles were in a box in the dry pantry, and she took out two packs of the vigil candles, which were slightly larger than tea lights but lasted longer. She also had larger decorative but functional scented candles scattered about that would lend a subtle scent throughout the house. Plus, she'd stacked plenty of firewood in the back room and next to the fireplace the day before, at least she hoped it was enough.

The suddenness of the temperature drop ran a chill through her whole body as she entered the laundry room. She'd never liked the room. It always gave her the heebie-jeebies for some reason. When the house was still under reconstruction, she'd overheard the men working in the area complain of the unexplained temperature drops. That had been at the height of summer. As it was now winter, the change was considerable. Frowning slightly, she headed for the dry cellar to grab more firewood, again hoping she had enough for the night. If they ran out, she could always send Luke to get more.

Back in her kitchen once more, she gave her purchases another survey before beginning the task of preparing her charcuterie board. But first, she needed a good-sized board on which to arrange the goodies.

She pulled out four boards from a drawer under the island and saw that each had a thin film of mold on the surface. Biting back a curse, she couldn't remember when she'd last cleaned them with a bleaching solution. She couldn't even remember when she'd placed them in the drawer. Until each board was thoroughly cleaned, none of them were safe to use. That would have to wait for another day. In any case, none were the right size.

A flash of insight, and she recalled the perfect board she had thought about earlier, which she knew was clean. She opened a cabinet on the far side of the kitchen and took down the old chopping board.

The adorable large board, with a thickness of about two inches and cut in the shape of a whale, would be perfect for what she had planned. One side showed faint carvings of letters and numbers along with various symbols and graphics that she couldn't decipher in a pattern she had never seen before. The flip side had a smooth surface showing fine-grained wood, which made it highly durable, able to resist bacteria, and gave it just the right amount of hardness.

One of the carpenters working on the house had found it. He'd volunteered to sand it down and smooth out the shallow designs. He'd returned it to her, saying he couldn't remove the etchings without causing damage. He even went the extra mile to rub food-grade mineral oil over it. Naya hadn't minded and had thanked the man for his efforts. Even gave him a tip. Besides, the designs would serve as a conversation piece.

Now that she was looking at it again, she couldn't help admiring the craftsmanship. It was truly beautiful and hand-carved, according to the carpenter. Flipping the board over, she smoothed her hand over the surface. Yes, it was the perfect board.

It didn't take her long to set up her phone at the right angle, making sure it never caught her face before clicking the option to go live. She continued to prepare the ingredients, keeping a close eye on the viewers. When going live, it was best to wait a few minutes before doing anything, giving those who received delayed notifications a chance to join. Delighted as the number of viewers rose, she waved a hand in front of the phone. She didn't say anything yet and instead continued to ensure all the ingredients were within easy reach. After about five minutes, the number of viewers reached a hundred thousand, and many happy followers were excited to know what she planned to show them.

"Hi, guys! Sorry for not making an announcement earlier, but there's a storm coming, and I've got friends and family coming in at a moment's notice. What's the best way to entertain without slaving over a hot stove? Let me show you how I prepare a charcuterie board for under a hundred dollars."

The comments flooded in, and many emojis covered the screen.

She chuckled. "Okay, guys. Charcuterie is basically a way of arranging cured meats, cheeses, and other good ingredients together on a board. I liked to start by putting out the cheeses, which are usually a combination of different varieties. Hard cheeses like Manchego and a sharp but flavorful favorite, the white cheddar cheese." She raised the cheese in question so it would get the camera focused. "Then there are the soft cheeses like artisan goat cheeses." She continued to show the ingredients one at a time while speaking to her viewers.

A glance showed there were now over two hundred fifty thousand viewers. "There are also the fruit-flavored cheeses that have recently become very popular, but with the fruits and berries I plan to place on the board, I feel like they would defeat the purpose. Plus, fruity cheeses can be quite pricey. So plain goat cheese is the way to go. Then there's the mozzarella. These come in blocks or balls. Whichever is available, but I prefer to crumble it between my fingers. However, if the presentation is at the forefront of the preparation, the balls are the perfect choice. Easier to pick up, too, with toothpicks or small forks. Oh, wait, let me grab those. Don't go away."

She scurried over to the pantry where she'd stored unopened boxes of cutlery. After digging through the pile, she finally found the box containing what she wanted and brought them out, then returned once more to her board. She'd give the small forks a quick rinse in the sink after she finished her presentation.

"I hope you didn't mind the wait. Another great choice is to have a soft, spreadable cheese like Brie." She quickly showed the cheese to the camera before placing it on her cutting board. "Guys, make sure to cut these into wedges. For some reason, I found that many tend to get nervous or shy about making that first cut into the block, so cutting these into eighteen slices is the way to go for easy access. My friend Carol—you know her, right?—well, she's staying over the weekend and absolutely loves triple cream cheese, which is perfect for crackers or toast. Its creamy, buttery flavor is oddly satisfying."

Naya had carefully placed each of the five cheeses on the board. As it was for her family and friends, and the board was large enough to hold the number, she left her five choices in place, liking the look of one type in each corner and the last in the center. The spaces between would soon be filled with meats, fruits, and other accouterments. Thinking of trimmings, she set her knife down and went to the pantry again, where she had a ready supply of honey, almonds, and marmalade that would do well for both the Manchego and Brie.

Naya looked up to check on the comments when a particular one caught her attention. She leaned closer to read it again before straightening, making sure the camera never framed her face.

"Manchego is my all-time favorite cheese. I'm telling you guys, biting into it, your palate gets swamped with strokes of fruits and nuts, resonating in clear unison. The zesty undertones add to its piquancy. Now, as I'm slicing mine, you guys should do the same at home, the aroma coming from it is delicious. It smells like dried herbs. The older it is, the sharper it gets, and it also gets harder. I chose a particularly aged one. So, look at my slice and check out how beautiful the granular texture is. You can clearly see the tiny pores that lace the flesh." She raised the slice in question and smiled as more comments came through. While she tried to answer as quickly as she could, she continued to slice.

For different textures, she diced small squares of the white cheddar cheese. "Now, guys, I know not many of you think about it, but really, presentation is a key factor when preparing a charcuterie board. Not only should it look pretty, but each ingredient must be placed in a manner that would not leave the diner confused as to what went with which. If I were lazy, I could just dump everything on the board and hope for the best, but that would defeat the purpose of the spread. A charcuterie is meant to make the experience easy and enjoyable but must also be satisfying."

She already had the Brie and triple cream cheese artfully arranged in their corners, so she grabbed the ramekin in the center of the board to show the viewers.

"Next, we have the marinated spicy mozzarella, which obviously still have liquid on them, so they go into a ramekin to keep the marinade from leaking all over the board." She showed off the cheese balls in the ramekin and returned it to the center of the board. "Now that the cheeses are all in place, let's proceed to the cured meats."

Naya grabbed a multi-pack and showed it to her viewers. "This is my ultimate choice because not only is it easier, but it's also less expensive. My grandmother always told me one does not need to break the budget to get satisfying and delicious results. These packs usually come with several types of meats like salami, coppa, and prosciutto. There's one meat my grandmother loved, Jamón Serrano. For me, a charcuterie board is incomplete without it. Although prosciutto is more readily available, its sweet, delicate, and moist texture is vastly different from the serrano's more intense flavor. Now let me show you how to present these on the board."

Taking up the thin meat rounds, she began folding the thinly sliced meats.

"Watch as I fold and shape these into florets. You can always leave the rounds flat on the board, but it's hard to pick up. This way, it's easier to pick up".

"I've seen many use a glass to form the roses or tulips, but I prefer the simpler method. Fewer things to wash."

Naya adjusted the camera before slowly folding the circles into triangle shapes. "Basically, you fold the slice in half and then another half. Arrange the folded meats like you would a deck of cards. That way, they can be easily layered onto the serving board."

Naya observed the passing comments while collecting the salami slices.

"The salami can also be folded in a similar way, but this time, I'll keep these more fanned out and less compacted. Once all the meat slices have been shaped, they can now be placed on the serving board." As she continued to place the meats around the cheeses, a sudden, loud thud caused her to raise her head.

The sound came from behind her, in the direction of the pantry. She frowned as she put down the circle of meat she'd been holding, swiped a paper napkin to wipe her hands, and walked over to the door. Light flooded the interior as soon as she opened it. She stepped inside and looked around, only to see nothing was out of place. It still looked exactly as it had when she'd last come in no less than twenty minutes before. A chill went through her, and she cursed under her breath. If the heaters were acting up that early in the day, God only knew how long it would last through the storm. She would have to call the contractor who'd installed it. Still thinking about the potential expense, she closed the door and went back to finish her board.

"Sorry about that, guys, I thought I heard something. Let's continue, shall we?"

She stepped closer to the phone to read the comments. To her horror, a lot of viewers claimed they had seen a shadow pass behind her. Gritting her teeth, she swallowed a curse and decided not to address the comments.

"My board doesn't have a rim, so I'm making sure to arrange the meats around the border. They'll serve as a barrier for the fruits that can easily roll off. Even with only twelve grams of meat slices, the manner in which they have been folded and layered makes the platter look full and abundant. Now that the meat and cheese are on the board, it's time for the accouterments."

The influx of comments that followed made Naya laugh. She sent a prayer of thanks that her viewers had gotten distracted. "Okay, slow down, guys. Let me explain. An accouterment, in this case, is basically anything else that pairs well with the meats and cheese. If one or two of these need to be placed in a separate dish, like a mini cast iron pan, place these down first and assess. If they fit, go for it. If not, change it to something that would better fit the space that needs to be filled. Gauging the space on the board should always be the first step before committing."

Naya started with salty things like green olives, kalamata olives, and pepper-stuffed olives, placing them in a mini-serving dish. "Do you know that one of my first mistakes when learning how to prepare a board was to use unpitted olives?

That was a lesson I will never forget. I ended up going to the dentist. So now, I always make sure to choose the pitted kind. That way no one breaks their teeth."

"Next, I'll add some pickles. Baby dills are a perfect choice, or if available, some gherkins, or maybe a combination of both. The more, the merrier, was what my grandmother used to say. Okay, guys, observe what I do."

Naya started by pouring the pickles into a bowl, then stacked them vertically into a ramekin for easy grabbing. Trial and error had taught her that it was the best method for serving the small treats rather than pouring them into a bowl with their juices or laying them flat on a mini serving plate. She also found placing the gherkins or pickles vertically in a ramekin made it possible to hold more in the container. When she was done, she stepped back and assessed her work.

"Now, doesn't that look cute and neater?"

One of the first things Naya had learned as an influencer was that presentation was the key to everything. And when it came to food plating, giving the diner easy access was everything that mattered, for it would lead to greater enjoyment.

Thanks to lessons she'd paid top dollar for, she'd learned how to properly pair things on the platter. Brie was simply irresistible when paired with honey, so she placed a small jar next to the soft cheese. She pulled open one of the drawers on the island and took out a disposable honeycomb server. Next to the honey, she placed two sampler jars of fruit spread, one of fig and the other of blueberry.

"Now it's time to reassess the board. You can see that it's filling up nicely, but there is still enough space to fit in more goodies. I like to add fresh fruits for a bit more color. My friend Carol introduced me to Chinese pears, and I've been ruined since." Naya smacked her lips dramatically. "They have the perfect hardness and texture that I really like. If these are not available, don't worry about it. You can use whatever seasonal fruits are available."

She took an apple from the fruit bowl and sliced it in half, then laid the flat sides on the chopping board and made thin slices. She then gently fanned and shaped the pieces into a heart. "Why hearts? Because I like hearts. So that's that. Also, apples are an inexpensive and delicious pairing with almost any kind of cheese. Remember, there is no right or wrong when it comes to a charcuterie board. What's important is it has to be playfully delicious and satisfying."

The muscats were next, and she cut them into smaller portions. Again, to make it easier on the diner. The strawberries and blueberries filled the leftover spots, and Naya made sure to place them next to the Brie as those paired perfectly well with it. Next, she added an assortment of nuts like walnuts, almonds, and pistachios, which really went well with all the delicacies on the board.

"We're almost done, but not quite. For a delectable variety, I love to bring in dark chocolate. It's the perfect break from the savory, salty, and fruity. Nothing quite beats the intense flavors."

"Now, for the final touch. Toast and crackers," she said, reaching for the bread and crackers.

She lightly brushed the diagonal baguette slices with olive oil and placed them in the oven at about four hundred degrees. Those would be ready in a few minutes or when they turn lightly golden, which was the extent to which Naya would be using the stove that night. Water and artisan crackers were fished out of the pantry and carefully arranged onto the already bursting board. There was no more room for the baguettes, so she took out a small serving dish and placed it on the island for when the baguettes were done.

"And there you have it," Naya announced in a cheery voice.

Something hit her foot, and she looked down to see that a

basket she normally kept on the top shelf for decorative purposes had rolled to the side of her foot. She stared at it for a long time before she realized the camera was still running.

"Send me some pics or clips of how your charcuterie board turned out. Thanks for staying with me, oh my gosh, almost forty minutes. Again, there's no right or wrong, so don't get anxious, and best of all, have some fun. 'Bye, guys!"

CHAPTER FOUR

Hoping no one thought it strange that a basket would randomly fall off the cabinet, Naya reached out and ended the live feed.

She had just pulled the baguettes out of the oven when a sudden shift in the atmosphere made her look up from her task. Only then did she realize it was getting dark outside. As for the basket by her foot, she bent and picked it up. Her house was free from drafts, so there was no reason why it should have fallen. She huffed a breath and placed the basket on the counter.

Sudden worry over Carol swept over her, and she quickly washed her hands before sending her a message. Thankfully, Carol promptly responded with a voice message.

"I've just crossed the gate as I speak. Also, I've got more food, just in case. I know you've got a full pantry, but I didn't see any marshmallows to go with the chocolate. Okay, got to go. This storm's going to be crazy, and it's hitting earlier than predicted. See you in a few minutes."

Naya breathed a sigh of relief. She might be a little irritated with Carol, but she didn't wish harm to fall on her or anyone. She left the charcuterie board on the island and went to gaze out the window. The sky was turning an ominous shade of gray, and she doubted the weather forecast was correct in their prediction the storm wouldn't hit until late that evening. Carol had said it was already getting bad, but it still looked calm enough outside not to worry too much. Either way, the sky could clear suddenly, just like it had earlier. Thunder rumbled in the distance as if nature tried to do its best to prove her assumption incorrect.

She felt intensely relieved that she would not be alone in the house. Socializing might no longer be among her top five needs, but knowing her family and friends would be safe around her seemed more important now.

Thinking of her family, she picked up her phone again to check where her mother and the rest were. She didn't have to worry long, for she had a waiting message saying they had crossed the gate and were driving up the private road. Relieved she wouldn't have to worry about Carol or her family and friends any longer, she sent a smiley emoji only to let out a shriek when lightning cracked above the house, closely followed by a boom of thunder.

Jenny yelped, and Naya dropped to a crouch with her arms over her head. Jenny crowded against her, shivering and whining. When nothing else followed, Naya got up, patting Jenny on the head. She went around the house to lock up the windows and draw the curtains, Jenny following her closely. Her actions were no help against Mother Nature, but the tasks made her feel better. She was standing in the middle of the living room when another solid crack of lightning sounded overhead, quickly followed by a thunderous boom. The lights flickered, and the house plunged into an ominous silence. Jenny yowled and scurried to get under the sofa.

Naya knew the power outage was most likely a safety measure, but she had a right to her frustrations. "Well, that's that."

"Jenny, it's okay, girl. Come to Mama." Jenny didn't move from her hiding place. "Great. Just what I needed."

Biting back another disgruntled comment, she carefully returned to the kitchen. There was no need to worry about the frozen perishables, as they were safe and secure in the ice cellar under the house. The refrigerators and one chest freezer she had in the kitchen had a separate generator that would automatically kick in when the power got cut off. A quiet hum coming from outside told her it had done just that. As for the rest of the house, there was no need to start the generator unless necessary, and she didn't find the need to turn it on. At least, not yet.

The matches and vigil candles she'd set on the island earlier were still in their packaging, so she only needed to unwrap them and place them on something to catch the wax drippings. She found a stack of coasters in the cupboard and took out two. She remembered the battery-powered candles in one of the drawers in the China cabinet and took those out as well. Those were safer, but the night called for the scented kind, which were already scattered around. On the top shelf, she found six kerosene lanterns. She took down three and checked to see if they had fuel. They did. She didn't need to light those yet but grabbed the package of matches so she could place one box near the lamps.

Next, she brought out extra candles and lamps and arranged them on the counter, island, and mantle over the fireplace. She included a box of matches at each location. Once she finished, she took one last look around and then went back to the window to peer outside.

She saw no sign of Carol or her family, not that she could make much of anything out. Snow had begun to fall like a thick blanket, and through the dimming light, she could see everything had quickly turned white outside. Whatever light was out there wouldn't last much longer. She looked at her phone again, but like before, no signal registered. Which meant calling or sending messages would be a futile effort.

Well, she hadn't wanted to cook, but her oven—thankfully a gas one—would help warm the house. She went down to the cold storage and pulled the lasagna from the freezer. She'd made it the week before, posting the step-by-step recipe on her social media. Once she had that heating in the oven, she returned to the living room and froze in her tracks.

A sense of a presence, of someone behind her, swept over her. She quickly turned, but no one was there. Shaking off the feeling and hoping her imagination wouldn't get the better of her, she tapped the flashlight app on her phone and began aiming it in different directions. Just like the previous times she'd felt like this, there was nothing or no one to be seen. One look at the topmost part of the phone still showed zero signal bars. Although she'd expected that, she couldn't hold back letting out a disappointed sigh.

She bent to place her phone on the ottoman when something dark, almost like a shadow, moved in her periphery. It moved too fast for a normal person and could barely be seen out of the corner of her eye, but when she looked up again, there was nothing. Startled, she moved closer to where she'd seen the movement and peered around the corner, but all she saw was an empty hallway.

"Carol? Is that you?"

She received no answer to her query and stifled a curse from escaping her lips. Of course no one would answer — she was alone in the house. The front door was ten steps away and had been within her line of sight the whole time, so she was sure no one had come in the last five minutes. She frowned deeply. So, who or *what* was that shadow all about?

Since she'd moved in, she'd noticed the shadows in the edges of her periphery, not to mention the man and the woman. Whenever she looked around, there was never anyone there. If somehow there had been, she found it highly unlikely they could disappear through a solid wall.

And then there was that laundry room . . .

An involuntary shiver ran over her body when a sudden chill settled inside the living room. With the growing storm, the freezing air from outside could easily seep into the house.

Naya dragged her damp palms down the side of her hips. Once upon a time, she hadn't been easily spooked, but those days had ended the same moment her life map had been shredded.

"Right. First things first, light the fireplace." Talking to herself helped break the ominous silence.

Naya returned to the kitchen and grabbed another box of matches and something to get the fire going. Her breath froze in the air, making her hurry to her task. She was kneeling by the fireplace about to strike the match when the memory of the ghostly apparition flashed through her mind. Her hand trembled, but she quelled her fears as she sat on her heels, staring at the fresh logs already set in the fireplace, which she couldn't remember replacing. Shaking her head, she proceeded to light the fire.

"At least you made sure to replace the ones that were burned. Uhm . . . thank you," she muttered under her breath, expressing gratitude to the unknown person.

The dry wood easily caught fire and soon roared happily. Once more, she was glad she'd resisted the urge to buy an electric fireplace. It wouldn't have done her any good if she'd caved into the marketing spiel of the salesman at that time.

The original fireplace had many issues, so she'd spent good money to get the whole thing overhauled. She hadn't used it before, not finding the need since she had been relying on the electric heating system she'd had installed.

She got up and watched as the fire crackled and popped. The flames jumped a little higher than she'd expected, but she waited until they settled into a steady blaze before replacing the fire screen. She held her hands out to the fire as she thought about lighting the fireplaces in the three bedrooms upstairs. A loud thump shook her out of her reverie. This time, it was coming from the second floor.

It must be the house shifting.

Naya rolled her eyes at her ridiculous attempt to pull logic out of nowhere. Who was she kidding? She closed her eyes briefly before glaring at the staircase. "Okey-dokey. Whoever's up there? You can kiss my ass. Stay out of my way because I need to light those fires."

Yes. She sure sounded brave. *Insert rolling eyes emoji.*

She set her lips in a tight line of grim determination and headed up the stairs. "Of all the houses to buy, I had to get one that has characters in its bones. Characters. Sheesh. Yeah. Okey-dokey. Let's get this over with."

CHAPTER FIVE

M ichael used the sleeve of his parka to wipe off the condensation on the windshield. He almost laughed when Luke Rollins let out a string of expletives under his breath as he carefully maneuvered their car through the thick blanket of snow. "You okay there, buddy?"

"The weather update said this storm wasn't going to hit until later tonight. They're hours off that prediction," Luke grumbled. "If I'd known it was going to be this bad, I would've recommended we postpone the drive to Naya's until it blew itself out."

Michael's lips twitched at the barely concealed snarl in Luke's voice. "We're going to be okay. Try focusing on the road. I can barely make anything out, but I do *see* the embankments on either side of us. You said we're already in her driveway."

"Didn't I tell you that Naya's driveway is at least half a mile long from the gate? Did I fail to emphasize *half a mile*?"

"I heard you the first time, Luke. Now come on, according to this map, we should be there in about five minutes." Michael raised said map.

"You said that ten minutes ago!"

"I know I did, but I read the map wrong. Now, I'm certain. You make it sound as though you've never been here before."

"Oh, I forgot to tell you." Luke turned to him with wide eyes. "I've never been here before."

Michael couldn't help chuckling. "Roll in the sarcasm, why don't you."

"You said you knew this place because you had a house here."

"I *do* know my way around Amber Ville. I just haven't been in *this* part of Amber Ville."

"Boys, please."

Luke lifted his head to look at the speaker in the rearview mirror. "Sorry, Mom."

Michael looked over his shoulder and grinned at the woman who spoke. Dr. Kelly Rollins, mother to Luke and Naya, had been like a second mother to him and his sister Rachel. "Sorry, Dr. Rollins."

"I swear, big brother. The way you and Luke sounded. It's like we were back in kindergarten all over again."

"And how would you know, little sis?" Michael turned to look at Rachel in the seat behind him. "You were not even born when I was in kindergarten. And you seem to have forgotten that Luke and I could never have gone to kindergarten together. Me being seven years older."

"Oh. I remember," Rachel grumbled. "Still, both of you sounded like kids to me."

"Rachel," Dr. Rollins warned. "Anyway, I was able to send a message to Naya that we were on her driveway before we lost signal. I still find it ridiculous why anyone would call it a driveway when it's practically a separate road all its own."

"Sorry, Dr. Rollins," Rachel said.

"Now, now, children. Did you both forget I told you to call me Kelly, like six years ago?"

Michael flashed her a grin. "I remember, but I can't bring myself to call you by your first name. You're too respectable to be called anything other than Dr. Rollins."

Kelly stretched out an arm and slapped him lightly on his shoulder. "Mind your manners, young man."

"As for why this is called a driveway," Michael continued, "we'll have to ask Naya that bit of detail. Mine isn't as long and winding."

"You're so easy to tease, Mom," Luke said, shaking his head.

Michael chuckled at the easy banter. He'd always felt a little envious over the easy-going relationship between the Rollinses. He'd known them since they'd first moved to Chicago sixteen years earlier. His mother had made him bring a welcome-to-the-neighborhood casserole to their new neighbors. He could still remember when Naya opened the door. Whatever resentment he'd felt about the task disappeared the moment he saw her. He'd been captivated ever since.

She'd looked him up and down before her gaze settled on the dish in his hands. "Wow, you're tall."

Michael gestured with the dish. "It's beef bourguignon. My mom's specialty. She told me to tell you welcome to the neighborhood."

"Thank you." Then Naya yelled over her shoulders. "Cancel the order, Mom. We got *food*."

Michael could feel his cheeks warm and couldn't wait to get away. "Here. Careful. It's hot."

"I got it." Naya took the dish from him. When she had it safely in her hands, she signaled with her head for him to enter. "Come on in. I bet you're hungry, too, big guy."

Michael had been so surprised that he'd been unable to say no to her invitation.

He found out later she was ten to his fourteen.

Naya had made quick work of introducing Michael to the Rollins family. He still couldn't remember how he found himself sitting with them for dinner, but it was the first of many happy meals he shared with them. Their parents were out working most of the time, and their friendship grew. Even though he was older than Naya and Luke, he had been proud to introduce them to his friends and made sure the new kids were treated fairly.

College had taken him out of Chicago, and he'd lost himself to his studies for a while. One day, a classmate showed him a video that had been going viral. To his surprise, it was Naya, and much to his friends' amusement, he immediately followed her YouTube channel. They only stopped teasing when they'd caught him on a video call with her. Naya had winked at him and set about charming his friends.

A powerful gust of wind rocked the car, pulling Michael back to the present. He turned to look at the road before them, or at least tried to make it out. Luke had turned on the headlights, and the light created a tunnel of radiance that barely reached beyond the narrow road. Large snowflakes fell in a steady stream, covering the hood with a thick white blanket.

"Luke?"

"Yeah, Mike?"

"Are we even close to Naya's house?"

"I think so, but with all this snow and the speed we're going, I can't really tell exactly where we' are."

Michael's stomach growled as he held on to the dashboard when the wind gusts from outside pushed their SUV to the side of the road. He shook his head and wondered why Naya would choose to live so far from civilization. His house was isolated, but not quite like this one was. He could at least still see the town from his window. Plus, he had neighbors.

The sound of the distant rumbling made him crane his neck to look up at the sky. What he saw was more snow falling and not much else. It didn't surprise him. There was something about storms in Amber Ville. Once a storm descended, it literally went from daytime to nighttime within minutes. Outside, the sky grew steadily darker, and the car accumulated more snow as it continued to creep up the road.

"How much further is it?" Rachel said, her voice laced with worry.

"It shouldn't be much further," Luke said, not taking his

eyes off the invisible road. "It just seems a lot farther away because of how slow we're moving. Keep a lookout for a cairn to our right."

"A cairn?"

"Came with the property, from what Naya told us," Kelly said.

"So, it marks what area of the property exactly?" Rachel asked.

Michael tapped the landmark on the map that came with the car. "It means we should be five minutes walking distance to the front door of the house."

"Oh, five minutes. So about two or three minutes by car?"

"Well, if you're implying that we're moving faster than walking through knee-deep snow, then yeah," Luke said.

"I can't reach Naya," Kelly said, tapping on the screen of her phone. "I'm still not getting any signal at all."

"Maybe the power's out?" Rachel said.

"That wouldn't be a surprise," Kelly said. "Luke, be careful, honey. The wind gusts are getting stronger."

As if the wind heard her, a particularly strong one hit them from their left. The car jerked and free-slid to the right and then immediately to the left. Despite the seatbelt, Michael's shoulder slammed into Luke's before he was thrown against the door. From the back seat, he heard Rachel's scream.

"Hold on, everyone. The car's lost traction." Luke didn't quite shout, but the panic in his voice was clear.

"Pump the brake, don't floor it," Michael snapped.

"I am, and I'm not," Luke said, his cheeks bulging as he struggled to regain control of the car. "God, you sound exactly the same as when you were teaching me how to drive."

"Be thankful *I* taught you how to drive."

The SUV came to a sudden stop, and Michael's head jerked painfully to one side. "Ouch." He closed his eyes and attempted to move, but a sharp pain lanced through his neck muscles. He held his breath for a moment before letting it out. After a moment, the pain abated. Only then did he open his eyes to check on the others.

Luke had his forehead on the steering wheel with his eyes closed, but he didn't appear to be injured. Michael slowly looked up, thankful to no longer feel pain in his neck. He could barely make out the SUV's hood because it was mostly buried in a snowbank. Thankfully, it didn't look like they'd hit anything too solid. Not that he could confirm it with any conviction.

He carefully turned around to check on Rachel and Kelly. "We hit a snowbank, but the airbags weren't' triggered. How are you two back there?"

"We're okay," Rachel said as she helped Kelly straighten up. "Barely got jostled, thanks to the pillows and bags around us. I think you two got the brunt of it. Are you okay?"

Mile breathed a sigh of relief. "We're fine. I think I pulled a muscle on my neck, but it's tolerable."

"Michael, wrap your scarf around your neck," Kelly instructed. "Like a collar. It's just a precaution until we get to Naya's. I'll check you out once we're there. For now, it'll have to do. We can't take any risks out here."

"Yeah, I'll do that." Michael grabbed his thick scarf and wrapped it snuggly around his neck. With the added support, he felt much more comfortable.

Other than disheveled hair, the two women didn't look as winded as he felt . . . or Luke looked. He tilted his head to the left, then right, but other than a slight pull on his neck muscle, he felt all right. Looking down at his cell phone, he still saw no signal. Glancing in the sideview mirror, he saw only snow behind them. Swallowing, he stared at the white blanket surrounding them, growing thicker with each passing minute. He knew they either could wait for a cell phone signal or get out of the car and walk up the rest of the driveway. If they stayed in the car, the likelihood of freezing was a fact, but if they walked, they could probably make it without freezing.

"I don't think we should stay in here," Luke said, echoing Michael's thoughts. "If we get out now, we can beat the worst of the storm and be at Naya's in no time."

"Luke's right," Michael said. "We'll be in more danger if we stay in here."

"What about our stuff?" Rachel said.

"We can come back for them once the storm clears. Otherwise, bring only what you can carry in your shoulder bags. Things you can't do without should the storm make it impossible to go down to the city. Like medicines." Michael proceeded to sort through his backpack.

"That sounds like a plan," Kelly said. "Rachel, place whatever you can carry in your bag, and I'll do the same. This isn't the full brunt of the storm, so we should take advantage of it now."

"It's so cold out," Rachel said. "What about clothes? And the wine. I brought it specially for tonight, now we'll have to leave it."

"I'm pretty sure Naya's got alcohol in her extensive pantry, Rach. It's either we brave the cold or freeze to death," Luke said. "As for clothes, I say we take whatever we can wear or fit into our packs. But don't bring anything that can weigh you down."

"I guess you're right. All right, let's get out of this thing." Rachel huffed. "Knowing Naya, she's got extras of everything."

Michael reached for the door handle and pulled the latch. He struggled to push the door against the snowbank until he finally managed to open it enough to get out. A cold blast of icy wind hit him in the face and made him gasp, which was a mistake. He immediately pulled the scarf higher over his face when the insides of his nose burned.

He heard Luke grunt as he did the same on his side. Rachel and Kelly were luckier, they had been spared dealing with the snowbank, but they also made sure to cover their faces with their scarves. All around them, the snow sparkled with ice crystals that were there one minute and blown into powder the next.

The four of them quickly secured the belongings they were leaving behind. Michael made sure the more valuable items were placed in the trunk for safekeeping. When they were done, Luke made a last-minute check and then closed the hatch.

"All set?" Michael said, looking at Luke.

"Yes. Shall we?" Luke said with a decisive nod. He pressed the fob, and the locks engaged with an audible click.

"Michael, secure that scarf around your neck," Kelly said.

"I did, and my neck feels fine," Michael said.

"I'll check you out as soon as we're at Naya's," Kelly said, pulling her parka around her. "Did you bring your medicines with you?"

"Yes, Dr. Rollins. I have them all here." He smiled, patting his satchel.

"Good. Naya is thorough. She'll probably have enough medical supplies and equipment to stock a clinic. Luke, you lead the way. Rachel and I will follow you and Mike after," Kelly said with quiet authority.

"All right. Let's move out." Luke winked at him.

Michael had to stifle a grin but didn't say a word. They all turned as one and started walking in the order Kelly stated. He looked up again and saw the heavy snowfall. Although they all wore thick padded clothes and heavy parkas, Michael didn't know how long they would keep warm should they lose their way.

He ducked his head, thoughts of freezing out in the snowstorm whirling in his mind as he trudged through the snow.

He could already feel his lungs burning from the exertion, but it wasn't something that alarmed him. COVID or not, this sort of weather was enough to hurt anyone's lungs.

After two minutes of ever-dropping temperature, Michael feared they would most likely not make it unless they got rescued. Despite his gloved hands and the scarf protecting his face and neck, his cheeks ached, and his fingers and toes were losing feeling by the second as they trudged forward.

A calm had settled around them, where before, he could hardly hear his thoughts over the howling wind. He welcomed the silence. At least they were getting some reprieve from the storm, but he knew it wouldn't last.

CHAPTER SIX

Time lost all meaning as Michael's thoughts momentarily drifted to his near miss with death. He'd been confident in his health and never imagined catching the damned virus and ending up in the ICU for just under a month. His physical therapist would burst a vein should he find out what he was doing at that moment. He was supposed to be staying warm and resting.

The snow glistened under the light from the phone app he was using, almost teasing him with its cruelty. The light shifted, making him look up to see a different light dancing on the low clouds. Looking over his shoulder, he hoped to see a car or a truck, maybe a snowplow. What he saw was two sets of glowing yellow eyes followed by the sounds of a growling engine and two sharp honks.

Do mirages happen in a snowstorm?

The pair of headlights pierced the darkness, getting bigger and brighter as they came closer.

"Am I imagining it, or is that a car coming toward us?" Rachel said.

"It's a car. It's a goddamned car," Luke shouted as he hurried to Michael's side.

Michael's heart beat a little faster, sending blood circulating through his extremities, delivering painful jabs into his fingers and toes. "We're not seeing things. It *is* a car, and it's coming up fast."

"Oh, thank God," Kelly said. "I hope it's Naya, come to rescue us."

"Wasn't she up in the house when you last spoke to her?" Luke said.

"Well, she mentioned that her friend Carol had driven in for the weekend," Kelly said, joining Michael and Luke.

"Whoever it is, I hope they stop to rescue us. I need to pee," Rachel said, hopping in place.

The tiny car continued to creep toward them, and Michael began waving his arms over his head. The car drew to a stop, and the window rolled down.

A shadowed face leaned out, and a woman's voice called out bright and clear. "Dr. Rollins? Is that you, Luke?"

Michael lowered his arms and turned to Luke. "I think she knows who you are."

Luke walked over to the car. "Yes, it's me. Luke Rollins. Who am I speaking to?"

The woman grinned brightly. "Hi, Dr. Rollins. Hi, Luke. It's me, Carol. Carol Sweetman. I'm staying with Naya for the weekend. She told me you lot were coming. I drove by an SUV by the side of the road a while back and thought you had somehow gotten stuck out here. Come on, get inside the car. It's small, but it's never failed me."

"Oh, thank God, Carol," Kelly said as she hurried toward the car. "I'm glad to see you,"

"I dropped in unexpectedly, as Naya expected me to do." Carol giggled.

Michael didn't speak as he followed Kelly, Rachel, and Luke to get inside the car. He didn't miss the fleeting frown on Luke's forehead as he opened the door. Rachel got in after Kelly and Michael took the seat beside her. Luke sat in the front with Carol. Michael's curiosity grew when Luke flashed Carol a quick smile. He'd known Luke most of his life, and that had to be the fakest cheerful smile he'd ever seen on his friend's face.

"Everyone set?" Carol gave them all an assessing gaze. "I

bet you're frozen. Let me adjust the heater."

Michael felt the hot air rise from the vents under the front seats and overhead. He immediately felt better, only to bite back a curse when pain radiated from his toes and fingertips again.

"Ouch," Rachel whimpered beside him.

Kelly moaned but held out her hands toward the waves of heat.

"You all should thaw out soon enough. The best news is, we're less than five minutes from Naya's front door," Carol said. "You all shouldn't worry about supplies. Naya's got loads of it, enough to last at least six months. I also brought supplies from town."

Michael blinked in surprise. If they were five minutes away from the house, that meant they'd been stranded much further than he'd first realized. Luke mentioned the driveway was about half a mile long, and they'd driven for a while, so how could that be?

"What about the perishables?" Rachel asked.

"Believe it or not, the house came with pantries, an underground cold room, and an ice cellar, where there's no need for electricity to keep the items frozen, especially during winter. She's also got a couple of generators set up for the main house and for her refrigerators and freezers in the kitchen, should it be necessary."

"I keep hearing about these pantries. How many has she got, exactly?" Michael said, unable to contain his curiosity.

"I'm not so sure, really." Carol chuckled softly. "She mentioned she had a truckload of ice blocks delivered last week, but her explanation of why she did that went over my head. Let's just say Naya loves to can and preserve, and she makes loads of them. She told me her goal this year is to can a thousand edibles."

Rachel gasped. "A thousand? What's she going to do with

all that food?"

"You'll have to ask her." Carol shrugged. "Maybe she's hoarding food."

"Naya has always been a non-conformist. While in therapy, she said her new life goal is to be independent of external resources," Kelly said. "If I were to take an educated guess, it's not that she's hoarding, just being self-sufficient. Now that she's got the ability to do so, she's making sure she continues to do so into the far future."

"And then she'll probably incorporate the canning and preserving into her company." Luke chuckled. "Naya never does anything without purpose."

"It's why she's a very successful businesswoman." Kelly's grin radiated wide with pride.

Carol huffed. "You mean making money out of hoarding food?"

Carol's question startled Michael, and from Luke and Kelly's expression, they were just as shocked as he was.

"Mind telling me what's wrong with Naya making money?" Rachel's tone held an icy hardness.

Michael clenched his hand, adding a mental fist pump, glad his sister was not one to tolerate bullshit, and what Carol said was exactly that . . . crap.

"It's nothing serious," Carol said, her voice high. "I just never thought of connecting what she's doing as something one can make money from."

"Well then, you don't know Naya at all now, do you?" Rachel challenged.

"Who does, really?" Michael observed how Carol's hand gripped the steering wheel.

Rachel opened her mouth to say something else, but Kelly placed a hand over Rachel's. Rachel closed her mouth, but her gaze never wavered from Carol's reflection in the rearview mirror.

"Carol, as Naya's friend, you should know by now how talented and business savvy Naya is. Everything she does has a purpose. Especially when it involves her business." Although Kelly's tone sounded neutral, it left no doubt that she didn't tolerate any insult to her daughter. "Now, how much longer before we get to the house?"

"Not long, Dr. Rollins. We're almost there." Carol said, her tone subdued, but the nervous tremor in her voice couldn't be missed.

"Very good," Kelly said. And that was that.

Michael's curiosity peaked. He'd always been aware of Naya's non-conformity to expectations. Her choice to become a social media influencer was a prime example. Both her parents were doctors, and Luke was in his fourth year in medicine. It had shocked everyone when Kelly stopped practicing. She now assisted Naya in running her fast-growing business, which had taken a completely different turn but was apparently very successful.

Luke had mentioned that he and Kelly had taken on bigger roles during Naya's recuperation. Even after Naya returned to work, Kelly remained involved. Michael couldn't find any fault in that. Time away from running the business apparently gave Naya the time to change focus. It appeared her focus was on her new home and making food. How she integrated it into her existing business would be interesting to learn.

His gaze shifted back to Carol. He could be wrong, but she appeared to be in her early thirties. Many would even call her attractive, especially with her fair skin and midnight black hair that flowed over her shoulders. Her personality had seemed bubbly when she'd first approached them in her car. However, her acerbic comments about Naya made him quickly change his mind about his initial impression of her.

He also wondered about the barely hidden and thinly

veiled hostility coming from Luke and Rachel. If it were only Rachel, he could fully understand, as she was very protective of those she considered family. Luke's reaction, however, was what had captured Michael's attention. Luke was an easy-going guy who was only truly serious when it came to his studies and his family. Michael deduced that Luke had some unfavorable knowledge regarding Carol, considering his previous response toward her. Kelly wasn't much different, either. She was almost clinical in her behavior toward Carol.

All this made him wary of the woman. Who was she really? And why did she act like she had authority or influence over Naya? As far as Michael knew, Naya was not someone to boss around or easily manipulate.

One thing he would give Carol credit for was her ability to drive. Not long after they were all settled, she was speeding up the driveway. She handled her little car well on the icy road. When it lurched forward, she was quick to react to maintain control. Michael couldn't wait until they reached the house so he could get out of the car. Powerful wind gusts rocked the small vehicle, making him feel nauseous. Luckily, Carol managed to keep them moving forward.

He breathed slowly through his nose and counted to calm his stomach but kept his focus locked on the road. He couldn't believe his eyes when a clearing suddenly appeared directly ahead of them. Then he caught sight of the house. The scene looked like it had been plucked straight out of a Thomas Kinkade painting.

The car's headlights barely cut through the heavy snow, but from what he could see, Naya's stone-clad Colonial-style home stood surrounded by a low fieldstone wall. A thick blanket of snow covered the roof and tops of the walls. The orange glow beyond the windowpanes shimmered delightfully, reflecting on the snow in millions of dazzling stars. The house looked old and new and so very warm and welcoming.

A fleeting shadow beyond one of the curtained windows on the second floor caught his attention. It seemed odd and out of place for some reason. The movement was too fast, and the dark shadow shape appeared too strange. His brows slowly furrowed as he kept staring at the window.

"Other than us, is anybody else staying in the house with Naya?" He asked no one in particular.

"No, it's just us," Carol said. "Why?"

The curtain moved slowly to one side and paused before falling back into place. It wouldn't have been weird if someone had been there, but Michael hadn't seen anyone. So who or what had moved the curtains?

"Just asking," Michael murmured, not wanting to speak of what he'd seen to the others. He also couldn't help feeling that maybe he was entering a situation he wasn't prepared for.

He couldn't help but feel nervous about seeing Naya again. He still remembered the chaos when the news of her disappearance had first aired and the horror he'd felt when Luke had called him in the middle of the night, asking him to help find her. He hardly recalled how he'd managed to catch a redeye flight to Los Angeles or how he'd found his way to the hiking trail where she'd been last seen. Hundreds of people, all of them strangers, had shown up. All had been prepared to do whatever it took to find her. Only then did he realize how beloved Naya had been by her followers.

He could never forget that incredible day when a follower had arrived with six of her friends and their search and rescue dogs. They hadn't stopped to rest after their long flight and had immediately hit the trails. It had taken them and their dogs six hours, but they'd found her, barely alive but still breathing and fighting for her life, her body broken and her face unrecognizable from the fall. It was only later they discovered that her ex-fiancé had viciously hit her face over and over with a brick.

The next day, the same group of women had gone out to search for her ex, only to find him face down at the bottom of a cliff, not far off from where they'd found Naya. The police had encountered no signs of a struggle and presumed he'd been ridden with guilt for what he had done and jumped.

And now Michael was here, about to see Naya again after two years.

What would she look like now? He knew she'd undergone a series of plastic surgeries to repair the damage. Of course, he did. He'd been the one to have the highly skilled surgeons flown in for her. Kelly was the only one who knew. Not even Luke or Rachel knew. Not even Edward, Naya's father. When Kelly had asked him why he didn't want anyone to know, he'd confessed to her about his feelings. Kelly hadn't even looked surprised. She simply thanked him for the help and promised not to say anything until he was ready.

As far as Michael knew, Naya still had no idea how he felt about her. He only hoped that two years was enough time for her to recover, maybe not fully, but enough for her to accept his involvement.

"The weather's cleared a bit," Carol said, stopping the car in front of the house. "I don't think this will last too long. We better move fast."

The wood-framed glass front door opened, and Naya's tall, curvy figure appeared. He couldn't believe how beautiful she looked, framed by the elegant rustic entry of mosaic stone.

"Mom! Luke! I'm so glad you made it. Just in time, too. It's warmed up a bit, believe it or not." Naya grinned broadly in welcome. "How was your trip?"

Although she wore a thick cable-knit sweater, she looked cold as she ran her hands up and down her arms. Michael wanted to rush out of the compact car, take her in his arms, and keep her warm, but he caught himself. Naya would get confused and wonder what had gotten into him. Besides, she was busy hugging her mother and brother. He could wait. He'd waited years for Naya to be free. Patience was key. It had to be. After all, Naya Rollins was the woman he'd been in love with since the first day he met her.

CHAPTER SEVEN

Michael opened the car door and immediately realized the outside temperature was tolerable instead of freezing. The weather of an incoming storm was incredibly temperamental. He was just glad he and the others were no longer in danger of freezing. With Naya, Kelly, and Luke still greeting each other, Michael thought to give them a moment to themselves and moved to help Carol with the groceries.

"I got it," Carol snapped, grabbing the paper bag he had in his hand.

He released the bag without uttering a sound, extending his hands and moving away. He hadn't done or said anything to warrant Carol's attitude towards him, but he couldn't exactly confront her about it. Carol didn't even look at him as she grabbed the two remaining bags and slammed the hatch closed. Without sparing a look or saying a word to anyone, she stalked into the house.

If he didn't know better, he'd think he had personally affronted the woman. Thankfully, the Rollinses were spared Carol's attitude, since they were preoccupied with their reunion.

Michael shook his head as he watched the woman disappear into the house. Something was truly off with Carol. He hitched the strap of his bag higher on his shoulder and took in the surrounding scene.

The beautifully restored colonial home immediately evoked a sense of charm. Luke had informed him that it was registered with the Vermont State Register of Historic Places.

Naya's restorations had been done in a way that honored the home's original style. He'd always liked the architecture, as the homes were solid structures that were built to last generations.

The main house structure was classically colonial in symmetry. The addition of right and left wings gave it a unique character. However, those also looked to be part of the original design, so it must have been an older structure than the more common Colonial Revivals.

"Naya," Rachel squealed as she finally staggered out of the car.

Naya laughed as she turned away from Luke and Kelly and held out a helping hand to Rachel. He'd never heard a more beautiful sound.

"Rach! Girl, I missed you so much." Naya gave Rachel a hug.

"Hey, I told you I was coming over as soon as I heard the house was done." Rachel laughed when Naya turned to glare at Luke. "No, it was your mom, silly. Don't you know we're phone pals?"

"Phone pals? I haven't heard that term since the eighties." Kelly shook her head, then nudged Naya. "You've improved on the house since the last time I was here."

"You did a good job. It's stunning." Luke threw an arm over Naya's shoulder as he gazed up at the house. "This is a lot of house for one woman. Are you sure you're going to be fine out here all on your own?"

Naya shrugged but grinned broadly. "I suppose it can be a lot to handle for some, but it's just perfect for me. As for help, don't worry. I'm not yet at the point where I'd need any, but once I start with the rest of the projects I have in mind, I will need that help. I've already talked to several people in town who said they can recommend some names."

Luke had told Michael about the changes brought about by

Naya's injuries and surgical procedures. He couldn't remember the medical terms Luke spoke of. All he knew was that nerves had been affected, and nothing could be done to fix it. Hearing Naya's voice sound deeper than it used to be would take some time to get used to, but it was still her voice.

As for the nerve damage, he could see some of it. The need to kill her ex all over again swept over him. What had happened to Naya still made him angry enough to lose all sense of logic. It was one reason why he'd stayed away.

Naya briefly leaned her head on Luke's shoulder before looking over her shoulder, and their gazes met. Michael smiled and walked over to her, but then she lowered her eyes.

"Hey, you," he said.

Naya immediately looked up, but she still hesitated to come to him. He couldn't have that.

"Come here, beautiful," he said, opening his arms.

Naya turned all wide-eyed, laughing like an excited child before flying into his arms.

He laughed as he caught her. She wrapped her arms around his torso and laid her head on his chest. He tightened his arms around her, closed his eyes, and breathed in her scent. Tears threatened to spill, but he swallowed them away and kissed the top of her head instead. He wanted to do more, but it wasn't the right time. When he finally opened his eyes, he met three pairs of all-knowing eyes. Heat rose to his cheeks, and he looked away.

"You came," Naya said. She leaned back and gazed up at him. "I missed your face, big Mike."

"I missed you as well. I'm on vacation for another two months and thought I'd make the most of Luke's invitation. I couldn't resist the opportunity to join him here. Hope you don't mind."

Naya's smile brightened, but the flush on her cheeks made him think she missed him as much as he did her.

"No. I don't mind at all," she murmured.

"Good to know. Now, let me look at you." He cupped his hands, keeping them an inch away on either side of her face, but didn't move to touch her.

She closed her eyes but stayed still. It was all the permission Michael needed to gently clasp her face between his hands and focus on scrutinizing her face. The plastic surgeons had done miracles to repair what they could. Other than a slight change to the shape of her face and a small droop to her left eye because of minor nerve damage, she looked exactly the same. He ran the tip of a finger down the affected side. She would bear the scars for the rest of her life, but he was certain of one thing . . .

"Beautiful," he whispered.

Naya opened her eyes, staring at him for the longest time until she finally broke their locked gazes by laying her head on his chest once more. "Don't disappear again, you hear?"

Michael felt his heart stutter. For the first time, he felt a possibility that Naya felt more than just friendship toward him. He drew in a deep breath and wrapped his arms around her again. "Never. I promise."

"That's good," Naya whispered into his chest. "I expect you to keep that promise, okay?"

"I promise to keep my promise," he whispered back.

"I'm sorry to break the reunion, darling, but I think we should get inside," Kelly said.

Naya stepped away. Michael wanted to hold on, but he reluctantly let her go.

"Oh, my God. What was I thinking? Let's all get inside." Naya looked out at the driveway and then turned a questioning look at her mother. "Wait a minute. What happened to your car? And where are the rest of your things?"

Rachel let out a sigh. "We had a minor accident on the way over. It was pure chance Carol got to us when she did."

"What? Oh my God. Here I was, making you stay out here and getting cold. Is everyone all right? No injuries? No, don't answer that. Come on. Let's talk inside." She hurried to the door and opened it.

A funny-looking dog gave a huffing bark and ran out the front door. It sniffed the car tires before running through the deep snow toward the perimeter wall.

"Jenny, come back here, girl," Naya called out, clapping her hands, but the dog turned mid-run and disappeared into the deep snow. "Ach, Jenny girl. You're a menace."

Jenny's head popped up from beneath the snow, surging up amid a shower of powdery snow. Still panting and running, she returned and sat in front of Naya.

"Jenny, come. Introduce yourself to Michael."

Jenny stood and walked over to him, and he couldn't help but stare down at the funny-looking canine.

"What kind of dog is she?" Michael leaned down, holding out the back of his hand.

Jenny sniffed at it for a long moment, her ears perked and her tail unmoving. Suddenly she got excited and placed her paws on Michael's legs. Unable to resist the charm, Michael patted her head.

"She's a Pocket Bully," Naya said. "Don't worry, she's more lapdog than guard and loves strangers to the point she'll welcome them."

Surprised, Michael looked at the mean-looking but adorable dog and then back at Naya. "I would think from the way she looks, she'd be more guard dog."

Naya rolled her eyes. "She's my deputy dog. Come on, let's get everyone inside. Jenny, inside now."

He chuckled when Jenny stayed close to his side. "I guess she likes me."

"You're going to be stuck with her for a while." Naya's grin disappeared when she looked up. "Let's get all of you inside."

Michael looked up to see the angry gray clouds that looked much lower than they had been ten minutes earlier. The wind picked up as well, and the temperature dropped.

"Let me show you around." Naya led them through the large entry.

The front door stood easily three feet taller than Michael. It felt odd to feel dwarfed, as that didn't happen often. Naya closed the door after Michael followed Kelly, Luke, and Rachel inside. He breathed in the lovely scent of warm spices mixed with the wood of the furnishings that perfectly fit the ambiance of the place.

They entered a foyer with a high ceiling and a uniquely beautiful light fixture above dangling from a heavy metal chain set into the crossbeam high overhead. To one side, elegant shelving built into the woodwork easily spanned eight feet with a bench, several storage areas, and hooks to hang jackets and bags. To the right was a louvered door that Naya opened to reveal a large closet. They all took off their heavy coats and hung them inside.

Rid of the heavy outerwear, Michael felt the warmth surrounding him. The smell of scented candles and wood-burning fire filled the air with such a homey, comforting scent that it lulled him to relax. The house had a welcoming feel to it, almost like he was being embraced. He closed his eyes, took a deep breath, and let it go slowly. A strange feeling flowed over him, almost like he was being observed. Feeling self-conscious, he opened his eyes only to see the others exiting the room and going deeper inside the house.

Curiosity piqued, Michael followed the others through the ornate French doors. He was greeted by an open and spacious main level. His gaze was drawn to the large living room at the bottom of the stairs and the wall of windows that afforded views to the front and side gardens. The windowpanes were frosted by snow, but he could clearly see the stormy weather outside.

Michael whistled under his breath, impressed by the understated elegance surrounding him. He was accustomed to the finer things in life, having grown up in Chicago in a house that had been in their family for over two generations. What Naya had designed would make anyone who stepped inside feel immediately like they had come home. The sense of welcoming that came over him felt different, though. He wasn't quite sure why.

The stone entry gave way to glistening wood floors, open rounded archways on both sides, and a large room beyond. Shabby chic and rustic furnishings, like the glistening wood of the tables in the sitting room, added to the lived-in feel. A large stone fireplace graced one wall, and Michael strode over to examine the craftsmanship of the mantel. It was filled with pictures of the Rollins family, and to his surprise, several were of him and Rachel.

The pictures were a mixture of old and new, some going back to sixteen years ago, judging from the one showing Luke as a toddler perched on Michael's hip. It was such a startling inclusion, and he still clearly remembered the day it was taken. Their parents had gone to a party, and as the eldest, Michael had been left to babysit. He hadn't minded and had enjoyed himself immensely. They had servants to watch over them, of course, but he'd taken his duties seriously.

He looked over his shoulder and sought Naya's attention. "Did this mantel come with the house?"

Naya walked over to his side. "Yes. It's original. There is one down here and one in each of the three bedrooms upstairs."

"I see you've included us." He kept his voice low as he gestured toward the pictures.

Naya touched one of the frames with the tip of a finger. "Of course. You're my family."

"Thank you."

Their gazes met and held for a moment. Michael's heart skipped a beat at Naya's expression. There was a sadness in her eyes he couldn't quite interpret. He'd never intended to be away for so long.

"I intend to keep my promise, Naya."

Naya didn't respond, but a soft smile formed on her lips. Somehow, that hit him harder than he'd expected.

He cleared his throat before asking, "How much restoration for those alone?"

Naya looked relieved at the change of topic. She blinked rapidly, but her smile broadened to a grin. "Surprisingly, not much. The historical society said the previous owners used the fireplaces to heat the house, so they were the ones to have them repaired and maintained."

"Lucky."

"Extremely. I saved a lot of money, thanks to them."

Michael looked toward the kitchen. From the bank of refrigerators set against the far wall and the largest limestone-topped island he had ever seen, he could only imagine it to be the kitchen of Naya's dreams. Her personal domain.

"Interesting." Michael wandered toward the kitchen.

"The kitchen is actually why I thought I should stay here for a week," Kelly said. "You have no idea what that kitchen does to me."

"It's what one would call kitchen porn for her." Rachel snickered.

Naya laughed out loud. "I know, right? You should have seen the faces of the crew when the limestone slab got delivered."

Michael joined in the laughter. "Can't say I blame them. That island is huge."

Kelly rolled her eyes, looking amused.

"As you can see, there's plenty of space, but it's not too big to handle or get lost in," Naya said.

"Everything turned out lovely, darling," Kelly said.

"Thanks, Mom. It's a little different from what you're used to in Chicago, but it's home."

"It's a little isolated, don't you think?" Luke said.

"It's the isolation that drew me here, Luke," Naya said.

"It's not that isolated, Naya," Rachel said. "I used to say that, too, when I first visited Michael here, but the town and its people are lovely."

Naya tucked her hair behind her ear. "I need to go down there more often. I'm getting to know more people here, though. And yes, the town is lovely."

Luke approached the coffee station and rubbed his hands together. "Now this is more like it. Don't mind if I fix myself some coffee."

"Go ahead. Help yourself." Naya waved a hand at him, then suddenly snapped her fingers and turned to Rachel. 'I have to take you to the diner I found there."

"Good?" Rachel asked, raising a brow.

"*Very* good," Naya said.

While Naya and Rachel talked about the diner, Michael walked up to the staircase. Located at the far left of the main floor, it curved upward to the second-floor landing, where he assumed the bedrooms were located. He stepped closer to the banister and examined the workmanship. It was most definitely hand-carved, not the smooth, almost too-perfect look of machine-caved spindles. The gleam of the wooden handrail also looked to have been stained and oiled by a craftsman. To his expert eyes, it was most likely the work of a local artisan and somehow made Michael proud of Naya's choice of workmen.

"Ah, perfect."

At the sound of Luke's voice, Michael turned from his examination to see Luke sipping from a mug.

"No, Michael. None for you," Rachel said.

Michael grimaced. "I know, but can't I just dream?"

"What did I miss?" Naya asked, looking from Rachel to him.

Michael took a deep breath. "I've been limited to two cups of coffee a day."

"Oh, no way." Naya looked horrified. "I could never . . . But how did that come about?"

"It's not a ban, just a precaution because of the medications," Kelly interjected. "He had to take a lot for a long time."

"Ah." Naya turned to face him. "Don't worry about it. It's not the end of the world. And it's temporary, right?"

"I know," Michael said, smiling at Naya. "But I miss it. I had the worst headaches at first, but I'm used to it now."

Their gazes met and held, then Naya lowered her gaze and turned away.

He decided to change the topic. "How much land do you have?"

"Not enough." A smile tugged Naya's lips, and she visibly relaxed. She tucked her hair behind her ear, a flush of red staining her cheeks. "I love how open it is out here.

"You're just greedy, Naya."

CHAPTER EIGHT

Michael startled with shock as he processed the boldness of the statement. Curious about the voice, he turned around, only slightly surprised to see Carol stepping off the stairs. She ignored everyone, headed straight to the coffee station, and poured herself a cup.

He turned to Naya and saw a flash of irritation cross her face. When she saw his gaze, she looked away. Whatever was going on with Carol didn't sit well with him. He wanted to snap at her but held back since he hardly knew the woman, who was supposed to be Naya's close friend. Instead, he chose to take the high road, but he wasn't sure how much longer he could hold onto his patience.

"That's quite a statement, Carol." Kelly frowned. "Are you throwing that declaration out to show your lack of support for her business endeavors, or are you implying something else?"

"Not accusing at all. I'm just saying—"

"I didn't say you were accusing her, but now that you mention it . . . ." Kelly let the comment drift off to an unvoiced question.

"She clearly said that Naya's greedy." Rachel stepped next to Kelly.

"That's not what I—"

"Just shut it, Carol, why don't you?"

"Rachel, be a dear and make me a cup of tea, please," Kelly said.

Rachel walked to where Carol stood by the coffee station,

stopping in front of her. "Do you mind?"

Carol raised a brow at her before stepping to one side and facing Kelly. "All I'm saying is there are lots of people out there who have no place to live, and here she is, buying up tracts of land that's most likely going to be too much for her."

"Who would've thought that with your profession, you'd still have that much time on your hands."

Carol turned to Rachel. "What do you mean exactly? Why don't you just say it?"

"What you just accused Naya of? It's how Sarah got her head bashed in." Rachel poured hot water into a teacup.

"Who's Sarah? What are you talking about?" Carol glared at Rachel, but when she didn't get an answer, she turned around to face Naya. "Naya? What is she talking about?"

Rachel shrugged as she placed the tea bag in the cup. "You're a Jamie, that's all. I love Yellowstone."

"What the hell does that even mean?"

"I'd take a breath and attempt to calm down, Carol," Kelly suggested. "You're working yourself up."

"But what is Rachel implying?"

"Nothing. Yellowstone is a particular Netflix series that is her favorite. You should watch it," Luke said. "Now, why don't the two of you drop this unnecessary drama? You're both forgetting we're guests in Naya's home."

"But—"

Rachel walked past Carol to hand over the teacup to Kelly. "Here you go. It's mint tea and chamomile. Cleanses the palate and settles the stomach."

"Rachel. Carol," Kelly said in a soft, warning voice. The soft smile she gave Rachel, however, ruined the reprimand. "Why don't we take a seat over by the window?"

Kelly and Rachel proceeded to walk toward the chairs by the front window, leaving a gaping Carol to stare after them. Without saying a word, she went over to where the two women now sat, pulled a stool, and sat by Kelly's side.

"I apologize," Carol said in a soft voice.

Michael unclenched his teeth and turned to Naya. He laid his palm on the small of her back and gently rubbed it. "I know what you meant. About the acreage. It's never enough around here, is it?"

Naya looked up at him, her eyes glittering with relief. "I know the acreage is extensive, but you know how I've always dreamed of running a homestead."

Michael threw a brief side-eye in Carol's direction before redirecting his gaze back to Naya. "I supposed *some* would see your need as greed, but that's not how I see it. I remember you talking about a homestead back when you were still in high school, way before you went the influencer route."

"You remember that?" A grin blossomed on Naya's face.

"Of course I do." Michael ran his palm down her back re-assuringly. "I have always believed that more would be better because then you always have something new to discover, a fresh challenge to get over. I think that living life without any challenges is uninspired. What would be the point of waking up every day if there's nothing new to look forward to?"

"Why don't you just enjoy what you already have?" Carol said.

Michael heard the obvious condescension in Carol's tone and didn't like it one bit. He also felt Naya tense beneath his hand and sensed her irritation. She'd clearly heard the same thing.

"Everybody's different, Carol." Kelly smiled.

Michael had known Kelly for a long time, so he didn't miss the glint in her eyes as she spoke.

"Naya's got more than enough. Why seek more land? What if she can't handle it?" Carol turned and smiled at Naya. 'You know I worry about you. All I'm saying is that you're all alone out here, and more land means more work."

Kelly walked over to Luke, took the mug he was holding, took a sip, and returned it to him, then she turned to Carol. "Some people are content once they get to their end goal. As a friend, you should know that Naya's not like that. She seeks, she enjoys, and she goes further by creating more goals. That is why she is very successful in what she does." She intently held Carol's gaze.

Carol shrugged and faced Rachel with a clear change of subject. "Rachel, I'm thinking you and I share a room. I'll show you upstairs?"

Rachel's eyes widened at the obvious snub to Kelly but she covered it up with a chuckle and turned to Naya. "Do you mind if I go upstairs with Carol? I really need to get out of these clothes."

Naya waved a hand toward the stairs. "Oh sure, go ahead. Your room's two doors from the top to your right."

"I'll show her where it is. No need to worry yourself about it," Carol said.

Michael could not believe the audacity of the woman.

However, Naya turned her back on Carol to face him. "While Carol takes Rachel up to their room, why don't you and Luke come with me? I'll show you where you'll be staying."

"How about me?" Kelly asked.

"You can stay in my room, Mom," Naya said.

"I know where it is," Kelly said. "Go ahead and show Luke and Michael their room. I'll go take a shower."

"I'm guessing our rooms are in the other wing?" Luke asked.

"Room. Originally, there were three bedrooms upstairs, but I joined the smaller middle one to the master's and turned the extra space into a master bath. And you're correct, your bedroom is in the other wing. It's quite large, so neither of you will feel crowded. It used to be the servants' dormitory, but it didn't come with a bathroom, so I had one installed."

"Sounds perfect," Luke said.

Naya and Luke walked side by side while Michael followed behind them. They crossed the main floor to get to a small hallway. Naya opened a door to reveal a steep and narrow stairway. On the landing, he peered out a small window that faced the back of the house, where he could see a barn. A sudden wave of dizziness hit him. The scene wavered, and for a moment, he swore the house heaved a sigh before it righted, and everything was normal again. The strange feeling made him straighten up wide-eyed and look around him. He shook his head, and a lancing pain pierced his temples. He closed his eyes, wondering what was going on.

"Michael?" Naya asked, her voice bringing him back to the present. "Are you all right?"

He feigned a smile. "A sudden headache."

"Your room's right here, so you can lie down for a while."

"No, no. Don't. It's likely because I'm tired and hungry."

Naya looked relieved. "Food isn't a problem. Why don't you change into something more comfortable and come downstairs? If the food doesn't fix your headache, I've got some tablets that can take care of it. Do you have clothes to change into?"

"Yes, we all took out spare clothes before leaving the car."

Naya looked at Luke. "We should discuss how to rescue your things, but I think we can't do anything until after the storm."

Luke nodded. "Do you still have spare clothes stored somewhere?"

"Yes," Naya said. "You know I always have extras."

"Just in case," Michael said in sync with Luke. He gazed at Luke, and they laughed.

Luke turned to Naya. "Don't ever change, sis. As for a shower, Michael, why don't you go ahead? I can wait my turn."

Michael nodded. "Thanks, Luke. Don't mind if I do."

"Nah, don't worry about it, man." Luke waved a dismissing hand. "Take your time. I'll go down with Naya and watch TV. Maybe play with Jenny."

"Thanks," Michael said, feeling self-conscious. "I'll see you downstairs when I'm done."

Naya smiled. "Food should be ready by then."

When Naya and Luke left him alone, he dropped his bag on the floor. He cautiously bent his neck to the left. When he felt no pain, he curled it to the right. Other than a slight pulling sensation, there was no discomfort. He'd have to get Kelly to check him out, but he knew that, physically, he was okay.

Looking around, he saw a typical guest bedroom with twin beds and a dresser placed between them. He glanced at the clock sitting there, which read half past five o'clock. It surprised him to see how early it was. He walked over to the window and drew the curtain to one side. There was still enough light outside, but unlike earlier, the barn was no longer visible.

It suddenly struck him that their venture up the driveway and Carol's rescue had happened within a span of fifteen minutes at most. But then, in snowstorms like this, time always seemed to slow down, and those fifteen minutes had felt like a lifetime.

A shiver ran through him. Only then did he realize that his clothes were damp. They must have thawed out from the heat in the house. One thing he knew for sure . . . He needed to get out of the clothes and into the shower.

He whistled his appreciation upon opening the door to the huge bathroom. The expansive counter boasted two wooden trays. One held an assortment of miniature-sized hand soaps, lotions, shampoos, and conditioners. The other had toothbrushes and shaving kits still contained in sealed plastic bags.

The shelf over the toilet held a stack of different-sized towels and extra supplies of individually wrapped toilet paper. With the addition of floral wreaths and scented candles, Naya had instilled the hotel-like bathroom with a cozy and inviting atmosphere.

He was in the middle of taking off his shirt when he heard footsteps outside the door. "Luke? Is that you?"

When he didn't hear a response, he shrugged it off. He was stepping out of his trousers when he heard the footsteps again. For a moment, he debated what to do, but he clearly heard someone in the bedroom. Finally, he pulled up his pants and buttoned them closed. He opened the bathroom door and peered out, but the bedroom was empty. His forehead twitched from fighting a frown and sensing something peculiar going on. Maybe the shadow he'd seen earlier when they pulled up to the house had a bigger impact on his psyche than he'd realized. Unable to shake off his uneasiness, he abruptly decided not to mention or acknowledge anything. Normally, he wasn't one to take on the attitude of *out of sight, out of mind*, but considering the events of the day, he needed to maintain his denial. He did not even want to think about anything strange.

What he needed was a hot shower.

He removed his pants, stepped inside the cubicle, turned on the faucet, and immediately let out a groan of pleasure when hot water poured over him. He was humming quietly and washing the shampoo and soap over his body when a sound made him look up. It was quite faint, and he had to tilt his head to the side to focus on the sound. The footsteps were light at first, but then they got heavier, and he saw something move beyond the foggy enclosure. He didn't know what to expect when he slid open the shower door, but he was alone in the bathroom. A soft thud came from outside the bathroom, adding to his unease as he recalled stories about old houses.

He heard more footsteps from the bedroom, getting louder and heavier, sending fear of the unknown coursing up and down his body. The rhythm changed, and the footsteps started pacing back and forth, then stopped just outside the bathroom door. The water temperature dropped, and he quickly turned off the faucet. He was not a man who was likely to show his fear to anyone, even himself, but this was something he couldn't shake off.

He grabbed a towel from the rack and hurried through the motions of drying himself. He'd planned to shave but had no desire to stay in the bathroom longer than necessary. With the towel wrapped around his waist, he entered the empty bedroom with no sounds of footsteps. He studied the ceiling as he pulled a t-shirt and a pair of shorts from his bag.

Old houses usually came with cavernous attics, and it was common for animals to crawl into such spaces. Yet Michael suspected the footsteps he heard were from a two-legged creature wearing heeled shoes.

He glanced through the open bathroom door at the clothes he'd dropped on the floor and then at the pair of sleeping shorts in his hand. Why he'd only thought to bring sleepwear beat him.

"T-shirt and shorts, it is." He knew the clothes were not enough, but he didn't have anything else. Still thinking over his lack of planning for proper winter wear, he suddenly remembered Naya's just-in-case attitude.

Curious, he opened the closet door and stifled a laugh when he saw two thick robes hanging on wooden hangers. On the shelf were four packs of white t-shirts and two pairs of thick sweatpants, one gray, the other tan. Said items were still in their original plastic. He also spotted at least ten pairs of disposable slippers in their plastic covers stacked on the bottom shelf. He grabbed the tan sweatpants and put them on. They were more decent and warmer than his sleeping shorts.

Naya had not changed. She always stayed one step ahead, thinking of others and making sure her guests never lacked anything. She was an incredible woman, and he couldn't help thinking how proud he was of her.

Not wanting to spend more time alone, he grabbed a package of disposable slippers and sat down on the edge of the bed. He was tearing off the plastic when the bathroom door slammed shut behind him. The suddenness of it made him freeze, his mind trying to comprehend what had just happened. There had been no draft to cause the door to shut like that.

I'm not going to freak out. I'm not going to freak out. I am too old to freak out. Just breathe. Get a hold of yourself. Maybe there was a draft. After all, this is an old house.

Even as he tried to tell himself it was nothing, he wasn't convinced. There was one thing he did know . . . He had to get out of the bedroom and join the others downstairs.

As he opened the bedroom door and stepped into the corridor, he saw a silhouette of a person standing at the end of the hallway. There was something odd about whoever it was, and he was still processing when the shadow zipped straight into the wall. It moved so fast that he thought he was seeing things at first. But then it reappeared before darting out of sight again . . . .into the opposite wall.

"Oookay." He placed his hands on his hips and stared at the empty hallway.

Nothing moved, not that he expected it to. The wall in question looked solid enough, but he still had to make sure. Gritting his teeth, he stepped up to the wall and peered at the architecture. There was nothing strange about it. Just a plaster wall, from the looks of it. A cold, gentle breeze blew past him, making him look around, but the sudden drop in temperature made him shiver. As he scanned his surroundings, the windows seemed tightly sealed, and he saw no visible exits leading outdoors. He couldn't think of a logical answer to what was going on.

Outside, perimeter lights cast a soft glow over the view, and he could clearly see the heavy snowfall. It took him a moment to realize he was standing at the exact window where he'd seen the curtain move. As he gave the view outside a last look, something cold brushed past him, not quite unlike the breeze, but it was enough to make his hair stand on end.

"What the fuck is going on?"

CHAPTER NINE

M ichael walked into the open space of the main house. His stomach immediately reacted to the delicious aromas filling the air. A quick inspection of the room let him know that none of the ladies were present. There was no sign of Luke either, and he wondered where the man went to watch TV.

"Hello," he called out, but there was no reply.

Nothing but a kettle sat on the six-burner stove in the kitchen. The island, however, had several dishes on it. He walked over to inspect what was on offer. In the island's center was a large wooden charcuterie board with an assortment of meats and cheeses and a variety of fruits and pickled olives. His mouth watered at the sight. It looked professionally made, but his gut told him Naya had been responsible for its preparation. He recognized her style—overly complex, yet simply done. The sound of footsteps coming from behind him made his heart race. He turned quickly, expecting an empty room, only to see Naya coming down the stairs.

"Did I startle you?" Naya asked.

Michael grinned. "You did, yes."

Naya's smile broadened. "I'm sorry. I should have said something when I thought I heard you call out earlier, so I came down to check on you." She glanced up at the clock on the wall. "What can I get you?"

"Don't worry about me. I don't mind serving myself," Michael said. "Besides, you've already laid out everything."

Naya gestured toward the coffee station. "There's a pot of

coffee ready should you want something hot. There's also tea. The mini fridge under the island has plain and flavored bottled water and sodas. There's also beer and wine."

"Thank you," Michael said. To his embarrassment, his stomach growled.

Naya laughed. "I'm hungry, too. Come on, let's eat."

"What about the others?"

"Luke's watching a DVD on the TV in my room. He told me to give him a yell when it was time to eat. Mom's reading a book. Carol and Rachel are in their room."

"Do you want me to fetch them?"

"You can just give them a yell from down here."

Michael shook his head. "Just like when we were kids."

"Exactly." Naya grinned as she walked to the coffee station and poured herself a cup of hot water from the electric kettle. "Tea?"

"Not now, thanks."

Naya dropped a tea bag into her mug. "The power came back when you were taking a shower, but I doubt it'll last long. You might have noticed the shift earlier. It sounds like a soft thumping."

Nick blinked at Naya in surprise. "Like footsteps?"

"Footsteps? No. It's more of a sharp drum sound, but it should have been muted, considering your room is on the opposite end of the house from where I installed the generators. Why do you ask?"

"Nothing, just asking. You have generators?"

"Yes. One for the house, two for the refrigeration units, and another one for the heaters for the water pump. They kick in automatically when the power dies."

Michael leaned his hip on the island and crossed his arms in front of him. "I have the same system at my house. Power outages are used as a precautionary measure whenever there's a storm. Aside from nasty snowstorms, we also have electrical storms. More often, those happen in the summer months, but not necessarily."

"I suspected the cut earlier was precautionary, but thanks for confirming it." Naya wrapped her hands around the steaming mug and blew on it. "So who's calling the others?"

"I'll do it. I'm louder." Michael walked over to the stairs and bellowed, "Let's eat!"

Naya chuckled when an answering yell came from upstairs.

"We're coming!" Luke yelled back.

Naya's girlish giggle made him turn to her. She was grinning into her cup and looking at him mischievously. "I haven't heard that bellow in years."

"I won't do it again." Michael walked back to the island, rubbing the base of his neck.

"What's wrong? Did you hurt yourself earlier?" Naya put down her mug and walked up to him.

"I pulled a muscle, that's all. Don't worry about it," Michael said, but he stood still when Naya placed her hands on his neck.

A light frown formed between her brows as she examined his neck. "Is there any tenderness?"

"None. But when I looked up the stairwell, I felt a slight pulling sensation."

"Hmm . . . Mom would have to give you a closer examination. When you move your head, is it painful?"

Michael turned his head to the left and then to the right. "No, no pain. Only when I stretch it."

"Is everything all right, Naya?" Kelly called from the stairs. "Is Michael's neck giving him problems?"

"Only when he stretches it," Naya said over her shoulder. "I'll go get a neck brace. I'm sure I still have some from my hospital stay."

"Do that, please, sweetheart. Now, Michael, I want you to

sit on the stool so I can test your range of motion. Let me know if you feel any pain and how painful it is."

"Okay." Michael pulled out a stool and sat on it.

Kelly proceeded with her physical examination, asking him questions, which he answered as honestly as he could.

Naya came back with a collar in each hand. "Mom, I have a soft and a rigid. Which one do you need?

"Just the soft one, Naya." Kelly held out her hand.

Naya gave Kelly the soft collar, which she carefully placed around his neck. "Is Michael okay? He won't need an X-ray or a CT scan?"

"I feel fine, Naya." Michael raised his arm, and Naya immediately moved close enough for him to curl his arm around her waist. Only then did he catch Kelly looking at them. To his surprise, she smiled and walked away.

Naya frowned. "Are you sure you're not in pain, Michael?"

"I'm sure," Michael reassured her. "Now, let me up so we can eat."

"Michael's going to be fine, Naya." Kelly didn't look up as she began to place food on her plate. "The collar is only a precautionary measure. And no, he doesn't need an X-ray or any sort of scan." She turned to face him again. "Wear the collar for two or three hours, but don't sleep with it on."

Naya left his side to get two plates from the other end of the island. He walked to her side and was about to get a plate for himself, but Naya handed him one she had in her hand.

"Thanks." Michae smiled down at her.

Naya waved at the island. "There's cheese lasagna, vegetable casserole, roast chicken, and three rice dishes. Rice pilaf, garlic rice, and biryani. I'd only intended to include the lasagna, but I wanted to give everyone more choices. There's also choice meats and cheeses on the charcuterie board."

Michael laughed. "When did you make all this?"

"Except for the charcuterie, just this week. I had a live

presentation earlier and showed my followers how to make a board for under a hundred dollars. I'm not sure I made the right choice of title, though. Food here is so cheap compared to other cities."

"You have more in your extensive storage system?"

"Oh, definitely. Enough to feed us for about a month."

"What will you do with the food you can't eat?"

"Most of what I make lasts from three months to a year frozen. The rest I take to the sheriff's station and the three churches here."

Michael wagged a finger at her brilliance. "Ahh, good call keeping the authorities fed."

"I hate waste, and have you been to the station? They survive on donuts."

Michael wanted to laugh at Naya's horrified expression but stopped himself. "I'm sure they appreciate whatever food you give them."

"Last week, I brought them a casserole, and the way those men dug into it made me think they're not being fed at home. When I told them it was a vegetarian dish, they looked shocked and horrified but then dove into it like a pack of hungry wolves. Good thing I made three. Two were meant for the church, but those poor deputies." Naya shook her head.

Michael rubbed her shoulder. "I've never seen you like this before. You're good at whatever you do, including cooking. So why sound so shocked? People like your food, Naya. I like your food."

"Who said your food isn't good?" Luke said from the stairs. He was carrying an empty plate and a wooden bowl. "Cool collar, Michael."

"No one's saying her food is bad, Luke," Kelly said. "Did you check on Rachel and Carol?"

"Yeah, knocked on their door and told them to come downstairs. Carol said Rach's still drying her hair."

"Let's go sit, then," Kelly said.

"Oh, lasagna." Luke rubbed his palms together as he reached for a clean plate.

Michael rolled his eyes only to break off into laughter when both Kelly and Naya did the same.

"What? I'm a growing child," Luke said as he started spooning food onto his plate.

"Don't they feed you in that dorm of yours, Luke?" Naya asked.

"The food served at the cafeteria is nothing compared to this."

"I just reheated everything, Luke."

"Exactly."

They were discussing the latest storm notification when Kelly broke off and looked toward the stairs. "Ah, finally."

Michaell looked over his shoulder to see Rachel stepping off the stairs, closely followed by Carol.

"Your hair looks good, Rach," Luke said.

"It should," Carol said. "She wasted so much time on it."

"She's just mad because she found out I don't dye or perm my hair to get it to look this way." Rachel didn't break stride as she headed to the island.

Luke leaned to whisper to Naya. "What did I miss?"

Since Michael stood between them, he heard what Luke said.

Naya pursed her lips, and a frown settled between her brows, but she didn't say anything.

Luke stood up and pointed at the chicken and rice dishes. "You'll really like those, Rach."

Carol joined them on the other side of Luke and made a show of studying the various dishes. "Did you order these, Naya?"

Michael blinked in surprise. How could someone who claimed to be Naya's best friend not know Naya had prepared everything?

Luke glared incredulously at Carol. "Are you serious?"

Michael heard Rachel's audible gasp even from where he sat.

"Really, Carol?" Rachel said. "Didn't you tell me, several times, that you're Naya's best friend?"

"And?" Carol glared at Rachel.

"And yet you don't know that Naya has been a superb cook for as long as I can remember. I grew up with her cooking."

"Really?"

Rachel laughed disparagingly. "Yes. Really. Luke, do you think I can abuse your lifetime friendship and love for me to fetch me a glass of wine?"

Luke gave her a salute and a smile.

Naya spoke up when Luke glanced at her. "There's a compact unit behind you."

"What do you like?" Luke asked as he turned and disappeared from view. "We have red, white, blush, and . . . oh, coffee liqueur."

"Red, please. Thanks, Luke," Rachel said. "It'll go well with the choices on the charcuterie board Naya prepared. Naya, this is gorgeous."

Michael smiled, conscious of the chemistry between his sister and best friend. Luke had always been a sucker for Rachel's attention. Even Michael's mother had privately suggested the two should date. He wondered what his parents would think when they found out he was in love with Naya.

Rachel lifted the charcuterie board in one hand and carried it over to the dining table. She placed the board in the middle of the table and then set her plate next to where Luke had been sitting. With Kelly seated at the end of the table, Rachel's choice left only the chair beside Naya empty. Luke came back with four bottles in hand. Naya started to stand, but Michael stopped her.

He placed a hand on her arm as he stood. "Let me. What did you want to get?"

"Oh, wine glasses."

Michael went to the cabinet where he'd spotted the wine glasses and took five out. He returned and placed them on the table before taking his seat again. Rachel started peppering Naya with questions about the preparation of the charcuterie board, and Naya answered them. Carol sat down and remained silent the whole time. Naya, Rachel, and Luke switched to discussing the best wines they thought would go well with the meats and cheeses. Luke got up again and came back with two more bottles because of a wine choice Kelly requested. Michael continued to eat as he watched the byplay, ever vigilant to the tension between Rachel and Carol.

It was clear Rachel and Carol's time together in the bedroom had resulted in female rivalry. What he couldn't understand was Carol's obvious jealousy of Rachel, though he'd seen it several times through the years. Rachel was a highly confident young woman, taking after their mother's great beauty and born into a wealthy family. Always an incendiary combination, in his opinion. Especially for those whose self-confidence and esteem were less than hers. It didn't matter if they were men or women. Jealousy didn't care about gender.

Thankfully, the bitchy contest had stopped, and everyone ate in peace, talking about the food and Naya's refrigeration units. Naya's cheeks flushed a bright red when they teased her about it.

"Carol mentioned you had several tons of ice blocks delivered, Naya," Luke said. "What on earth for?"

"Let me tell you about ice cellars," Naya began, but a distant rumbling interrupted whatever she planned to say. It was followed by the flickering of lights.

Luke began a countdown. "Three, two, one . . ." The power

cut.

"The generator should kick in about now," Naya said. They waited and waited in the dark, but nothing happened. "Why didn't the power shift?"

"It could be a number of things," Michael said. He grabbed his cellphone, turned on the flashlight app, and stood up. "Luke, come with me. Let's go check the generators."

"Hold on, let me grab flashlights," Naya said. She came back with two flashlights and a box of matches. "Rach, Carol, do you mind lighting the candles? Michael, are you sure it's okay for you to go outside?"

"I promise not to make quick movements that could aggravate my neck muscles, but yes, I'll be okay."

"He'll be fine, Naya. I'll make sure he behaves," Luke said, laughter lacing his words.

"Be careful out there, you hear?" Naya handed both of them the flashlights.

"We will. Don't worry," Michael said. He turned to Naya. "Where are the generators?"

"It's just outside the side door," Naya said, pointing to the door in question.

"Okay, let's get this done," Luke said.

He and Luke went to put on their parkas and gloves before exiting the house. The temperature change from warm to cold somehow made the cold outside worse than he'd anticipated. Already, the chill easily penetrated through the thick layers he wore.

"It's freezing out here," Luke said, warming his hands by breathing into them.

Michael did the same, but his throat already felt raw. "Let's get this over with quickly."

Luke nodded and pointed at a wooden shed about ten feet from where they stood. "That's strange. The door's open."

Michael frowned as he looked at Luke but didn't say

anything, lengthening his stride to plow through the snow as fast as he could. Luke matched him stride for stride. They both reached the shed at the same time, and Luke pulled the door wider.

"Well, I'll be damned," Like said and glanced back at him.

"What is it?" Michael peered inside and stared at the four generators standing side by side, all gleaming white. Against one wall was something draped with a tarp. "This makes no sense. These are all brand new."

"I remember Naya saying she'd checked on these earlier."

"Let me see. I have the same ones installed, so I'm familiar with the specs. These are highly reliable, and I've never had a problem."

"Go ahead," Luke said.

The first thing Michael checked on was the oil levels. One look and he had the answer he needed. He turned to Luke. "They're all empty."

"How can that be? Naya isn't the type to make a mistake like this." Luke went from one machine to the next. "She's not that absent-minded."

"No, far from it. Someone did this on purpose." Michael checked the floor but saw no signs of oil spillage. "Do you know where she keeps the extra fuel?"

"Yes. She was telling me about that earlier. It's in the barn. The safest place to store it, since it's far from the house."

"It may be, but it's going to take a while walking over and hauling the cans back here."

"Naya does have a snowmobile."

Michael met Luke's gaze and burst out laughing. "Why do I keep forgetting Naya's penchant for the just-in-case scenario? All right, do you know where it's parked?"

Luke thumbed over his shoulder. "Should be under that tarp. The shape fits."

Michael looked beyond Luke. "Of course, she'd park it

here. All right, let's get this done."

Luke threw off the tarp to reveal a gleaming red, two-seater snowmobile. "Help me attach the sled."

"She thought of everything, didn't she?" Michael said.

Luke chuckled. "She wouldn't be Naya if she didn't think of everything. Come on, the temperature's dropping."

He and Luke quickly bolted the sled in place and were on their way to the barn in no time. The temperature continued to drop as they loaded four containers onto the sled.

"We'll need to come back to fill up the other two generators," Michael said.

"We better hurry, then," Luke said.

Neither of them spoke much as they hurried through their task. They left the containers outside the shed before going back to the barn. Although they worked fast, Michael could feel his earlobes burning. By the time they had refilled the tanks of the four machines, half an hour had passed.

"Let's go back to the house," Luke said.

"I'll move the mobile back inside, and then we can lock up." Michael straggled the mobile and walked it inside to its parking spot. As he got off, he felt something under his foot and looked down to see what he'd stepped on. To his surprise, it was a key with a tag attached that read *SHED* in dark, bold print.

Luke and he closed and locked the door of the shed. As they walked back to the house, he played with the keys in his pocket.

"Luke?"

"Yeah?"

"I found the key to the shed. It was on the floor." Michael pulled his hand from his pocket and opened his palm.

"Fuck. That makes it look like someone went in there and purposely emptied the fuel tanks."

"As we came in together, and Naya is not the type to

sabotage her own safety, I'm thinking of two things."

"Naya told me Carol dropped in at two this morning. Unannounced. She didn't like it." Luke frowned. "I know for a fact Carol hasn't been around since before the accident."

"Either Carol did it, or someone else did. I don't like pointing fingers, but there's no other explanation. Someone in the house did this. Someone who was here before us."

"When I called Naya from the airport, she said she was at the store buying supplies."

"What time was that?"

"Just before we boarded," Luke said.

Michael stopped in front of the side door but didn't reach out to open it. "I don't know what's going on, and I hate pointing fingers at someone we hardly know."

"We'll have to talk to Naya, but not now."

"I hate keeping this from her, but you're right. I think we should tell her when the others are not around."

"I'll signal you when I can get her alone, all right?"

"Deal. But if I get her alone before you do, I'm going to tell her. I hate keeping things from her."

Luke nodded. "In the meantime, let's not mention the key in your pocket either."

CHAPTER TEN

Naya put away the last of the dishes she'd hand-washed when she heard the generators kick in. The lights flickered for a moment before steadying.

"Ah, we got power," Rachel said from where she sat at the table.

"That's the generator, Rach," Naya said. She picked up a rag and wiped down the counter.

"Sweetheart, now that I can see my way around, I'm going upstairs. All that food and wine made me sleepy." Kelly stifled a yawn as she stood up. "Excuse me."

"Go on ahead, Mom."

Kelly paused. "I wonder what's keeping the boys?"

"I heard the snowmobile earlier."

"Ah." Kelly grinned and shook her head. "Boys will be boys. Goodnight, girls."

"Goodnight, Mom," Naya said, not pausing from her cleaning.

Carol and Rachel called out their goodnights at the same time.

Naya cleaned until satisfied, then she washed and hung up the rag to dry.

"Naya, will you please sit down? Come here and join us," Rachel said.

"Listen to Rachel, Naya," Carol said. "The food will keep. Have some wine."

"Naya doesn't drink, Carol. You ought to know that."

Naya faked a smile. The bickering between Rachel and

Carol was beginning to wear on her nerves. Luke and Michael still hadn't come in, and she was about to go outside to check on them when the side door opened, bringing in the chill from outside.

"Finally," Naya muttered to herself. She pasted on a bright smile and faced them head-on. "Did you guys have fun with the snowmobile?"

Luke grinned broadly, but the look he exchanged with Michael didn't make sense. Naya frowned and was about to ask what she was missing when she heard someone approach from behind her. She looked over her shoulder to see Rachel joining them.

"Luke, what took you so long," Rachel said.

Naya noticed Carol pouring herself another drink. She'd lost count of how many glasses Carol had already consumed. Yes, she knew Rachel and Carol could handle their alcohol, but having finished two bottles within an hour, it was clear they had drunk more than enough.

"Your friend drinks like it's a competition," Rachel whispered as she walked past to help Luke out of his parka.

Michael hung his parka in the closet and turned to her. "Is there still hot water in the kettle? It was hell out there."

"Yes, but you go ahead and sit. I'll make you some tea."

"Forget tea. Have some wine with me, Michael." Carol's husky voice sounded closer.

Naya couldn't believe what she heard and turned to see Carol walking up to them, holding a glass of red wine out to Michael. Infuriated over Carol's blatant flirting, Naya started to walk away, only to be stopped when a hand grasped her elbow.

"Thank you, Carol, but I don't drink red," Michael declined in a polite tone.

Speechless, she could only stare when Michael placed a hand on the small of her back and gently directed her to the coffee bar at the other end of the kitchen counter.

"Can I have some brandy instead?" He spoke conversationally as they walked. "It was brutal out there, and I think I need something stronger than tea to heat my insides faster."

Michael met her gaze, a soft smile curling his lips. His eyes, though, were what captivated Naya. He was looking at her with an intensity she couldn't quite interpret, and it was doing funny things to her insides.

"I . . . Of course," she said. Then her mouth dried when Michael bent near her ear.

"I need to talk to you privately if you don't mind," he whispered. "Smile and pour me a drink."

All thoughts of his captivation flew from her mind and imagination. "What happened out there?"

They reached the bar, and Michael picked up a bottle and began to study it intently. He looked up and spoke over Naya's head. "Luke, I need your opinion. Can you come here for a second?"

"Sure thing, bro." Luke bent and said something in Rachel's ear before leaving her side.

Naya gritted her teeth. She did not miss the horrible acting, and it appeared that Rachel hadn't either. She got up with Luke, grabbed Carol's arm, and led her out of the kitchen.

"Why don't we go enjoy the fire in the sitting room?" Rachel suggested, taking up the half-full charcuterie board in one hand and her wineglass in the other.

"Sure," Carol said, shrugging. "Looks like Luke and Michael want to talk to Naya in private. Let's bring the wine, too."

The two women walked away without a backward glance.

When the girls were out of hearing distance, Naya turned and glared at Michael and Luke. "That was very subtle, boys. Your acting sucks as much as ever. Now tell me, what's going on? Speak."

Michael leaned a hip on the counter. "Someone sabotaged the generators."

Naya gaped and quickly turned to seek confirmation from Luke.

Luke nodded. "All four were empty. I remember Mom saying that you told her you'd checked on them this morning and that they were full. When Michael and I got to the shed, not only were they empty, but whoever emptied them also took off with the canisters. We had to go to the barn to get more fuel. Took us two trips."

Naya stared out the window of her downstairs office. Jumbled thoughts left her feeling confused. Finding out that someone had deliberately sabotaged the generators made her stomach turn. After Michael and Luke narrated what they had discovered, she quietly excused herself, leaving her brother and guests to their own devices.

She'd tried so hard to stay strong, to show the world she had moved on from the tragedy and on to a new and hopefully happier life. How was she supposed to tell anyone that her fears persisted? Or that she continued to be haunted by thoughts of what she could have possibly done to provoke Andrew's murderous actions?

Andrew's death had clearly not stopped the threat. It was becoming more obvious that he might not have been the only one who had wanted her dead. If she were to go by Luke and Michael's theories, only one person had the chance to empty the fuel tanks after she'd left for town that morning. Carol. Maybe they were right, but she had her doubts. Her property was not the only homestead in the area, and short of putting up a wall or security fence, anyone could come in and out on foot or by vehicle.

She stared at the phone Sheriff Ferrise had made her install, as it was the most reliable form of communication, especially during storms. He had pointed out that, considering her history, it would make his job of safeguarding her easier. She picked up the receiver and listened to the modulating tone of an available line. As she dialed the number, the nervous fluttering in her stomach made her realize just how anxious she was about what had happened.

The Sheriff answered after the third ring. "Ferrise here."

"Sheriff, it's Naya Rollins. You told me to give you a call should something happen." She quickly relayed what Luke and Micheal had told her.

"It'll be difficult with the storm, but do you want me to send a car over?" Ferrise asked after she finished her story.

"No. I mean, it could have been anyone." Naya briefly closed her eyes. "I don't want to point fingers with no proof."

"All right, I'm going to make a report for documentation. With your history, it's best we record everything that happens. Whatever it may be."

"What do you mean by *whatever*?"

"Anything out of the ordinary."

Memories of the ghostly figures she'd seen came to mind. "This house is strange, but it's not something I'd call in to report."

"Why not?"

The question startled her. "I mean, I can't call you every time . . ."

"Every time something strange or weird happens up there?"

For a moment, Naya didn't know what to say. "I wouldn't want to waste your time, sheriff."

"Nothing is more important to me than ensuring the safety of the people in this town, and I never consider it a waste of time."

Naya chuckled. "Even invisible visitors?"

"Let me tell you something, Ms. Rollins. I grew up around

these parts. Been sheriff for over twenty years and in the service ten years before that. The things I have seen, nothing surprises me anymore. I'm going to disconnect now. In the meantime, be safe. The landlines are still working, but who knows what will happen once the brunt of the storm hits us? Be safe, Ms. Rollins. Goodnight."

Her conversation with the sheriff replayed in her head as she closed her office door. The kitchen was empty when she entered, but she heard Rachel and Carol's voices coming from the sitting room. Indecision rocked her. Logic told her that Carol deserved the benefit of the doubt. However, she couldn't deny what she suspected, no matter what she'd said to the sheriff. Deep down, she knew Carol was involved, but the extent of that involvement eluded her. As for going into the sitting room and playing host . . . there was no way she could avoid anyone, even if she wanted to. The storm made sure of that.

Pasting on a smile, she went into the sitting room only to stop in her tracks. Rachel and Carol sat on the floor facing each other, with the ottoman between them. On it was the now empty charcuterie board, which both were studying intently. Naya stepped closer to see what they were doing. What she saw filled her with a sense of unease. Even from where she stood, she could see the shallow depressions where she knew letters used to be. They were barely visible, but the light from the fire and candles around the room somehow emphasized the carvings. Carol and Rachel had the tips of their fingers over the upended shot glass she'd used for the almonds and were staring at the glass with an air of expectation.

"What are you two doing?"

Carol and Rachel looked up at her, wide grins spreading across their faces.

"Naya! You didn't tell us you had a Ouija board." Judging

from the way Carol's words slurred, she was drunk.

Naya gaped at Carol. "Say again?"

"Ouija. You used a spirit board for your charcuterie board."

"I did?"

"Don't tell me you'd never seen one?" Rachel asked. Her flushed cheeks were a sure sign of her inebriated state.

Naya saw an empty bottle lying on the floor near Rachel's feet, and another stood beside Carol. Fearing the wine would stain her carpet, she bent to pick them up and placed them on a nearby table.

"No, I never have. You say the charcuterie board I used is one?"

"Yes. Come on, let's test this out," Carol said. "We have set the mood. The lights are out, the fireplace is flickering, and scented candles have been lit. We can play a game."

Uncertain of what to say or do, Naya hesitated. Her hesitation apparently made Carol think she had agreed to a game, for she scooted over to one side.

Carol patted the space beside her. "Come sit beside me. We'll teach you."

Naya looked from Carol to Rachel, uncertain about what to do. Her grandmother had cautioned her against using spirit boards, so she was familiar with how they operated. But she didn't know what to expect because she'd never consciously sought one out or joined calls for a game.

"I don't think we should do this, Carol. Why don't you give me the board so I can clean it."

"Aw, come on, Naya," Rachel said, pouting prettily. "We're stuck here with nothing to do until the storm blows over. It'll keep us occupied."

"Rachel, Naya has already said she doesn't want to play."

Naya turned toward the voice coming from somewhere behind Carol. The shadows had hidden Michael well, and she hadn't seen his tall form sitting on the wingback there. She had been in the house for two months but wasn't completely familiar with the layout just yet and had forgotten the chair was there. Relying on other interior designers had its pros and cons. Not knowing exactly what was where was one of those cons.

"Killjoy." Rachel grimaced, but there was no resentment in her voice. She threw a bright, albeit somewhat forced grin at Carol and motioned toward the shot glass. "Come on, let's continue. Michael, I take it you don't want to play with us?"

Michael stood and walked toward Naya. "It's not my thing, Rach. Come on, Naya, let's leave these two to their game."

Naya nodded and looked at the empty glass of brandy in Michael's hand. "There's more of that in the kitchen."

Michael looked down at his glass. "I can do with more. It's cold in here. But what I'd really like is some dessert with it."

"Oh? I thought you said you didn't want any."

"True, but that was earlier. I find I'm craving something sweet."

She reached up and touched his bare neck. "You took off your collar."

"Kelly said to keep it on for only three hours."

"How does it feel? Any pain?"

"None. I kinda miss it whenever I make a sudden move, though." He flashed her a wry grin.

Naya chuckled. "I'm just glad you didn't hurt yourself seriously out there. Mom told me what happened. Now, about dessert. What kind do you have in mind?"

"Luke mentioned this crazy thing you do."

Naya gave Michael a side-eye as she led the way to the kitchen. "Oh, he did, did he?"

"Yes," he said in a playful tone. "That you always make two or three of the same dishes when you film your recipe videos."

"And he's correct. Would you like me to give you a tour of my pantry?" Naya flipped her hair and froze.

She didn't know why she'd done that exactly, but Michael's gaze briefly lowered to her exposed neck. Her breath caught in her throat when his gaze met hers, trapping her in his smoldering intensity. It made her think of naughty things. Suddenly self-conscious, she turned on her heels and hurried toward the kitchen.

Michael followed her through the dark house. "Luke and Kelly were talking about this pantry of yours."

She grabbed onto the comment like a lifeline toward regaining her composure.

"It's not like any regular pantry," she said, glancing at him over her shoulder. When their gazes met this time, she didn't feel the same intensity. Had she imagined it?

"Ah, I think I heard something about you having several kinds," Michael said. "I don't really know anything about pantries other than it's where I place my groceries."

"I'll show you. Follow me." Naya nodded to the door leading to the basement. They were almost at the door when the temperature dropped. It was always the same spot. She shivered and turned to face Michael. "You know what? The tour can wait."

It was all she could do not to run. Unfortunately, Michael had other ideas.

"What's in the basement?"

"The ice room. I keep most of my frozen items and sweets in there, like meats and hams, but I believe you might prefer something else. Something to pair nicely with the brandy."

Michael looked around, his face not revealing his thoughts. "All right. Where do we get this dessert you're promising?"

Naya chuckled, but she waved her hand in the general direction of the room they'd passed along the way. "In the cold room. It's just off the kitchen."

"I'm confused. You mentioned an ice room earlier. What's the difference?" Michael's forehead creased in a frown.

"You mean the cold room from the ice room?"

"Yeah."

"Well, the ice room is the frozen locker. It's self-maintaining, thanks to the ice I put in there. In the old days, they used to go to the river to cut ice. I relied on the ice plant."

"How long does the ice usually last?"

Naya shrugged. "Give or take a year."

"Wow. Saves on electricity costs, I guess?"

"I'm trying. I'm just beginning to get it all together, so the costs are a little wild."

"And the cold room?"

"It's where I keep more refrigeration units."

When they reached the cold room, she opened the door and turned to grin at Michael when she heard his low whistle.

"How many units do you have in here?"

"I've got seven."

"Ah, that explains why you have four generators."

"They're crucial for perishable foods like sweets and other foods that need freezing or refrigeration. As I tend to make a lot of those, it made sense to invest in the units to hold them."

Naya opened the third unit and took down the cheesecake nearest the door. There were two others covered in plastic wrap. Homemade preserves she'd bought at the farmer's market covered the top of the cake she held.

"I know you'll like this one. I baked it yesterday."

Michael stepped closer to peer at the delicacy. "That's New York cheesecake, isn't it?"

"Blueberry." Naya grinned.

"That's my absolute favorite." Michael grinned back, taking the dish from her.

Naya closed the door to the refrigeration unit and turned

to follow Michael back into the main kitchen. An overwhelming urge to look over her shoulder came over her. Nothing was there when she looked, but the feeling of being watched persisted. Wide-eyed, she scanned the room one last time before hurrying after Michael.

Michael stopped and looked at her over his shoulder. "Hey, what's the matter?"

Naya shook her head. "I don't know. This house is still so new to me. I've been here two months . . . I guess I still need to get used to its quirks."

He lifted a brow. "What do you mean by quirks?"

"Don't mind me." Naya ran her fingers through her hair. "It's nothing."

"It's not *nothing* if you're scurrying after me in the dark like a frightened mouse. You're no mouse, Naya."

Naya briefly closed her eyes before huffing a lungful of air through her mouth. "I don't want to sound like a scaredy cat, but I'm really glad you're here."

"This has nothing to do with the generators, does it?"

Naya shook her head.

Michael gazed at her for a moment before tilting his head toward the island. "Let's go sit down and talk about it. If it's bothering you this much, then maybe you need to listen to your feelings."

CHAPTER ELEVEN

Naya looked over her shoulder as Michael placed the cheesecake on the island, pulled out a chair, and gestured for her to sit. She didn't want anyone to overhear their conversation, but with the open layout, it would be next to impossible to prevent it. After a moment's hesitation, she decided that whatever conversation they were going to have would best be done behind closed doors.

"Not here." She grabbed two clean dessert plates and spoons she'd left on the island before tilting her head toward her office. "Come with me."

Michael silently picked up the cheesecake and followed her. She opened the well-hidden door and ushered Michael inside, then closed the door behind him. Only then did she feel secure.

"I didn't notice there was an office here," Michael said, curiously looking around as he set the cake on the desk. "Or the jib door."

"It was a selling point, actually. Whoever built it was a talented artisan. This is my safe room. Not quite an escape room, but it'll do. Other than Mom and Luke, you're the only one I've shown it to."

Michael pointed at the phone. "I have one at my house here. They made you have one installed, too?"

"Yes. I called the sheriff earlier and told him about what happened."

"What did he say?"

"That he would document the report and would send over

a car, but I refused. I didn't want those poor men to come over for nothing when they're already dealing a lot."

"I agree." Michael looked around him. "Does this come with a bathroom?"

"Yes." She pointed to a door behind him. "That leads to it, and right next to it is a passage that will take you outside and upstairs."

Michael opened the door to the bathroom and gave it a brief inspection before disappearing into the passageway. Naya sat at her desk and took the time he was away to slice the cheesecake. Not long after, Michael reappeared and closed the door behind him.

"This is all very interesting. Knowing you have this room assures me of your safety," Michael said as he sat across from her. "Now that we're here, can you tell me what is bothering you?"

Naya placed the knife on a plate and thought about what to say. It didn't take her long to decide it was best to tell him everything. She needed to tell someone, and she felt safe with Michael. She always had.

"It may be my overactive imagination, but I can't get rid of this feeling that someone's watching me. At first, I thought it was because the house was so old and bound to be creepy. But things have been happening lately that I can't easily dismiss as anything other than a haunting."

The frown deepened between Michael's brows. "I didn't want to say anything earlier, but when we first drove up here, I saw a shadow in a window on the second floor. For a while, I thought you had another guest staying over, but you've made no mention, and no one's here other than the six of us. Also, when I was in the shower, I thought I heard footsteps in the bathroom and the bedroom. As I was coming down, I thought I saw someone in the corridor. Then the shadow shifted and flew straight into the wall and disappeared."

Naya blinked. "Why would you think I'd be hiding someone?"

"No, no. I said I saw a shadow on the second floor. Twice."

"I don't have any other guests." Naya shook her head. "But when I was preparing the charcuterie board, I swear I heard something upstairs. I thought it could be the house shifting or something."

"Naya, this house has a stone foundation, and the floorboards are pretty solid. Plus, the ground's frozen."

Naya took up the knife and used its flat side to serve the cheesecake. She carefully placed the slice on the dessert plate before pushing it toward Michael.

Michael took the plate and picked up a fork. "I can hear the cogwheels in your head turning. Spill it."

"I'm having doubts about this house."

"What about?"

"Did I buy a house with character? Or did I buy a house with *characters* in it?"

"That is a useful perspective to have. I've read that hauntings don't always mean something evil is still present. Or that a ghost is automatically a demon. Most often, it is just a restless spirit or a spirit that cannot move on."

Naya chewed on a piece of cake as she pondered Michael's words. "You're absolutely right. For two months I've lived here, and not once have I felt afraid. Lately, though, something doesn't feel right, and I can't shake it off. It all started gradually. At first, there were random noises that I chose to ignore completely. But then I started seeing strange shadowy creatures in the middle of the night. Sometimes in my room, but mostly in the corridor outside the bedrooms. It has happened enough times I can now identify two that keep coming back. One man and one woman. I know there are others, but they were too fleeting."

Michael moaned and pointed at the cake. "This is so good."

He nodded before taking another piece out of the slice. "Shall I tell you what I know about Amber Ville?"

"Yes, please." Naya sighed, relieved that perhaps Michael could provide her with some answers. "Obviously, I didn't research about the town. I should have, but I desperately needed to get out of LA."

"You could have moved back to Chicago."

"No. I wanted a complete change."

"By moving here?"

"Can you blame me?"

"No. I understand why you moved and why you came here, actually. Remember, I have a place here, too, and I usually come here when I need to get away from the noise of the city."

"From the city, yes, but also it's far from where people can connect me to my life before. Now my followers only know I moved to a new place, but they have no idea exactly where." *I haven't shown my face either.*

"You wanted anonymity."

"That, and the need to not be reliant on anyone ever again."

Michael nodded in understanding. "You moved here when exactly?"

"Two months ago, but I've been in and out with the renovation since I bought the place. Not as frequently as I wanted to. Preparations for the move kept me busy in LA. I had to do a lot of maneuvering so I could relocate and continue running the business without needing to go back and forth."

"No, that wouldn't have worked out. Have you ever gone out to check the nightlife here?"

"Never. Haven't even thought about it."

"All right," Michael said, shifting in his seat. He placed his empty plate on the side table next to his chair, folded his arms over his knees, and leaned forward. "For starters, there is no nightlife."

Naya's mouth fell open. "None at all?"

"None."

"But I've seen bars around the city."

"True. They're open during the day and part of the night. Everything in town closes by ten in the evenings on week-nights. After that, all the residents stay indoors. I once went out around eleven when I made an emergency trip to the pharmacy, and I was the only one in the area. Everything was lit up like any town, but everything was closed. No one was walking on the sidewalks, no cars driving around, no signs of teenage kids . . . The streets were empty."

"That's so weird."

"Do you remember that one time when we took that Universal tour with Luke and your mom? I think you were still in high school." When Naya nodded, he added, "Well, imagine the lots emptied of people."

"Yeah. I went there a few years back for a shoot when the park was closed. It felt strangely oppressive being out there in all the emptiness."

"Well, Amber Ville is like that. Around nine in the evening, people start preparing for last calls or packing up whatever they need to. When the clock hits ten, it's like all the actors and crew left the area."

"That strange silence . . . It was oppressive," Naya recalled how scared she'd felt and how she had hurried her crew to get their filming done in under an hour.

Michael's brows briefly raised. "That same type of silence is equally, if not more, oppressive in Amber Ville beginning at ten at night."

"So, you're saying the whole place turns into one large ghost town?"

"More so during the winter months." Michael picked up a fork and placed it on Naya's untouched plate. "Eat."

Naya smiled. She picked up the fork and started eating. "Why winter?"

"I once Googled it and got a weird answer from Quora."

"I don't trust that site, but tell me. What did they have to say?"

"That Amber Ville is on the list of the top ten most haunted cities in all of America."

"You're not serious," Naya whispered.

"Very. I checked it several times and even talked to some of my staff here. They said it's all true."

"But why? How?"

"I'm guessing it's due to all the deaths that happened here back in the day."

"From a plague?"

"Mining. Mining communities established Amber Ville."

"Oh. That's terrible."

"All the mines have been shut down, but what's left of the tunnels is deep and extends for miles."

"Even here? On my mountain?"

"You're on the mountain opposite mine, but yeah. Even here."

"But your house is half an hour away from here."

"Exactly."

"Oh, this is so bizarre."

Michael raised a brow at her.

"What?"

"Eat your cake."

"Oh." She took another bite. "Go on."

"Just like any other mining community, dying in the tunnels was part of the norm. The companies didn't care much for the miners and pushed them hard so they wouldn't lose money, and those old blokes loved their money. Human lives didn't matter much."

"What happened to those companies or their owners? Were they sent to jail?"

"Ha! Nope. Although a journalist under the guise of a

miner wrote a series of articles about the situation. It caused a stir in some places, but the companies were never called out. One morning, people woke up to get to work, only to find out they'd been shut out. And that was that."

"But the city survived."

"Yes, well, there is another story behind that. One involving prostitution."

"That's quite a jump, isn't it? From mining to prostitution?"

Michael smirked. "Mining town Amber Ville saw not only the boom of silver but also a boom in prostitution as a source of entertainment for the miners. Post-mining, the prostitution trade grew, and the old town was frequented by outsiders for their exclusive services. Of course, all that was held under a cloud of secrecy. Fortunately, that all ended in the thirties when the then-governor put a stop to all illegal activities. These days, Amber Ville is a tourist attraction. And of course, there's the green environment."

Naya nodded as she chewed. "That's how I discovered this place."

"You came here on your own?"

"I just wanted to be alone. I didn't tell anyone what I was going to do. In fact, I left the house without telling Mom or Dad where I was going. Before I knew it, I was at the airport buying a ticket. I boarded the plane, and when it landed, I rented a car. I only had my handbag and wallet with me. I'd even left my phone behind."

Michael stared at her briefly before dropping his gaze to the cheesecake and helping himself to a second serving. "Your mom called me, asking if I'd heard from you. You'd been gone for a week."

Heat crept across her cheeks. "I know. I'm sorry she had to go through that."

"You want to talk about it?"

Naya lowered her gaze from his penetrating one. "All I can say is I got overwhelmed by everything that had happened. I felt so guilty about putting my family through it all. My followers."

"I'm sorry I wasn't there when things got rough with your ex."

Naya shook her head. "No one, not even you, has said his name since that day."

"Have you? Said his name or thought of him since then?"

"Andrew Schwandt. There, see? I can say his name. And yes, I've thought about him. More than I would care to admit."

"Does saying his name bring up bad memories?"

"The memories come anytime, Michael. I remember everything that happened to me, how he came to my hotel and . . . I know I shouldn't have gone with him. Of all the stupidest things I'd ever done, why did I go with him?"

"Did he ever hurt you before then?"

"No. In fact, I'd have said he was the gentlest man I'd ever known. Loving. Loyal to a fault. He moved heaven and earth just to get me what I wanted, even when I didn't ask for it."

"And yet you broke up with him."

"He was getting too intense. There was never a day when he wasn't there. I found it romantic the first couple of months, and happy I had this man in my life. But then his behavior changed. One night, I was having drinks with some of my girlfriends, you know? Girl's night out?" Michael nodded, and Naya continued. "I hadn't been alone with my friends for weeks, so I had been looking forward to seeing them all again without someone hanging over my shoulders.

"I guess I had a little too much to drink, and I went to the restroom. There he was, sitting at the bar. I confronted him about it, and he said he wanted to make sure I got everything I needed. I felt suffocated. I told him to at least give me some space and that maybe we needed to have a break from each other. He didn't argue, and then I thought I might have made a mistake because things only got worse.

"One night, I was at Carol's place. I woke up in the middle of the night, and he was there, standing at the foot of my bed, staring at me. He said he wanted to make sure I had a good night's sleep. I screamed, and Carol came into the room. She immediately called the police."

"I sense you're blaming yourself for not recognizing the red flags."

"It's not as if no one had warned me, but I ignored them. As I mentioned before, I thought it was so romantic."

"Yet you went off with him that last time."

"I did. He was waiting for me at the hotel bar. We argued, and he got overwrought, and people were staring at us. I was stupid, I know, but I would never have guessed."

"What happened next?"

"He took us to this place we used to hike a lot. I knew where he was taking me, but I thought he only wanted to talk. I didn't even see the brick until I felt my face explode. I blanked out, and next thing I knew, I was on the ground and in so much pain."

"Did he say anything before he hit you?"

"No."

"When I heard you were missing, all I could think about was not being there to protect you."

Naya closed her eyes. She couldn't bear to see the pain on Michael's face. "Michael —"

"No, it's time you hear what I have to say."

"Okay." Naya opened her eyes.

Michael's gaze never left her face. "You know how I feel about you, have always felt about you."

"I know."

"That has never changed, Naya."

"Michael."

"You don't see me that way. Look, I know, okay? I just—"

Naya shook her head. "You're wrong."

"What do you mean?"

"At first, I was so scared, and when I thought I was ready, I heard about that woman you were dating and got scared all over again. As for Andrew . . . I guess I settled on him because I couldn't have you? I know. It was stupid of me."

"What woman?"

"Luke told me she was just a colleague."

"What woman?"

"Ugh, someone sent me this pic of you attending some big event, and a woman was gazing hungrily up at you." Naya grimaced and pulled out her phone. She flicked through her gallery, found the offending image, tapped to zoom out, and held it up for Michael to see. "This one."

Michael flinched, blinking rapidly before taking the phone from her. He peered at the image for a long moment before looking up, baffled. "This woman is the wife of a colleague of mine. She's not gazing hungrily up at me."

"She is, too." Naya stood, pushing her chair back with a loud scrape on the tile and moving around the desk to peer over Michael's shoulder. She tapped the tip of her nail on the woman's face. "Look at her expression. She's drooling all over you."

Michael took a deep breath and let it out in a huff. "Naya?"

"Yeah?

"She's sixty."

"So what? Age is just a number. You're denying she's hungry for you?"

"She was not hungry for me."

"Doesn't change the fact that she's a cougar."

"A what? A cougar? What are you even talking about?"

"Is she talking about that woman again? The one in the

117

picture?"

Naya whipped around at the sound of Luke's voice. She hadn't heard the door open. How much had he heard?

"He's denying that she's got her sights on him," she said as she moved away from Michael.

"Oh, come on. She's sixty years old." Michael said. "And hold on. Why did you keep this picture in your gallery? If I remember it right, that event was back in September — *three years ago.*"

"Yeah, do tell, sis. I want to know, too." Luke folded his arms in front of him and leaned on the doorway.

Naya sputtered and looked from her brother to Michaell. Both were smiling at her.

"No reason." She shrugged.

Luke smirked. "Three years, Michael. If you were to ask me —"

Naya leaped across the short distance and slapped her hand over Luke's mouth. "Shut up!"

Luke laughed under her hand and tried to talk, but Naya pressed her hand tighter against his mouth. She widened her eyes at him in a silent warning and had just opened her mouth to speak when a piercing shriek came from the sitting room.

Chapter Twelve

Naya dropped her hand, turning toward the sound. Luke sprinted off, leaving Naya standing there until another scream followed. She ran out of the office after Luke, who was already way ahead of her. He'd always been a fast runner. She heard a chair scrape behind her and knew Michael was following her.

"Rachel?" Luke yelled at the top of his lungs.

Rachel came running toward Luke, her eyes wide with fear. "Luke! Naya!"

Luke wrapped his arms around Rachel. "What happened? Are you all right?"

Rachel buried her face in Luke's chest. "There's something . . . There's . . . There's someone . . . something . . ."

Rachel was shaking so much Naya started to worry. She looked around but didn't see Carol.

She placed her hands on Rachel's shoulders and gave her a gentle shake. "Where's Carol? Rachel, talk to me. Where's Carol?" Her heart was in her throat, but she tried to speak as calmly as she could.

Rachel pointed a trembling finger to the room she'd just left. "She's . . . she's . . . fuck . . . she's still there. I left her in the sitting room. We were playing the board, and I went to get some . . . wine . . . and then Carol screamed and . . . she . . . She said something came after her."

Naya gently shook Rachel again. "Something? What do you mean, Rachel? Talk to me!"

Rachel grabbed her head and shook it. "I don't know. I'm

sorry, I don't know. She said it was a shadow. And then she fainted."

Naya stared at Rachel.

"Naya, you stay here with Rachel. Luke, come with me," Michael said as he walked past her.

Luke dropped a kiss on Rachel's head. "Stay here with Naya, okay, sweetheart?"

Rachel wrapped her arms around her torso, but she nodded and didn't move.

Naya placed an arm around Rachel, who was trembling so hard that she led her to a chair. "Here, sit down. Do you want some water?"

"No, I'm okay. Naya, please. You can leave me here. Check on Carol. Please."

"Fainted? Who's fainted? I heard screaming. What's going on?"

Naya turned around to see her mother hurrying down the stairs dressed in one of her nightgowns. "Mom. Are you okay?"

"Yes, I'm fine. I was in bed when I heard the screams."

"Mom, take care of Rachel, please. I need to check on Carol and find out what's going on." Naya didn't wait for her mother to reply. She hurried toward the sitting room, her insides shaking from the fear she'd seen in Rachel's face.

When she walked into the sitting room, she sighed with relief when she saw Carol seated on the wingback Michael had vacated earlier. Luke stood beside her, rubbing her back as Carol looked down at her shaky hands. Michael was nowhere to be found.

"Carol? What happened?"

Carol looked up, and the expression on her face made Naya stop in her tracks. Carol's eyes were wide as saucers, her face pale as a sheet.

"Naya. Where did you get that board?"

The unexpected question puzzled her. "The charcuterie board? During the repairs, one of the men found it. The wood was of good quality, so I had it sanded and cleaned.

"It came with the house? This house?"

"Yes."

"You do realize it's not a charcuterie board? Right?"

"I don't know where you're going with these questions. It's just a chopping board." What was Carol implying?

Carol stood up, bracing her arms on the chair. "No. No. I told you earlier it's not *just* a chopping board. The symbols on it are faint, but they're clearly Ouija markings."

"And I told you I don't believe in those things, and I also remember telling you I don't play with things like that." Naya let out a heavy sigh. "But you wanted to play because what harm would it do? What's your point?"

"But you failed to mention that it came with the house."

She should be commended for holding on to her patience. Unclenching her jaw, she pasted on a half-smile. "What has that got to do with anything, Carol?"

"Because if I had known it came with the house, I wouldn't have played." Carol sliced the air with a hand.

"Hold it." Naya held up her palm, closed her eyes briefly, and opened them to meet Carol's gaze. "Why are you blaming me for a personal decision you made? I don't even *know* what happened here. While I was with Michael and Luke, you and Rachel played with the Ouija board despite my warning and have yet to reveal what took place. So, pray, tell me how I am to blame for what happened. Which, *again*, I have zero knowledge of."

"Something came at us, Naya! Something that the board brought out."

"At both of you? Rachel said you told her something came at *you* when she wasn't in the room."

Michael stepped up beside her and placed a hand on the

small of her back. The touch comforted her, but it failed to lessen her rising anger.

Luke stepped between Naya and Carol. He looked at each of them before settling on Carol. "Carol—"

"No, Luke.," Carol said, but her gaze remained focused on Naya. "You don't understand. Rachel and I hadn't even begun to play. Don't you understand? We were just talking about playing, but neither of us could recall how to go about it. We were on our phones looking up the rules when something came out of the board."

Michael spoke up. "Wait, you keep talking about this *something*. Can you just tell us exactly what it is that you saw?"

Carol grabbed onto her hair, her hands visibly trembling. "It was a shadow, like a black mist, almost thick as soot. It came out of the board itself . . . like it oozed out. And then it rushed at me and . . . and I had this terrible feeling that it was about to crush me. That's when I screamed, and when I did . . . I don't know what happened, but the next thing I knew, Luke's helping me onto the chair."

Luke looked at Carol and crossed his arms over his torso. "Was it evil?"

"No. Not evil. Desperate. Like it wanted to get out, but it was trapped, and somehow I knew it was trying to get to me, to try to escape by using me. I was paralyzed in that moment, and . . ." Carol turned a pleading look toward her. "It was absolutely terrifying, Naya."

Naya didn't know what to say or how to react, but she could feel her anger abating. She turned when Kelly entered the room carrying a glass of water.

Kelly walked over to Carol and handed her the glass. "Drink this. It's just water, but you'll need it for the headache later."

Naya watched as Carol took the glass with shaky hands. She wanted to comfort her friend, but something bothered her. Something about Carol's story didn't add up.

"Carol, you said you and Rachel were looking up the rules of Ouija. How'd you do that? There hasn't been any signal for hours," Michael said.

Naya moved closer to Michael, and as if by instinct, he moved his hand from her back to encircle her waist. Naya immediately felt a little calmer.

Carol lowered the glass, and her eyes widened more, if possible. "But we had a signal."

Michael took out his phone and shook his head. "Nope. I got nothing."

Naya took her phone and checked. Nothing. "I don't know what's going on, but the power's been out for hours, and so has the signal. How'd you two get any?"

Carol looked down at the phone in her visibly trembling hands. "I don't understand. I swear I could open the browser, and I was getting results. Here, the page I opened is still up."

Luke took the phone from her and checked. He raised his head and met Naya's gaze. "She's right. The results came in."

Michael met Naya's gaze. "Maybe there was a momentary signal, but it supports what Carol's been saying."

"Can you please forget about the signal? What I can't understand is how it even happened. You need at least two people to open the board and activate it," Carol said, taking more sips of water. "Rachel and I were still discussing who was to ask the questions and who would be the medium when that black smokey thingy came oozing out of it."

The sound of a throat clearing made Naya look over to her mother, who had her hand over her mouth, staring intently at Carol. Kelly looked up and met her gaze. A silent communication passed between them, and Naya clearly read the concealed doubt in her mother's gaze.

Kelly lowered her hand and cleared her throat. "As far as I know, a board can only respond in that manner if someone had left it open. Or someone had activated it before you and Rachel could, and it reacted to your presence."

"But, Mom, no one's lived in this house for decades. It's been empty for at least fifty years," Naya said.

"Time has no meaning. What we need to do is find out how to close it," Kelly said.

"How do we even do that?" Naya felt a headache building from the events and fatigue slowly creeping in. "What do we do in the meantime?"

"I suggest we go to sleep," Kelly said. "There's nothing we can do in the middle of a storm and no way to contact anyone who might have an idea who to call who would know how to handle these situations."

"I wish I had sage," Carol mumbled.

"Not much good that would do," Kelly said with a huff. "That's just a fad that influencers like to brandish about because it's a *thing*. My mother told me that, in situations like this, professionals such as priests, pastors, or religious individuals should be consulted. We can't mess with the supernatural or paranormal or whatever it is we're dealing with. Best we go to bed and handle this in the morning."

"Hopefully, the storm will have passed us by then," Naya said.

"I would suggest we go around in pairs," Luke said. "We shouldn't wander around alone and risk an attack."

Naya raised a skeptical brow. "Attack from what, exactly?"

"From whatever it is that attacked Carol and Rachel." Luke shrugged and met her gaze.

Naya immediately caught onto Luke's attempts to pacify. "Shouldn't we all stay together, then?" Naya asked. "My room's the biggest, and we can drag extra mattresses in there."

"Your room is big enough for six people?" Michael asked.

"It takes up half the entire second-floor area, actually,"

Naya said. "I had two rooms made into one and a smaller third converted to a walk-in closet."

"A walk-in closet? In a mountain home?" Michael's raised brow was enough to make her cheeks heat up.

She tucked her hair behind her ear. "I consulted a designer, and she said no one can live without it." Her cheeks got hotter when Michael chuckled. Thankfully, he didn't say anything else.

"Well, I certainly am not staying alone," Carol said. She stood up and placed the glass on the table beside the chair. "I'm sure Rachel isn't ready to be left alone, either."

Carol looked around. "Where's Rachel?"

Kelly motioned toward the doorway. "I left her in the kitchen."

Worried, Naya turned and hurried to the kitchen. She felt rather than heard Michael join her. They both stopped when there was no Rachel to be found.

"Where is she?" Michael said. He started to walk away but stopped and looked back at her. "I think we agreed none of us should go around alone."

Naya nodded and turned to her mother. "Mom, do you mind if the rest of you stay here with Carol while I go with Michael to look for Rachel?"

"I don't want to stay here," Carol said, looking around anxiously.

"You go ahead," Kelly said. "Luke, Carol, come upstairs with me. Rachel may have gone up. Let's take care of the mattresses, too."

"Thanks, Mom," Naya said. "Wait a minute. Where's Jenny?"

"Don't worry about her. I left her in your bedroom."

"She didn't want to come down with you?"

Kelly laughed. "She did, but I thought it was too dark to look for her if I allowed her to come down."

"Oh, okay. Anyway, just push Jenny's bed off to the side. If it gets too crowded, place it in the hallway. She won't mind."

"Don't worry about us. Call out if you find Rachel before we do. We'll do the same if she's upstairs."

Worry gnawed on Naya, and she kept glancing at Michael as they moved around the first floor. By the time they circled back to the kitchen, they still hadn't found any sign of Rachel.

"That leaves the basement," Naya said. She really didn't want to go down there, not with a power blackout, and most definitely not after what had happened in the sitting room.

Michael poured himself a glass of water and drank it down. "How far could she have gone? She could just be up-stairs."

He poured water into another glass and brought it to her. She took it from him gratefully. She hadn't noticed how thirsty she was until the first sip.

"I sense your hesitance to go down there. Care to tell me about it?"

Naya grimaced. "It's my least favorite area. It's the coldest, and I don't like basements."

"Why turn it into an ice room, then?"

"It was part of the house, and the historical society didn't allow for any of my alternate proposals. Also, that's where the men found the board."

Michael let out a low whistle. "Understood. If that was the original ice room, I think there is a huge possibility that it wasn't just a meat locker.

Naya gaped at the implication. She struggled to say some-thing, opening her mouth multiple times without success. Fi-nally, she found her voice. "You really had to say that, didn't you?"

"You started it. Look, I don't really believe in the paranor-mal or supernatural, but certain things are happening in this house that I can't explain."

"Ah. Okay then."

Trepidation gripped Naya. She didn't want to go down to the ice room. But they needed to find Rachel, and there was no way she could leave Michael to go down alone. The man was robust enough, but she knew he was still suffering from his lung infection.

"How's your breathing? Are you okay?"

"I'm fine. Thanks for asking."

"Why would Rachel go off on her own?"

"That's what I want to find out," Michael said, his voice grumbly and low.

Naya recognized that tone. Michael never got mad. She'd never seen the man or boy lose his temper in all the years she'd known him.

A loud thud came from somewhere in front of them, making Naya jump. Michael's muffled curse only made her more nervous.

"Rachel?" Michael called out.

They didn't get any response, and Naya took a deep breath before letting it go.

"Let me go grab flashlights and matches," Naya said. *It's better to be ready in case someone tampers with the generators again.*

"Do you have candles down there?"

"I'm not sure, but let me grab a pack. Oh, and batteries."

"We're not staying down there the whole night, Naya."

Naya shook her head. "Best be prepared for anything."

"All right," Michael said with curiosity in his tone.

Naya went over to the cupboard where she kept her supplies and grabbed extra batteries for the two flashlights and a couple of candles and matches. She tucked the items in her pockets and handed a flashlight to Michael.

She took a deep breath. "Shall we?"

"How far down is it?"

"Down three flights of stairs," Naya said. "It's quite deep."

"It's three floors down? For real?"

"Just two, but three flights of stairs. Steep ones. The ice needs to be deep underground to stay frozen."

"Is there any other exit from there? Or is this the only way out?"

"There's another exit. It opens to the root cellar, but that hasn't been finished yet. Thankfully, it's accessible and clear of any debris, so if we can't get out the way we're going in, we have another safe exit."

"Where does the root cellar open to?"

"The backyard. So not far. I just hope a snowdrift didn't block the exit."

"Good luck to us, then," Michael said as they headed down the stairs, his mouth set in a thin line. "I swear to God, if Rachel left through there, I'm going to give her a good shaking."

"She was scared, Michael."

"So she left the house in the middle of the storm? I don't think so."

"We can't panic now, Michael. We still have to go into the ice cellar."

"I'm not panicking. Not yet. By the way, you're right about one thing. Something's different down here from the rest of the house."

"I'm glad I wasn't imagining it. I felt it the first time I came down here. When the workers were here, they said they didn't like it either, but we dismissed it to the temperature and the fact that it's set pretty deep underground."

When they reached the bottom of the stairs, Naya immediately saw that the cold room door stood open.

"Fuck, she went through here," Michael said. "Why would she do that?"

"Rachel? Are you in here, hun?" Naya called out, flashing the light into the dark room. "She's not here. She can't even hide in the ice, as the blocks are stacked close to each other against the wall. It's impossible to get to the back or move it without causing the rest of the blocks to fall."

Michael whipped the light across the space in the middle of the room. "Where's the exit?"

"Through there," Naya said, pointing the light to the far end on her right. "Why is that door open?"

"God damn it, Rachel. I'm going to kick your ass." Michael almost growled the words as he stalked toward the door.

A powerful gust of wet wind blew in. Naya closed her eyes and averted her head as she staggered against the onslaught. It died down as suddenly as it had started. She peeled her eyes open, only to grimace at the debris stuck to her lips. Michael rubbed his right eye, cursing softly under his breath.

"Don't rub your eyes." Naya pointed at the door. "That shouldn't have been possible. The door leads to another stairwell that would take us up. It's not on ground level."

Michael plucked some debris off his shirt. "Then how did this stuff get in here?"

"I don't know enough physics to explain it, but I know it shouldn't be possible."

"Unless she left the root cellar door open, too?" He raised his hand up to his eye again but quickly dropped it.

Naya sighed. "Now why would she do that? Why would she go outside through here? If she wanted to get out of the house, she could've just left through the front door."

"You know, this isn't like Rachel at all," Michael grumbled.

Naya followed him into the stairwell, keeping the beam of light ahead of her, making sure they could see through the piercing darkness. She flashed the beam overhead and saw the emergency lights she'd had installed.

"I don't understand it," Naya said, flipping the switches off and on several times, to no avail. "The emergency lights should be on, but none of them are working. It doesn't make sense. These are all brand new."

"They've been tampered with. I hate to say it, but it looks like someone is really out to get you. The question is why."

A surge of anger came over Naya. "Are they trying to scare me out of my own home? Well, they're not going to."

"We'll have to call the sheriff. Give him an update."

Naya ran her fingers through her hair. "Why are they doing this?"

"We'll have to discuss that upstairs, not here."

"Yeah." Naya stared at the emergency light and mentally went over the electrical plans. "If I remember correctly, there should be a control panel here."

She searched the walls, trying to remember the placement of the panel.

"I think I found it," Michael said.

She turned around to see him opening a panel behind the open door. "You found it!"

Naya hurried to Michael's side just as he began flipping the switches up. One by one, the emergency lights turned on.

"Did it trip?" Naya frowned up at Michael.

"That, or whoever attempted to meddle with it had little knowledge of circuits. They simply turned it off."

"The fact remains, someone tampered with it." Naya breathed a sigh of relief. "At least we have light."

She turned off her flashlight and gave the room another visual examination before they headed up the stairwell to the root cellar door.

"Hey, do you notice that it's not as cold down here as I thought it would be?" Michael said. "In fact, it's kind of warm."

Naya shook her head. "I thought I was imagining things, but you're right. It *is* warmer here."

"I don't smell any smoke, so there's no fire."

"This is all so confusing." Naya stopped short when she

saw the exit up ahead. "The door's closed."

"Stay here. Let me check if it's locked," Michael said.

Naya nodded and watched as Michael walked up to the door.

"It's latched on the inside," Michael said, testing the knob and pushing against it with his shoulder. "It's not budging. I don't think Rachel went out through here."

"There's no other exit."

Michael nodded. "Let me check outside and see if there's anything out there that can clue us in what's going on."

He moved the bolt, and the door opened easily. Naya held up a hand in front of her as a gust of wind and debris blew in, just like it had earlier in the ice room. She blinked through the onslaught and saw Michael struggle briefly with the door before he slammed it shut and bolted it again.

"Well, there's nothing out there but snow and wind. From what I could see, there's no one out there either."

"So where did Rachel go?"

"Good question. I'm quite certain she didn't go this way. Let's go back to the main floor. Maybe the others are already with her."

"Yes, let's. I'd rather discuss our next steps for finding Rachel up there than down here. I never did like this part of the property."

"It's not the only part that's creepy."

"I know."

"Let's get out of here." Michael reached out and took hold of her hand.

Naya's heart skipped a beat the moment their skins touched. She nodded slowly and followed his lead. Michael had always affected her on a visceral level. The first time she'd felt it had confused her twelve-year-old mind. As she grew older and spoke to her friends about it, instead of gaining confidence, she had felt insecure. Michael *was* older. Why would he even consider looking at her other than as a nuisance?

Michael led her quickly back up the narrow stairs to the kitchen. The tip of her right foot snagged on the edge of a step, making her lurch forward. She quickly righted herself but then felt herself falling backward. Michael quickly yanked her toward him and wound his arm around her waist. Naya tried to pull away from his firm hold, but her body betrayed her, and she found herself leaning against him.

Michael smelled like brandy, soap, and man. His scent made her want to press closer, but she fought against the urge. When she made to pull away again, Michael tightened his grip.

"Stay close and mind your step," Michael said in a firm voice.

She tried not to think too much about how her breast was pressed up against his muscled side as they carefully made their way up the staircase. The bright beams from their flashlights cut through the darkness, and they reached the kitchen door with no further incident. They didn't speak as they entered the kitchen, and Michael closed the door to the basement behind them.

Michael made no move to drop his arm.

Naya cleared her throat. "I think I should go upstairs and find out if the others have found Rachel."

"I'll come with you." Michael still made no move to drop his arm.

"Michael . . ."

"Naya . . ."

CHAPTER THIRTEEN

Michael's eye itched like a bitch, and it took a lot of self-control not to rub against it, but it didn't stop him from gazing into Naya's green eyes. He gently stroked his hands up and down her arms. Her skin felt so soft and smooth that he couldn't help but feel a mixture of relief and tension. He'd never found the courage to touch her like he was doing at that moment, and yet it felt right that he was. Also, Naya had pressed herself closer to him, whether she was aware of it or not. Her gaze kept lowering to his lips and back to his eyes. Around them, the house seemed to sigh.

I want her. He knew he could lower his mouth over hers, and she wouldn't back away, but the timing wasn't right. On the other hand, with only their clothes between them, his whole body felt like a tightly wound coil. Naya's eyes closed, and he could tell she was struggling like he was. He moved his hands up to her shoulders and gently shook her to gain her attention.

"You first," Michael said. Even to his own ears, his voice sounded gruff.

A soft sigh escaped Naya's lips, and she closed the distance he had created. It was a clear invitation, and she was hard to resist. Her lips were rosy pink and slightly pouted. Her dark lashes framed her bright eyes.

Alarms blared in his mind. *Don't do it. Now is not the time.*

But Naya pressed closer, and Michael's resistance fell. This lush, beautiful woman had always had a grip on his heart. Logically, he knew he could accept what she offered. They were both single, and she was sending clear signals that she wanted him to make a move. The realization made him hesitate. What if she rejected him? That possibility always existed, but he'd never know for sure if he didn't try.

To his disappointment, she stepped away.

"I need to call the sheriff," she said. "Follow me."

"Can we get to your office from here?"

"Yes."

Naya hurried toward a wall and pushed with her hand. There was an audible click, and a door opened.

"Neat," Michael said.

"I thought so, too. Through here." Naya turned on her flashlight and walked ahead of him.

The narrow but thankfully short passageway stopped at a dead end, which turned out to be another door system like the previous. The lights came on as soon as they stepped into the room, and Michael immediately recognized it as the office they'd been in before.

Michael closed the door behind him and breathed into his palms. Naya went over to the phone, picked up the receiver, and frowned. She tapped the switch several times before replacing the receiver.

"It's dead," she said, her shoulders slumping.

"It was worth a try, but the storm has been building up," Michael said. "Come on, let's get out of here. We have to find the others and tell them what we discovered."

"Don't speak in front of Carol," Naya cautioned, her tone sharp.

"I wasn't planning to."

Naya closed her eyes briefly before opening them again. Her eyes shone with impending tears. "I'm sorry I snapped at you. I don't know why I did that."

He walked over to her and took her in his arms. "Hey, it's no big deal."

Naya leaned her forehead on his chest. "I don't know why this is happening, but I'm glad I'm not alone this time."

Michael tightened his arms around her. "Remember my promise earlier?"

Naya nodded but didn't lift her head.

"I'm not about to break it."

"You have your life, your work, and your own house."

"You also have your work, and as for the houses, we can talk about that later. Just accept the fact that I want you in my life. I always have."

Naya looked up, wide-eyed and uncertain, but she didn't speak. A tear escaped and trickled down her cheek. He looked down into her green eyes, gently stroking a hand over her spine. When she arched her back, pressing a little closer to him, his libido kicked up a notch. He gently touched her lips with his, and she parted her lips, which allowed him to deepen the kiss. Tremors of desire made him grip her ass tighter, pulling her closer. She moaned into his mouth. Her intoxicating sweetness made his heart thunder and his muscles taut. Lust tore through him like molten lava.

"Naya? Michael? Where are you?"

Kelly's voice doused the embers growing between them like a bucket of iced water. Michael groaned and buried his face in her hair.

"They're looking for us," Naya whispered, her hands dropping to her sides.

Michael sneaked a kiss on her neck before straightening. "We can use the door or retrace our steps. Up to you."

"No. I don't want Carol to know this office is here. We go back through the basement."

"All right. Let's go."

He helped Naya ensure the jibs were closed and hidden from unfamiliar eyes before they quickly returned to the kitchen through the basement door.

"Naya? Michael? Is that you?"

"We're here, Mom," Naya called out, glancing at him with a blush filling her cheeks.

He smiled and ran the tip of his finger down the side of her face. "Later."

Naya's eyes widened briefly, but she smiled and straightened her back. "Yes."

Entering the kitchen proper, Michael saw Kelly, Carol, and Luke waiting for them. He heard slurping and turned to see Jenny drinking from her bowl.

"I take it she wasn't downstairs?" Kelly placed her hands on her hips.

"No," Naya said. She crouched to the floor. Jenny, tail wagging and mouth dripping with excess water, walked up and huddled up to her.

Michael looked away from the reunion and walked over to the sink to wash his hands. "There were no signs anyone had gone that way, either. Also, the door had been locked from the inside."

Michael caught himself from rubbing on his eye.

Naya apparently noticed. "Michael, wash your face. We need to take care of your eyes."

Michael sighed but didn't argue with her as she opened a drawer next to him and pulled out a first aid kit. She handed him a small plastic bottle of eyewash.

"Thanks," Michael murmured as he took it from her.

"Do you need help?"

Michael shook his head. "I got it."

"What do we do now?" Carol asked.

Michael winced at the sting from the eye wash, cursed under his breath, and lifted his hand to rub his eye.

Naya grabbed his wrist. "Don't even think about it."

"No, ma'am," he said and grinned at her. He screwed the lid back on and handed it over to her.

She shook her head and rolled her eyes at him. "Keep it. Just in case you'd need to use more later." She replaced the kit in the drawer.

"Thanks." Michael slipped the tiny plastic bottle inside his pocket.

"If she didn't go outside through the cellars, where could she have gone off to?" Carol continued.

Luke leaned his hip on the edge of the island. "While you and Michael were downstairs, the three of us searched here and upstairs. I also went outside and checked the driveway and the garage. Other than my footprints, I found nothing out there."

"Where could she have gone to?" Naya said.

"We checked everywhere." Luke shrugged. "Even under the beds when we moved the mattresses."

"I shouldn't have left her alone," Kelly said.

"Don't blame yourself, Mom," Luke said. "Are there any hidden rooms or doors in this house that we should know about?"

Naya shook her head. "None."

"You know, I once saw this show where this guy created a series of corridors within the walls of this woman's house, where she was living alone."

Luke rolled his eyes. "That's no help, Carol."

"But it could be possible, right?" Carol's gaze bounced from one person to the next. "That some stalker who recognized you constructed hidden corridors so they could stalk you while living in the house undetected?"

"That does not explain the *something* you were talking about when you attempted to play with the Ouija," Naya snapped.

Carol jumped and stared warily at Naya before slowly nodding. "You're right. No man did that. That was totally paranormal."

Naya turned away and placed the flashlights and candles back in the cabinet and drawers. "Let's not talk about the paranormal, okay?"

Michael crossed his arms in front of him and met Luke's gaze. From the way Naya closed the cabinet door without making a sound, he could tell she was hanging onto her patience by a thread. To him, it seemed like she would have preferred to slam them shut.

"I'm getting worried," he said. It wasn't like his sister to disappear without a word. "We need to find Rachel quickly. She could freeze to death."

"Her parka is still in the closet. I saw it when we were searching earlier," Kelly said. "I don't think she'd have left the house without it."

"Which may mean either she's still inside the house or she walked out without any protection," Luke said. "But I know Rachel. She wouldn't do that. She's not the type."

"We need to call the police," Carol said.

"And just how do we go about that? All the lines are down." Naya's voice rose a fraction. She crossed her arms in front of her and closed her eyes.

"Well, we had a signal earlier. Maybe it'll come through again?" Carol said.

"It's possible," Michael said.

Naya opened her eyes and lowered her arms. "I agree". "We should keep checking for a signal. In the meantime, does anyone have ideas on where to look for Rachel? Other than yelling our heads off, hoping she responds?"

"I was ready to go to bed earlier. Now I'm just hungry," Luke said. When Michael threw a glare at him, Luke threw up his hands. "I'm sorry, but I get hungry when I drink and am stressed. Rachel's disappearance is stressing me out, so I need food."

"There's plenty of food," Kelly said. "Let me get some of

that ham I saw somewhere. The thing is, I can't remember where I saw it."

"It's in unit two, Mom," Naya said. A movement outside the window had her walking over and leaning over the sink to see outside. A shadow moved by the side of the car and disappeared into the dark. The perimeter lights flickered, making it difficult to see outside clearly. She turned slightly, not taking her eyes off the spot.

"Michael?"

"Yeah? What is it?" Michael moved quickly to stand by her side.

"I think I saw someone outside," she whispered.

"Let me go and check," he said, already turning toward the kitchen door, only to stop when her hand held on to his arm.

"Don't go out alone," Naya said.

Luke joined them. "I heard. Did you recognize who or what it was you saw?"

"No. I just saw a shadow. But it moved too fast, whizzing from left to right, by the side of the car."

"Did it come from the direction of the garage or somewhere else?"

"I think the garage, but I can't be sure. I just saw the movement."

"Luke, we have to go," Michael said.

Luke nodded. "Naya, stay here with Mom and Carol. Don't separate or go anywhere until Michael and I come back. Is that clear?"

Michael dropped a kiss on Naya's cheek and hurried to the foyer, pulling on his parka for the second time that night.

Luke stepped up beside him. "I take it you and Naya have come to your senses?"

"Yes."

"Finally. All right, I'm ready."

Michael checked to see if they were alone before stepping

closer to Luke. "Do we have anything to fight off whoever it is outside? What if they have weapons?"

Luke put up his fists in a boxer's pose. "We got these."

Michael nodded. "I guess we run."

Luke nodded sagely. "Live to fight another day. We are going out there purely for investigative reasons only."

Naya bit on her lower lip. She didn't like that both Luke and Michael had to go out in the dark, but what else could they do? This whole thing felt like a script right out of silly horror movies, and they were following it to the letter.

"Naya? Did you see someone out there?" Carol said, coming up from behind her. "Did you recognize them?"

Naya frowned, suddenly unsure of what she'd seen. "No. Just a shadow."

"All right, this is creepy, but I didn't want to sound crazy or anything," Carol said, pursing her lips.

"What are you talking about?"

"Well, when I talked to you while you were in town this morning, I thought I saw someone outside, but when I looked out, no one was there. The thing is, Jenny didn't react either."

Naya remembered what had happened that morning and pulled out her phone. "Guys, I want to show you something."

Carol leaned closer. "What is it?"

"I posted on *IG* this morning."

"You did? I thought I got a notification, but I haven't been able to open the app all day. What did you post?"

"This." Naya clicked on her gallery, bringing up the first image she had taken that morning. "I didn't realize there was a problem at first until the notifications went crazy. But yeah, this is what I took earlier."

She held out her phone to show Carol the image. Kelly moved closer, and Naya shifted her phone to give her mother a better view.

"That's Jenny and you," Kelly said, her brows furrowing. "What's so special about it?"

"Can I?" Carol asked. Naya handed her the phone. Carol began zooming in and out of the image. "Is it a CCTV pic?"

"No. I took that myself."

"But you're the one sitting outside —"

"Like I said, I took that pic, and that's what came up."

"You took a pic of yourself," Kelly said, peering at the screen.

"No, Mom. I took the pic of the dog. That isn't me sipping tea outside. I was inside the house the whole time. Sitting on that chair when I took that picture." She pointed to the furniture and jumped when the front door suddenly opened.

"What the hell?" Michael walked in, looking wild-eyed as though something had frightened him.

"You're back fast," she said. "Did you see something outside?"

"I'm not sure," Michael said, shrugging off the heavy coat. "Luke and I had just stepped outside to check around where you saw the shadow by the car. I heard a sound from the woods and saw two glowing eyes. Large as saucers. Most likely reflecting the perimeter lights. I think there may be a catamount outside. A wild one. So, I got back inside as fast as I could."

Naya frowned. "A catamount? No, that can't be. They're extinct."

"Are there any other predatory wild cats in Vermont?" Carol asked.

"Not that I'm aware of," Michael said.

"It could've been a cat," Luke said, coming in calmer than Michael had. "Or a bear."

"Look, it could have been anything, but what I saw past the window was no cat," Michael said. "Last time I checked, cats don't walk on their hind legs."

"Luke, have you seen this?" Kelly took the phone from Carol and passed it to Luke.

"No, what is it?" Luke took the phone from Kelly. "Hey, Michael, have you seen this?"

Michael placed his parka over the back of a chair. "Seen what?"

Michael joined Luke, and Kelly and Carol repeated what Naya had told them. As the group huddled over her phone, Naya took a deep breath and sat on a chair. It had been a long day, and she could feel the fatigue seep in.

"All right. Maybe we're seeing things because of something else entirely," Carol said.

Naya's curiosity rose. "Like what?"

"Carbon monoxide poisoning?"

"None of us are displaying any signs or symptoms of that kind of poisoning. You're a nurse, you should know these things. Besides, Naya has all those sensors," Kelly said, pointing a finger at the ceiling. "I counted. There's about fifteen of those around the house."

Carol made a face. "Okay, so that one's out." She started to pace. "If it's not carbon monoxide, what else could it be that's affecting me? Us?"

"It's not poisoning," Kelly said.

"How come you're so sure?" Carol glared at Kelly.

Carol's look was so unlike her usual politeness toward Kelly that Naya's previous doubts about Carol's character resurfaced.

"Because of that damned picture Naya showed us, Carol. No one can poison digital cameras." Luke's low growl made Naya tense. Things were escalating and quickly getting out of hand.

Carol shrugged. "Oh. If you say so. I know you don't believe in the paranormal, but I know what Rachel and I saw.

We had no idea that the charcuterie board had been an already active Ouija. But what I do know is, as Kelly has mentioned before, we need to close it."

"How do we even begin to do that?" Luke looked at all of them, one at a time.

When his gaze landed on Naya, she threw her hands up in defeat. "I have no freaking idea, Luke. Maybe we can search the internet and hopefully get in touch with someone who knows."

"That's not possible right now," Kelly said.

"No, it's not," Naya said. "What we can do is stay together and get through this storm until we can contact someone."

"I propose we all stay down here," Carol said. "Everything's within reach, plus the exits are immediately accessible. The fireplace is lit, and it's also warmer."

Naya raised her brow. "Excuse me. I lit the fireplaces upstairs."

"No, you didn't. It's cold as ice upstairs," Kelly said. "I lit the fire in your bedroom."

Michael raised his hand. "When we got here, Naya gave us a quick tour and showed us to our rooms. All the fires were burning brightly."

"Thank you, Michael." She looked at her mother and Luke. "That's what I was doing before you all got here."

"Look, I know something strange is going on, Naya. Do you remember when I told you I saw someone upstairs when we drove in?" Michael said. "Maybe what we're dealing with here is a combination of things. Our imagination, maybe some paranormal whatever, and someone pranking us, although I use the word prank loosely."

"You mean someone's in the house with us that we don't know about?" Kelly asked.

"It's the only logical explanation," Carol jumped in.

Naya gave Carol a side-eye. Carol had spoken casually, but

it was the momentary smirk that betrayed her. A stray thought came to Naya, but she immediately pushed it away. Instead, she faced Michael.

"I saw a man lighting the fire in the living room this morning. This happened after I took the picture I seem to have miraculously taken of myself earlier."

"I did say a combination of things, right?" Michael raised a brow at her. "I suspect this house may be haunted simply because it's very old and too many people had lived and most likely died in it. However, the tampering and sabotage of the fireplaces, emergency lights, and the human presence outside the window — all suggest someone living and breathing is responsible. And let's not forget that Rachel seems to have disappeared and is nowhere to be found inside the house."

"Suddenly, that TV show is not so farfetched," Carol said.

"Oh, my God. Can you all stop panicking?" Luke threw up his hands.

"We're not panicking, we're discussing all the possibilities," Kelly said, crossing her arms in front of her. "At this point, too many things are going on that are not logical. One of which is — what the *fuck* is that sitting on the car outside?"

CHAPTER FOURTEEN

Naya jumped at her mother's use of the F word. "Mom?"
Kelly pointed to the window. "There's something out there."

Luke and Carol hurried to the window to look out.

"Something is sitting on top of Carol's car. It doesn't look human," Luke said. "I am not going outside again."

"A cat?" Naya squeezed herself between Luke and Carol.

"That's no cat," Carol groaned and rolled her eyes. "That's a tarp. It's just a tarp. Talk about panic, God."

"Look, it's clear to me we're all getting a little overexcited," Naya said, her hands up and palms facing everyone. "I think we should all try to get settled. You don't have to sleep, not if you don't want to, but at least take time to chill out and relax."

"I can't relax, not without knowing where Rachel went." Michael rotated his neck from left to right before letting out a deep breath. "But you're right. We should all try to calm down and think this over logically."

"I have to be honest . . . I *am* scared and confused." Naya let out a heavy sigh. "There must be some sort of explanation for all of this." The day had been long, and she was exhausted. All she wanted to do was lie down and close her eyes.

"You're right." Kelly crossed her arms in front of her. "Right now, there's nothing we can do. She's not anywhere in the house. We can't go outside looking for her without risking our lives, either."

"What if she's just hiding?" Carol said, gazing at each of them.

Naya frowned at Carol. Something nagged at her, telling her to suspect Carol knew something, but she couldn't think what. "Why would she hide from us?"

"Naya, you had to have been there." Carol shivered.

The action was a little over the top, in Naya's opinion.

"That black, shadowy stuff that leaked out of the board. It wasn't normal. And it scared the hell out of me. I told you how it felt when it rushed at me. There's no way you can convince me I imagined that."

"I'm not doubting you, Carol." Well, she did, actually, but she just couldn't say that out loud. She met Michael's gaze and saw the same suspicions in his eyes. "You all can go on ahead. I'll clean down here and join you in a few minutes."

Kelly let out a sigh, walked up to Naya, and hugged her. "It's going to be all right, darling. I'll go on up ahead."

"Okay, Mom." Naya kissed her mother's cheek.

Kelly stepped away and faced Carol. "Carol, you're coming with me."

"I'll stay down here and help Naya."

Naya shook her head. "No. Go on up with Mom. You went through a shock earlier. I'll be all right."

"If you're sure?" Carol looked hesitant.

Naya didn't want to encourage her. She wanted to be alone with her thoughts. "Quite sure."

Kelly took hold of Carol's arm and led her out of the kitchen. Naya watched them walk through the door until they both disappeared from her line of sight. Only then did Naya let go of the breath she'd been holding.

"Michael and I will help you down here," Luke said. "There's not much to clean up, but I don't think we should leave you alone down here."

Naya opened her mouth to argue but then closed it. "All right. I just need to check and secure the fire down here. The generator may need refueling."

"Michael and I will go do that," Luke said. "You stay here, okay?"

Naya nodded. "Thank you. Take the flashlight with you. Take two."

"We got it," Michael said, smiling gently at her before turning to Luke. "Shall we?"

Naya watched as Luke and Michael went out the back door. Alone in the kitchen, she began loading the dishwasher with dirty dishes and serving plates. She double-checked the room and then remembered she had yet to return to the living room. Conflicted, she debated with herself whether it was wise to go into the living room or not. The need to clean up won.

"Might as well get over it," she muttered.

She paused at the living room entrance and surveyed the room. It looked much like it had when they'd left it earlier, and nothing seemed amiss. It was easy to spot the wine glasses, plates, and charcuterie board, thanks to the light from the fireplace.

"Get a grip, Naya." She quickly grabbed the items and left as fast as she had come.

Luke and Michael had yet to return, and she stared down at the charcuterie board in her hand. She had loaded the dishwasher, but she hadn't switched it on. Running the machine would have to wait until the morning when, hopefully, power will be restored.

As for the charcuterie board? It would have to be washed by hand and sanitized before she could put it in the cabinet. She ran the tips of her fingers over the wood, tracing the faint designs. The letters were barely visible, but now that she knew what they were, she couldn't ignore them.

The board felt heavy in her hands, the wood smooth to the touch, and she wondered who could have made it and what had made them hide it under the floorboards. No answers came. Frustrated at the day's events, she muffled a curse and turned on the tap.

She was drying her hands and scanning the room to check if she'd missed anything when, finally, to her relief, she heard the back door close.

"Luke? Michael?"

"Yeah," Luke said. "It's us."

Naya hurried to pour the hot tea she'd gotten ready. "It's Chamomile." She handed him the cup, noting his reddened cheeks.

"Ah, thank you," Michael said. "Just what I needed."

Luke appeared right behind Michael, and Naya quickly grabbed a second cup.

"Here," Naya said and handed him the tea. "Everything set for the night?"

"Yes. We refilled the tank and brought in more firewood. You'd be happy to know we saw no signs of further sabotage."

"That's good. Very good," Naya sipped from her mug. "We should get the both of you upstairs. There should just be enough hot water left."

Luke took a sip from his mug and grimaced. "Michael, if you don't mind, I'll shower first this time."

"You go on up. Take your time."

"'Night, Naya." Luke raised his mug to salute them before he walked away. He paused and turned around. "I think I'll use your bathroom tonight, Naya."

"Go ahead. 'Night, Luke."

Left alone with Michael, Naya felt her heart flutter, but fatigue hit her just then, and she yawned.

Michael leaned against the coffee counter and smiled. "Tired?"

Naya covered her mouth and nodded. "It just hit me."

"It's been quite the adventure for all of us, hasn't it?"

Another yawn hit Naya, and to her amusement, Michael yawned wide as well.

"Let's go on up. I think the tea hurried things along." Michael chuckled. "Let me check the fire in the living room."

"Done that. It'll burn itself off. I also locked all the doors and windows while you and Luke were gone." Naya stood and placed her cup on the island. She inwardly debated briefly whether to wash it or not before shrugging. "It can wait."

"Come on, let's go upstairs."

They held hands as they ascended the stairs, neither saying a word. When they reached the landing, Michael yawned again.

He chuckled as he swung Naya into his arms. "If things had been different, I would have revealed my feelings for you long ago. I've wanted you in my life for a long time, and I still feel the same way. But my eyes are crossing, and I can't think straight."

"I wanted to talk to you about us earlier, but I can barely keep my eyes open." Naya quickly stifled another yawn. "Damn. That tea was potent. Let's agree that our talk will have to keep for a bit."

"Tomorrow then?"

Naya nodded. "Tomorrow's good."

Michael kept his arm around her waist as they walked the rest of the way to her room. The door was slightly ajar, and she saw Jenny curled up in her bed, which someone had set by the doorway. Together they silently tiptoed their way into the room so as not to wake the others. Guided by the firelight, Naya went to her walk-in closet to change into a tank top and sleeping shorts. She returned to the room to see Michael standing in the center, looking down at her mother on the mattress next to Carol on the floor.

Michael looked up and met her gaze. "I guess we sleep

together tonight?" he whispered, laughter lacing his words. "Not the plan I had in mind, but there's nowhere else to lie down."

"I'm sure Mom didn't realize she had taken over your bed. I don't mind if you won't."

Naya got into bed, slipped her phone under her pillow, and settled under the covers. She watched the fire dancing happily in the fireplace and shivered. Her toes were cold. Jenny normally slept at her feet but must have felt put out with so many humans in the room. Naya lifted on her elbow to check on Jenny, tut-tutting her tongue to gain the dog's attention. Jenny didn't stir. Naya lay back down again and turned onto her back, wondering how she would be able to sleep without Jenny's comforting weight on her feet.

"Your turn," Luke said, walking out of the bathroom.

Michael got up and disappeared behind the closed door.

"Goodnight," Luke said, stifling a yawn.

"Goodnight, Luke," Naya said. She stared at the ceiling above her, willing sleep to come. But she couldn't help hearing the muffled sounds of Luke settling down and listening to the sounds of water splashing in the bathroom.

She didn't look away from the ceiling when Michael came out of the bathroom. Didn't dare take a sniff of how good he smelled from the soap and shampoo. Not even when he slid into bed next to her.

Michael moaned softly as he settled. "God, I am positively exhausted. Goodnight, Naya."

"Goodnight, Michael," Naya said, her lips curving into a smile and finally closed her eyes.

Michael's proximity should have made her feel some sort of nervousness, but the truth was, she only felt at peace. Being in bed with Michael was not something she had thought to be doing when she woke up that morning, but it sure felt right. She tried to pace her breathing and began to count imaginary sheep. Maybe that would help her relax enough to get some sleep.

"Naya?" Michael whispered in the dark.

"Hmm?"

"Would you mind terribly if I kiss you goodnight in the presence of your family?"

She broke into a wide grin and opened her eyes, turning her head to face him. "I'm sure they wouldn't mind."

"I mind. I can hear you two," Luke said.

"Sorry, Luke." Michael leaned forward until he brushed a kiss over her lips. "That's all I can manage without my neck hurting." He winced as he lay his head back on the pillow.

Naya reached out to touch his hand. His bigger one clasped around hers. It was what she needed. She moved closer to him until her body flushed against his side. Michael moved his arm, allowing her to lay her head on his shoulder.

"Let's try to get some sleep." Michael dropped a kiss on her cheek.

Naya let out a soft sigh and closed her eyes. The soft thud of Michael's heartbeat sounded like a metronome, a steady tempo playing in her ear. She felt herself sink into the lulling rhythm, hazily aware that around her, the house shuddered.

The next time she opened her eyes, it was still dark, but the light from the fireplace made it possible to see around her. Only the sounds of animal and human snores broke the silence. The dream had been so vivid. Heart still pounding in her chest, she reached under her pillow for her phone. She blinked rapidly to adjust to the LED light. Three a.m. Like clockwork.

She placed her forearm over her eyes, stifling a groan. It felt like mere minutes had passed since she had closed her eyes and started dreaming of Rachel. Then Michael's advances joined the dream, and her body still thrummed from her reaction.

She glanced at Michael and saw he was deep in sleep—lying on his stomach, his cheek on the top of the pillow he clutched close to his chest. How she wished she could go back to sleep.

With a sigh, she swung her legs over the side of the bed. A soft tap tap from the doorway made her look up. Even in the minimal light, she could see Jenny's erect ears, her eyes focused on her, her tail thumping away.

Tiptoeing so as not to wake the others, she walked to the doorway and signaled to Jenny to follow her. Jenny stretched and grumbled, but her tail never ceased wagging. Grumbling turned to an excited whine and a scurry of feet as Jenny followed her down the stairs. Naya looked out the window and saw nothing but a blanket of thick snow.

A whine at her feet made her look down on Jenny. "It's freezing out there, girl. Are you sure you want to go out?"

Jenny dipped her head, her gaze never leaving Naya's. Naya checked outside again. The perimeter lights reflected on the snow, making it look like someone had sprinkled the garden with silver dust. Jenny let out a garbled part bark, part grumble, and a smidgen of whine.

"Do it fast, you hear?" The moment Naya opened the door, Jenny dashed out. Naya closed the door and watched through the window, observing Jenny leaping into the snow. After a while, when the dog showed no signs of coming in, she turned the doorknob and left the door partially open. The heat would seep out, but it was either that or leave Jenny stranded outside. There was only one choice, and that was Jenny's convenience. Besides, that's what the generators were for. Thinking of the generators, she wondered if they had enough fuel. But it was too early, too cold, and she really didn't want to go out there alone.

Rubbing her eye with the heel of her hand, she

contemplated what to do. All around her, the house was silent, as if even the spirits had gone to sleep. After some thought, she decided a good workout would ease the stress that kept her awake. She'd made a promise to her physiotherapist, and she intended to keep it.

Still in her tank top and pajama bottoms, she stepped into her indoor gym, opened her playlist, and got down to the business of exercising. The routines they'd assigned her were tough, but the adrenaline rush never failed to lift her mood.

She pushed herself through the crunches and cardio workouts for a solid hour. She paused at one point when she heard the door creak and the sound of the dog lapping up from the water bowl in the mudroom. No signs or sounds came from upstairs, so she focused again on her routine. Just one more leg workout, and she'd be done. Jenny walked into her line of sight and immediately gave her a slobbery smooch.

"Jenny!"

Naya wiped her face and stared down at her hands. She glared at Jenny, who walked away with her tail wagging, leaving her with no option but to stop her routine and head to the bathroom in her office.

A hot shower followed, and once again, she was glad she'd paid the extra dollars to guarantee the supply even without power. She dressed in a pair of sweats that she kept in the office closet. The workout and Jenny circling her with her rapid-wagging tail put her in a better mood. Unfortunately, it had not been enough. Glancing at the clock showed her it was barely past five. She abandoned the idea of going back to sleep and turned her attention to coffee.

CHAPTER FIFTEEN

"Hey."

Naya looked up to see Michael leaning against the doorway, looking rumpled and half asleep, his shoulders slumping forward as he stifled a yawn. He wore a loose gray t-shirt and plaid pajama bottoms. His hair was a mess.

How can the man look so good with bed hair? Naya looked him over and noticed he was barefooted.

"Hey, back." She pointed to his feet. "In case you'd forgotten, there's an active storm, and the floor is cold."

"The smell of coffee drifted upstairs. Of course I had to respond to its call. As for my feet, I don't like slippers. I swear I slipped them off beside the bed, but they weren't there. Poof and disappeared." Michael pointed to his face and made a circular motion. "I'm guessing you had a rough night, from your dark circles."

"Uh-huh. My eyes may have been closed, but my mind was too busy. Not even my workout could shut it up," Naya said, gently pressing the heels of her hands against her eyes. When she opened them again, she picked up her cup and took a sip. "I couldn't stop thinking about what's been happening or wondering where Rachel went. I dreamed about her last night. How'd you fair?"

"Just as bad."

"I swear I heard you snoring last night."

"I could've been." Michael stepped deeper into the kitchen, shrugging nonchalantly. "Mind if I have some coffee?"

"Help yourself. No need to ask," Naya said. "Perhaps your

lungs are still weak. That could be one reason you were snoring."

"My lungs are still kinda weak, yes."

"The cold could have severely affected them. And you were out there for quite some time yesterday. Several times."

"Don't have to remind me. And anyway, you couldn't have stopped me. My sister is still missing." Michael stood back, staring down at the coffee station.

"I've been thinking about that all night. We don't know if she's truly missing or not. She could just be somewhere around here. We didn't get the chance to check in your bedroom . . . and I didn't think to ask Mom . . ." Naya frowned. "What are you doing?"

Michael turned around, his expression bewildered. He held the aluminum pot in one hand and the filter sock in the other. "What are these?"

Naya opened her mouth to respond, stifling a laugh when Michael peered into the sock only to flinch back.

"Should I throw this out?" he said. "It looks nasty. Don't you have any coffee pods?"

Naya's contained laughter backfired into a snort. "They're not good for the environment, so nope, no pods. That's a sock, or rather, a coffee filter. And that pot isn't where the coffee is. It's in the other one."

"A sock." Michael's frown deepened. "You brew coffee using two pots and a sock?"

"Traditional coffee socks are the OG of filterless filters, and yes, I do like brewing coffee the old-fashioned way. And guess what? Contrary to popular *modern* belief, old-fashioned is still the best way to go. Go ahead, have a cup."

"No need to get defensive." Michael replaced the filter and poured himself a cup from the other pot. A soft moan escaped him after taking a sip. "You're right, this is much better than the pods I'm used to."

"Of course it is. It's also free of hormone-disruptive chemicals."

Michael's cup stopped midway to his mouth. "Hormone what?"

Naya opened her mouth only to jump in her seat when Rachel walked into the kitchen. She looked fresh from a shower, as evidenced by her damp hair and the scent of baby powder soap.

Her forehead convulsed as she gaped in awe at her friend. "Rachel?"

"Oh my God, that coffee smells so good! I was taking a shower and wondering how to go about getting coffee without having to go out to buy some." Rachel rubbed her palms together. "I think the power's up 'cos there's hot water. Good morning, guys."

"Rachel?" Michael said, looking just as shocked as she felt.

"Yeah, what?" Rachel went to the coffee station and poured herself a cup.

"Where have you been?"

"Me?" Rachel looked over her shoulder.

"Yes, you." Naya slid off the stool.

"I went upstairs last night and got into bed."

"No, you didn't," Michael said, his voice accusing.

"Excuse me?" Rachel put down the coffee pot with a clatter, her voice rising. "Yes, I did. You were all down here taking care of Carol, and I felt so mucky after what happened. I was also kinda in a panic, so I thought going to bed to sleep it off was the best thing to do."

Naya threw a glance at Michael, then turned back to Rachel. "We were calling for you. We were all looking everywhere for you."

Rachel raised a skeptical brow. "Did any of you think to check in on me in the bedroom?"

Naya began to nod but stopped herself, frowning. "Well,

no, but Mom said she and Luke did."

"Could've fooled me, 'cos I was tossing and turning for a long while until sleep finally took over."

"So you didn't hear us calling for you?"

"Nope. I could've sworn, though, that someone was outside the window."

"What do you mean?"

"I heard this whistling. At first, I thought it was the wind, but when I looked outside, I realized the storm had died down and there was hardly any wind, so it couldn't have been that."

Michael held up a hand. "I'm sorry, but can you two stop talking for a minute?" He jabbed a demanding finger at Rachel. "You were not in the house last night. We searched the everywhere inside. Where were you?"

"I already told you. I went up to the bedroom and got into bed after I took a shower. And to reiterate, no. I didn't hear anyone calling for me, and I was awake for a while, wondering what the rest of you were doing before I fell asleep. Other than the whistling man and the creepy shadows, I didn't hear or see anyone."

"Naya and I even went downstairs through the cellars looking for you," Michael growled.

"And? What is that supposed to do with my going to bed?"

Naya shared a look with Michael before repeating, "You weren't there, Rachel."

"We didn't find any sign of you down in the cellars either," Michael added.

"Exactly. That's because I wasn't downstairs. I was up in the bedroom," Rachel said in a tight voice.

Naya briefly glanced at Michael again before returning her attention to Rachel. "How could that be, Rachel? Mom, Luke, and Carol checked upstairs, and they said you weren't there. None of us could find you anywhere."

Rachel placed her mostly filled cup on the island and straightened. "Look, I don't know what else to say. I went upstairs and got into the shower. I was in there for a good long while, crying my heart out because of the scare I went through before I got into bed. Stop making me feel like I'm lying or that I did something wrong." With that, she stared at each of them with an expression that was hard to read and left the kitchen.

Naya stared after her, mouth hanging open. She had known Rachel for a long time and considered her a sister. She turned to Michael. "I'd swear she's telling the truth. So who's lying and why?"

Michael didn't respond, but Naya could see the white-knuckled grip around the handle of his mug.

"I also know that Mom and Luke would never lie about this. That only leaves Carol." Naya looked down, mentally tracing the grains of the highly polished wood tile. "But why? What would motivate Carol to lie about Rachel's disappearance?"

"I hate to ask this, I mean, she's my sister and all, but could Rachel be lying?"

"Her motive being?"

"Fuck." Michael set his mug on the island and remained silent for a lengthy period, uncertainty shining in his eyes.

"I think I should go after her," Michael said in a low voice. "Apologize."

"We both should." Naya took in a deep breath at the same time as Michael. The incident had cast a dark shadow over the already gloomy morning.

"Hey, guys, what's going on?" Carol walked in, thumbing toward the doorway. "And am I hallucinating, or did I just see Rachel go up the stairs? I called to her, but I don't think she heard me."

"You weren't imagining things. But I think we were all

imagining that she'd disappeared." Naya turned around and took Rachel's abandoned mug to the sink.

"What do you mean?" Carol grabbed a cup from the cabinet and poured herself a cup of coffee.

Naya turned on the tap and began washing. "Well, that's the thing. According to her, she was in her bedroom."

Michael added further details as Naya finished washing the mug and dried her hands.

"No way I could've missed her," Carol said, her tone insistent. "She wasn't in the bedroom, and no way in hell was she in the bathroom, because I went in there to check. She was not there."

"*She* says otherwise," Michael said, his mouth twisting. "I believe her."

"So, you're saying we all imagined that she had gone off and disappeared somewhere? The entire night?" Carol gazed at Naya and then Michael, looking incredulous. "Look, Michael, I know she's your sister, but why would she lie like this?"

"*She* has a name." Naya threw a glance at Michael. "And for the record, I also believe Rachel."

Carol grunted and twisted her mouth to the side. "Okay, so let's say *Rachel* never left the house. We couldn't find her, so where'd she go? We raised our voices, calling out to her, but she didn't respond."

Naya took in a deep breath. Her suspicions about Carol had not abated, so she had to be careful about whatever she said in front of her. "I don't know, Carol, but why would Rachel lie? What good would that do?"

"I don't know." Carol's brows furrowed and her lips set in a tight line. She looked just as bewildered as Naya felt.

"Look, none of this makes sense." Michael started pacing. "None of what happened last night makes sense. Rachel disappearing and reappearing makes no sense at all."

"I know." Naya sat on an island stool and scratched her scalp, barely holding back from pulling on her hair. The whole situation was confusing, and a headache was blooming at her temples.

Carol broke the silence that had fallen. "What do we do now?"

Naya sighed. "I suggest we accept Rachel's version of things but also try to figure out what's going on that is making all of us see and hear things."

"Mass hysteria?"

"I refuse to believe that. And no, there is no poisoning."

"I didn't say anything about poisoning. I just threw out that possibility last night."

Naya put up a palm toward Carol. "Just covering the bases."

Carol gazed at her, her face devoid of expression.

"What do we do now?" Michael repeated the question, breaking another round of silence.

Naya placed her hands on the island and eased off the stool. "I am going to hunt for a signal, any signal, and hopefully get a chance to call in someone who can help us as soon as we're cleared from the storm."

"You're not going out there alone, Naya," Michael said.

"You're welcome to join me." Naya raised a brow at him.

"I will."

Carol looked at Michael and then at Naya. "Are you two sure that going out there in this weather is a good idea?"

"I'm well aware getting off this mountain right after the storm may not be possible. However, we must confirm the roads are clear enough to drive on." Naya struggled to maintain a steady voice, hiding her frustration with Carol. The act was becoming increasingly difficult to sustain in Carol's presence. "If I can't find a signal, we'll have to wait for the roads to be cleared. Once we're able to get to town, we can ask for some help, or at least suggestions about who can help us."

"I don't think they'll have the roads cleared by tomorrow, if at all," Michael said. "There's likely to be fallen trees barring the roads, which could take days to clear out."

"Don't even think about walking down the mountain." Carol pointed to Naya.

"I'm not saying we walk all the way down the mountain to the city," Naya said, her cheeks heating under Carol's glare. The woman had a point. "I just want to investigate the extent of the damage. At the very least, it'll give us an idea of how long we're going to be trapped up here."

"I guess we can do that. But not until after breakfast," Michael said. "How are you with supplies?"

"I told you, food won't be a problem." Naya rolled her eyes. "I had supplies delivered before I moved in and did more shopping before you guys showed up. We can survive up here for several weeks, even a couple of months if need be."

"You're a survivalist, Naya. Just admit it," Carol said, her face brightening.

"I never denied it." Naya grinned.

They made quick work of breakfast, and an hour later, Naya and Michael walked over to the generator shed.

"Michael, look."

"What is it?" he asked.

"Sunshine." She spread her arms, raising her eyebrows for effect.

Michael glanced up and groaned. "We got sunshine. That's got to be a good sign, right?"

"We'll have to see."

Once they refilled the generator tanks, they attached the sled to the snowmobile. Michael took the driver's seat and revved the engine while Naya handed him one helmet and placed one over her head. They had been driving for about ten minutes when Naya spotted several fallen trees in the forest, but only one lying across the road. But she saw no sign of the rental. She tapped on Michael's shoulder and signaled for him to cut the engine.

"Did we miss the rental? I didn't see it." Naya got off the sled and checked her surroundings. "Hold on, I see something up there. I think we just passed it."

She started walking, but Michael stopped her. "Get in."

They turned the snowmobile around and retraced their route. They stopped right next to a large lump of snow that Naya had spotted. She got down and dragged the snow away to reveal the metallic silver paint of the SUV.

"There goes my idea of driving the car back up to the house." Michael shook his head. "I'll dig out the trunk and try to open it. At the very least, we can get our luggage. And Rachel's precious crate."

Naya joined Michael in wiping the snow from the back of the car.

Michael fished out the car keys from his pocket with a smirk. "I brought them, just in case."

"Good call," Naya said. "Try it out."

The key fob didn't work the first two times Michael aimed it at the car, but on the third try, it finally clicked, but the trunk didn't open.

"I guess it needs a little help," Naya said, looking at Michael.

"It must have frozen or something. I'll go dig out the front door. See if I can get it to open manually."

Naya helped Michael dig out the area where the door would be. It took some time before they finally found the handle. She stepped back to watch Michael tug at the door handle several times before the driver's side door finally opened. Michael leaned in and fiddled with some controls. Naya pumped her fist at the sky when the trunk opened.

"It's open," she called out.

Michael joined her at the trunk, his cheeks red from the cold and effort. "Let's do this."

With some maneuvering, they managed to transfer the luggage and crate onto the sled. By the time they were done, they were both panting.

"Did you happen to bring water with you?" Michael said.

"I did." Naya opened the seat and pulled out two bottles of water. "They're cold but not frozen."

"It'll have to do," Michael said, taking one bottle from her.

Naya took a sip from the bottle, only to wince at the icy temperature. She warmed it in her mouth before swallowing. All the while, she continued to check out their surroundings.

"I see one tree lying across the road," she said.

"At least it's only the one," Michael said.

"Yeah, but what about the rest of the way down there?" Naya looked at her phone. "Let's keep going. Maybe we can get a signal further out."

"Okay, but not too far," Michael cautioned.

The rest of the drive was relatively easy, considering the chaotic storm the night before. At one point, they abandoned the snowmobile and walked. They took their time, ambling through the snow, knee-deep in some parts but mostly only came up to a few inches above their ankles. Overall, it wasn't as bad as Naya had thought it would be.

Despite her gloved hands and the thick scarf protecting half of her face, her cheeks ached from the cold. Her fingers and toes were getting numb from the frigid temperature.

"Naya? Are you all right?"

Naya shook her hands and pressed them to her face. "I'm surprised how cold it is. I thought I had dressed properly for this walk. Apparently, not good enough?"

Michael quickly came closer to check on her. "Damn it,

you're freezing. You should've said something earlier. Did you even put on thermal underwear?"

"I didn't really think about it until just now." Naya groaned. "Don't say it. I should know better. Especially up here."

"We better start heading back." He pointed toward the sky. "There's no way of knowing how long that's going to hold, so we shouldn't risk it."

"I've yet to find a signal," Naya said, flexing her aching arm when the blood flowed through it again. She'd been holding her phone higher up in search of a signal but to no avail and now suffered the consequences.

"Look. Gray clouds are forming quickly. That's always an ominous sign of the storm not being over yet." Michael linked his hand with Naya's. "Come, let's get going. I don't like how the temperature dropped just now."

They hurried back to the snowmobile. Michael revved the engine and drove as fast as he could. After ten minutes, with the house still not in sight, Naya decided to address the elephant in the forest.

She leaned closer and spoke in Michael's ear. "About last night . . ."

"What about it?"

"I'm sorry if I embarrassed you."

"You didn't. Why? Were you uncomfortable about what happened?"

Naya looked ahead. "No."

Michael slowed down the snowmobile, the sound of the engine humming softly. "Look at me."

Naya gritted her teeth and turned her head. She met Michael's gaze and felt her heart melt. His gentle expression and the softness in his eyes were all too familiar. As far back as she could remember, Michael had always looked at her like that. She'd often hoped it would become more than just friendship.

Looking at him now, she recognized it as reined-in emotions. Of what, exactly, she'd have to discover.

Michael cupped her cheek. "I think we've always known we had feelings for each other, but the timing has never been right."

Naya nodded. "You think the timing is right this time?"

"I think so."

Nodding once more, Naya took a deep, icy breath. Her nostrils flared, and she coughed. "I'd like to get more into the romance of things, but I think we should take this up in the house."

Michael's laughter echoed around them. "I hate to say it, but I agree. We'll talk later, okay?"

"You said that last night."

"Yes, but again, the timing wasn't right. Let's get home before that cold front drops on us."

"I hate it that we don't know what's going on. We need a working weather app."

"Do you have a radio?"

Naya thought about it. "There should be one somewhere. I just can't remember where I placed it."

"You've got a lot of storage in that house. Where do you usually keep those types of things?"

"It could be in one of the cabinets or one of the pantries." Naya cherished her cupboards and pantries, but they eventually become too crowded for her to recall what belonged where. Well, other than her food items. And she'd only recently moved, too.

Michael chuckled. "Problems of the modern world. Too many cabinets. Too many pantries. All right. Once we get home, I'll hunt for that elusive radio. Maybe we can get some news the old-fashioned way."

Naya's teeth were chattering by the time they arrived back

at the house. Michael didn't let her go, holding onto her arm until they reached the front entrance. Kelly opened the door, let out a gasp, and ushered them inside. To Naya's embarrassment, Michael quickly divested her of her thick clothing. Kelly closed the door behind them, tut-tutting her worry. Naya noticed her mother didn't seem to question Michael undressing her in the foyer. She was actually helping him.

"Thank goodness you're back. We were getting worried," Kelly said as she draped a thick blanket over Naya's shoulders.

Luke entered the foyer just then and handed Naya a cup of steaming hot cocoa, which she accepted gratefully.

"Thank you," she said, wrapping her hands around the ceramic cup. She couldn't stop shivering.

"Michael, bring her over here. Let her sit by the fire," Kelly said, frowning worriedly.

"I'm okay, Mom. Just cold."

"Don't talk. Just sit here by the fire and drink your cocoa." Kelly's frown deepened as she turned to face Michael. "What took you so long?"

"We hurried as fast as we could, but the snow began falling heavier, making it difficult even for the snowmobile. When we first went out, the snow wasn't as thick."

Naya gratefully sank into the chair beside the fire, which roared happily, crackling and spitting. Soon her shivering stopped, and she felt herself finally able to relax and sink deeper into the chair. The fireguard kept the flames within the confines of the firebox, and the clock on the mantlepiece ticktocked in a soothing rhythm. Kelly, Carol, and Rachel sat on the three-seater opposite her while Luke took the wing chair on the other side of the fireplace.

Michael surprised her, though it really shouldn't have. What he did was just as familiar as the look she finally accepted as his special way of looking at her. He approached her chair, kneeled, and placed a blanket over her lap. He continued to talk, telling the story of their descent from the mountain before sitting on the floor and leaning his back against her chair's leg. No one called him out or asked him questions.

Naya sensed the curious look Carol sent their way but didn't have the energy to comment. Fighting to keep her eyes open, she listened to the low drone of Michael's voice, but her battle to stay awake was in vain. The marvelous warmth from the fire made her defeat all too easy. Soon, her world faded to sleep. Her last thoughts were how thankful she was to have her family and friends, *and* Michael, surrounding her.

She would almost swear she heard the house around her take a deep breath and settle.

Chapter Sixteen

The softness of the warm fur felt good against Naya's cheek. Unable to resist, she rubbed her cheek against the hefty body. She didn't need to open her eyes to know it was Jenny cuddled next to her. As if sensing Naya's waking, Jenny took a deep breath before letting out a huff and a grunt.

Naya's eyelids fluttered open, and she gazed into Jenny's dark orbs. "Hey, sweetie. You know you're not supposed to get on the bed. What're you doing here?"

Jenny rolled on her back, exposing her belly before stretching her short legs above her. It was a blatant request to stroke her belly. Naya had never been able to resist such a thing, smothering a giggle into the thick neck and rubbing the palm of her hand over the soft fur. She closed her eyes and took a deep breath.

The next time Naya opened her eyes, she didn't know where she was. Everything was dark except for the roaring fire. The shadows shifted around her, and she couldn't hear any sounds other than that of the fire and the wind beyond the walls. She turned toward the window. Beyond it was a deep darkness. Her stomach twisted in hunger.

Raking her fingers through her hair, she looked around for any sign of Jenny, but she wasn't in the room. The bedroom door was closed, so someone must have shown her out. Out of the corner of her eye, she noticed her clothes lying over the bed's footboard. Peeking under the quilt, she found herself wearing only her panties and tank top. She racked her brain, trying to think of who would've removed the rest of her clothes.

Her last memory was sitting in the wing chair downstairs with Michael sitting by her feet, speaking in his deep voice. As her mother and Carol had been there, too, she hoped it had been one of them who had removed her clothes. As for taking her to bed, there were only two possibilities, and one of them made her blush.

Her stomach grumbled loudly, enough for her to realize she'd slept long enough for her body to seek sustenance. She looked to her right and left, searching for her phone. She spotted it on the night table, and two taps lit up the screen and the time. No wonder she was hungry. It was past midnight.

She put on her sweats, slipped on her fleece-lined slippers, shrugged into her terry robe, and was out of the bedroom in less than a minute. She took a moment to consider what was different before continuing down the corridor. The nightlights gracing the lower part of the wainscotting were all glowing, which meant power had been restored while she'd been sleeping.

She hurried down the stairs, and Jenny caught up with her from somewhere. Downstairs, she checked the circuit panel behind the panel by the restroom. The switches were all up, and no red lights flashed. That also meant that someone had checked on it—only none of her guests knew the location of the panel.

"Thank you, whoever you are," she murmured.

Her stomach made another loud grumble, and Jenny looked at her askance, her tongue lolling to the side of her mouth, making Naya giggle. "You're so funny. Come on, let's grab something to eat."

Jenny's tail wagged a mile a minute as she trotted beside Naya on the way to the kitchen. Expecting to see at least someone there, Naya stopped short at the doorway. She looked down at Jenny, who tilted her head. Her wagging didn't waver.

"Do you know where everybody went, Jenny girl?"

Jenny licked her chops and sat on her haunches.

"I guess not."

Naya's stomach made another loud rumble, and she decided she needed to eat quickly to avoid further discomfort. She went to a refrigerator and pulled out a container of sliced meats. She was assembling a sandwich, sharing nibbles with Jenny every so often when she felt a presence. She looked up and saw Michael leaning on the doorjamb like he had that morning.

"Hey," he said, a smile tugging on his lips.

Naya grinned. "Hey, back at you. Where is everyone?"

"They went down to the town to connect with the outside world."

"Oh, the road's already cleared?"

Michael straightened up and walked toward her. "Surprisingly. A crew came up while you were sleeping and informed us they'd cleared that one tree off the road. Other than that, they said there wasn't that much damage downtown. We bore the brunt of it up here. It didn't take them long to restore the power. However, the internet signal was greatly affected, but they assured us they should have that settled soon. Otherwise, it's as if the storm had just been a hiccup."

"Wow. I would have thought it would take longer than several hours. I'm grateful, though." Naya started slicing her sandwich. "You want some? I can make more."

"I had dinner a couple of hours ago. But, yeah, sure. I'd like a slice."

"Coming right up."

"I thought you'd sleep through the night."

"I'm surprised I slept as long as I did."

"It's only eight. Still early."

That caught her by surprise. She checked the time on her phone again. "This says it's almost one a.m."

Michael frowned. "The lack of signal shouldn't have affected the time. The only way that could happen is if you reset it or it's set to a different time zone."

Naya checked the settings and frowned. "It's set for a different time zone."

"I hate to ask . . ."

"How did I even change the time zone when all this time I was asleep? Everything was fine until I woke up."

"Someone tampered with your phone." Michael met her gaze. "Change your passwords."

"I hate this," Naya muttered, quickly doing as Michael suggested. She ate her sandwich while changing all her passwords. It took some time, but she got through it.

"All right. All done." She checked the time again to make sure. "So it's almost nine now, which means I slept over six hours?"

"Stress can do that to you. Plus, we did quite a bit of hiking."

"It wasn't as bad as I'd feared."

Michael cleared his throat.

"I'm not used to this kind of weather," Naya said in a hurry.

"It's temperamental, I give you that," Michael said, raising a brow.

"It is." Naya licked her lips.

His deep laughter shot through her, making her hyperaware of her body's response. She bit the inside of her cheek and concentrated on making the sandwich Michael had requested.

Michael move behind her, his heat radiating into her back. "I think the sandwich is done." His voice, sounding right next to her ear, almost made her smash the sandwich.

She recovered quickly and cleared her throat. "Is one enough?"

"Never."

It wasn't difficult to miss his double entendre, especially given how her nipples stiffened beneath her robe. She drew in a shaky breath, quickly picked up the plate, and turned around, offering it to him.

"Eat your sandwich. If one is not enough, it's easy enough to make another."

"I'm sure it is." Why did Michael's lopsided smile have to look so sexy?

Naya's gaze locked onto his, and she couldn't move. She started when he took the plate from her.

Michael's smile grew. He turned and walked around her toward an island stool. "Let's eat."

Naya's breath caught in her throat. Her gaze lowered and locked on Michael's tight ass as he sat. *Why did it have to be so tight?*

"What are you doing standing there?" Michael raised a brow at her. "Come sit with me."

The breath she didn't realize she'd had been holding her breath erupted as she moved to sit next to him. She lowered her head to cover her rapidly heating cheeks, allowing her hair to fall on either side of her face.

"This is good," Michael said between bites. "I hate to ask, but can you make me another?"

"Sure. But here, take this first." Naya picked up a have sandwich from her pile. "I don't think I'll be able to finish these."

Michael took the sandwich from her and immediately took a bite. "Are you sure?"

"Pretty sure."

They didn't speak much as they focused on eating. To Naya's surprise—and Michael's—they finished the sandwiches she'd prepared and had room for dessert. She pulled out the tiramisu she had made for one of her live shows the previous week, and they both dug in.

"I don't know why this tastes so different."

"I've discovered that some recipes taste better when they've had at least two or three days to marinate in their juices."

Michael stared at the bite trapped in the tines of his fork. "Huh. Mom used to say that, but I was always impatient."

"Patience is key to deliciousness."

"And you're absolutely right."

"Changing the topic, I was wondering about the others. Shouldn't they be back by now?"

"Let me check." Michael pressed the side of his phone and furrowed his brows. "It's almost ten. No messages. And the signal's strong."

"I'm calling Mom," Naya said, picking up her phone.

"I'll call Rachel," Michael said, quickly tapping his phone.

Naya sat there, watching Michael. Their gazes met.

The number you're dialing cannot be reached. The number you're dialing cannot be reached.

She gritted her teeth at the repeating message and pressed the red disconnect icon. "It's not going through."

Michael raised his index finger, frowning as he listened. He started to lower his phone when he suddenly sat up. "Rachel? Where are you? Wait, wait. Let me put you on speaker."

Michael pushed a button and placed his phone face up on the granite surface. "Go ahead. Naya's here with me."

"Oh, okay. Hi, Naya. Luke and your Mom are here with me."

"Naya, what's up?" Luke's voice spoke up.

"I woke up, and other than Michael, all of you were gone. Where are you guys?"

"We were on our way back, but the weather suddenly turned, and Mom got nervous about going back up in case things worsened. I suggested we go to a hotel here in town, but Rachel said she had the keys to Michael's place, so that's where we are."

"Why didn't you tell us sooner? I was getting worried."

"Naya, we tried calling several times earlier, but the calls wouldn't connect," Kelly said. "Things are fine down here. We went to grab my prescription, but as Luke mentioned, the temperature suddenly dropped, and people were closing their shops. The weather app says something about a large area of low-pressure system developing."

"A blizzard?"

"Yes," Kelly said. "Another blizzard. Apparently, it's common around here this time of year. It's understandable why there are no people around town right now."

Michael gazed at her and leaned over to whisper in her ear, "I've never told Rachel about the town and the weird curfew. I don't think your mom knows. Or Luke." His breath ticked the side of her neck.

She swallowed a gasp when her insides twisted in a delicious quiver. "Oh, that's normal, I guess . . . the early shut-down," she bluffed. "You know, small towns and all. Well, if you're staying at Michael's place for the night, I guess we'll see you tomorrow?"

"All right, we'll see you tomorrow, darling."

"'Bye, Mom."

Naya disconnected the call and then faced Michael. "Looks like it's just us for the night."

Michael grinned. "I'm thinking if I have to be stranded in the mountains in the middle of a temperamental snowstorm, what better place than here with you. Because you, my dear, are sexy as hell."

Naya put her palms on her cheeks, unsure of what to say. Much to her consternation, she felt the growing heat there. From the gleam in Michael's eyes, she knew he could tell how badly she was blushing.

Michael took a step toward her, one small step that brought him closer than he already was. "Come on, Naya, I think it's time we had that talk."

Swallowing, Naya turned away. She didn't want to avoid the subject but didn't know how to be upfront about it either. Instead, she picked up their plates and turned toward the sink.

"Let me help you with that," Michael said. "You wash, I'll dry. Does that work for you?"

"Yes, thank you."

They worked together in silence, Naya deep in her thoughts, Michael silently drying the dishes with a clean dish-rag he'd fished out from a drawer. When they were done, Michael turned toward the coffee station and switched on the water heater.

"Coffee or tea?" Naya asked when she stood beside him.

"Tea's good."

"Chamomile, then?"

Michael dipped his head in acquiescence and leaned back to observe Naya as she went about placing tea bags into two mugs. When the heater switched off, he picked the pot up and poured the hot water, then grabbed both mugs and gestured with his head toward the living room. "Why don't we sit in there, where the fire's cozy and warm."

Naya led the way toward the hearth and sat on the wing chair she'd fallen asleep on earlier in the day. She took the mug Michael handed her and wrapped her hands around the ceramic. Even with the roaring fire, she felt the deep chill that had settled outside. A loud banging noise from upstairs startled her.

She shivered. "I thought the storm was over."

"No idea. I haven't checked the weather station." Michael placed his mug on the side table and went to get the throw from the sofa. He carefully placed the soft blanket around her legs before settling on the floor beside the chair, just like he'd done earlier that day.

Naya curled into the chair and stared into the flames. When Michael occasionally moved to drink some of his tea, his chest would brush against her legs. Each incidental touch warmed her insides.

"I've always wondered . . ." she said.

"About?" Michael asked when she paused.

"What if I hadn't been such a coward and asked you out? Would you have said yes and dated me?"

"I wouldn't have hesitated. I've always wanted to go out with you."

"Why didn't you say anything?"

"I've thought a lot about that over the years. And honestly? I have no idea why I never did ask you out. Maybe I was a coward. I don't know. But it didn't feel it was the right time."

"When would have been the right time?"

"Now."

"What makes *now* different?" She held up a hand when Michael opened his mouth to respond. "No. Don't answer that. I feel the same way. That somehow now *is* the right time." She stared directly into his eyes. "The right time for . . . us."

"When you went missing, your fans trended that hashtag, *WheresNaya*. I thought my world had ended. And then your mom called, and I feared the worst."

"I wasn't ready to die. Not even when I saw that brick coming down at me, felt it smashing into my face. I remember thinking *I'm not ready to die. Not yet.*" The memories flashed, and Naya briefly closed her eyes but immediately opened them again. Her therapist had encouraged her to face her fears with open eyes whenever they came up, and she'd been right. The first time she'd kept her eyes open during an episode, she'd screamed until her throat hurt. Not anymore.

"When they found you, they thought you were dead.

Instead, you opened your eyes and told them to take you to the hospital."

"I've heard that story, but I don't remember much about that time. I think I was trying to tell them to take me home. I just wanted to get home and feed Jenny."

"You almost died, but I had to leave and fly halfway across the country, trapped in an unending marathon of meetings I couldn't get out of. I got a call from your mom. She said she needed my help because you needed emergency plastic surgery, and the local hospital had no plastic surgeons on hand. I then turned to the hospital president, who was signing papers for a new building I was constructing for them, and requested his assistance. I didn't even ask him if one could come or not." Michael gazed up at her, his eyes suspiciously glistening with unshed tears. "They did a good job."

Naya reached down and cupped one of Michael's cheeks. "There's not much scarring, but they couldn't do anything about the nerve damage. I'm just glad I have my face back . . . most of it."

"You're beautiful, Naya."

"I don't think I've ever thanked you." She blinked back the tears that threatened to spill.

Michael moved to a kneeling position and placed his arms on either side of her. "You survived. That's all I prayed for. And I prayed very hard."

He was so close. Close enough for his scent to cloud her thoughts.

"There's something I need to confess. I've loved you for a very long time, and I remember the exact moment I realized it," Michael said. "I felt a kick inside my brain when I saw you for the first time."

Naya chuckled and widened her eyes in pretend shock. "I was ten years old. How could you?"

"And I was fourteen. Heck, I was confused. I even tried to

deny it. Felt all sorts of guilt. So instead, I became your big brother, your best friend."

"My protector. Don't think I didn't know about all those boys receiving a talking-to from one senior high student."

"I did my best." His large hand gently palmed the back of her neck, pulling her closer until their lips met. He had always been confident and showed no hesitation in his approach.

Michael tasted like chamomile as his tongue teased her lips. Naya leaned in, willingly allowing him entrance. Moans and whimpers echoed in her ears as his touch skirted under her tee, touching her braless breasts and taunting her nipples.

He leaned back and gazed down at her. "May I?"

Michael's request left no room for doubt over what he meant. Naya barely nodded, and Michael pulled her shirt over her head and threw it somewhere over the back of the chair.

His breathing deepened as he stared down at her. "It took every ounce of my restraint not to do that on your eighteenth birthday." He leaned down and sucked one nipple and then the other.

Naya groaned as soon as his lips moved between nipples, feeling the cool air attack the moist tips. She closed her eyes, relishing the sensation of her nipples hardening to almost painful levels under his double assault.

Blood rushed to her breasts, making them feel heavy and swollen. His stubble grazed her tender flesh, the kind of abrasion she had never welcomed before.

"Michael." Naya couldn't articulate any further. She opened her eyes when he placed a finger over her lips.

"All you need to say is stop, and I won't go any further."

Naya nodded against his finger. Opening her lips, she took the digit into her mouth and sucked.

"Fuck." Michael growled out the word. His head dropped, and he began kissing her diaphragm, moving over her ribs and her stomach down to the waistline of her sweats.

The room blacked out. For a moment, Naya stared into the darkness, blinking her eyes as she tried to accustom them to the situation. "God, did we just lose power again?"

The glow from the fire cast shadows into the corners of the room. From the doorway, Jenny stepped in, her nails scraping loudly against the stone floors.

Michael let out a sigh as he lay his head against Naya's breasts. "Not only do we have a blackout again, but we also gained an audience."

Naya couldn't stop her giggles from escaping. The more she tried to stifle them against her hand, the more she lost control. Michael apparently couldn't help it either, because he muffled his laughter against her stomach.

"I'm sorry, but this is so funny." Naya bit back her laughter and set her hand over his larger one. A memory hit her in that instant, and she sobered quickly. "I'm sorry. I was stupid and allowed myself to get into a relationship with a psychopath."

Michael let out a sigh as he turned his hand over. "Something my father said to me comes to mind."

Naya ran her fingers over his palm. He didn't have calluses, but his hands were anything but soft.

She looked up and met his gaze. "What is it?"

"Sometimes a painful experience can lead us to a better future."

"I believe it makes sense to think of coming close to death as agonizing."

"I thought I'd lost my chance when the reports first came in."

She let go of his hand and reached up to palm his cheek. "I—"

A blunt force pushed her from behind. Caught unprepared, she lurched forward, straight into Michael's arms.

Michael wrapped his arms around her, but something took

hold of her hair and pulled from behind.

Naya screamed.

CHAPTER SEVENTEEN

"Michael!" Naya flew backward and scrambled to stand on the chair when whatever had taken hold of her suddenly let go. She stood there, uncertain of what had just happened. Her gaze met Michaels as she began to pat her head, but nothing was there.

Jenny started barking aggressively and ran to the back of the chair. Gasping for air, Naya twisted around on the chair, trying to get her bearings, when she felt herself sway. She would have fallen off the chair had Michael not caught her in his arms.

He carefully set her down on the ground, panting and gasping for air from his effort. "What the hell happened?" He tightened trembling arms around her.

"I ... something ... something .... what the fuck!"

"Shh, it's all right. Whatever it was, it's gone now."

"I want to get out of here." A sob caught in her throat as she buried her face in Michael's chest. "Please. Get me out of here."

"Okay, okay. Let's get into the car and drive to town." Michael looked down at her and stepped back. "Where's your shirt?"

Naya searched around for her shirt, huffing a frustrated breath when she saw it had fallen under the chair. "Got it."

She was pulling it over her head when the sound of a howling wind followed by the rattling of the windows made her look up. "If we can even get out of here."

Jenny whimpered, drawing Naya's attention. The dog sat

in front of the fire, ears flattened to the back of her head. Jenny lowered her head and let out another whimper.

"She's frightened." Naya turned from Michael, crouched low, and opened her arms. Jenny crawled up to her until Naya could hold her. The poor dog was trembling like a leaf.

"Whatever it was that grabbed you was not of this world, Naya." Michael scoffed. "Jesus Christ, I can't believe I'm acknowledging the paranormal."

"It's the only logical explanation. Something doesn't want me ... us, here." She lay her cheek on Jenny's head. After a moment, Jenny turned and licked Naya's chin. Naya dropped a kiss on Jenny's head and huddled her closer.

"But what has changed?"

Naya gazed up at Michael. "I don't know. This is the first time this has happened."

"Do you remember when this started?"

"This is the first time something has attacked me."

"So you've always known or sensed they were around?"

Naya shrugged. "Since I moved in, I guess. I've always sensed them, but they always stayed in the periphery. A movement here and there, things falling, but Jenny never seemed nervous. Wary, yes, and suspicious. Never scared like she is now."

"So, what has changed?"

"I don't exactly know."

"When you were alone here with only Jenny around, you sensed their presence, but they never did any harm."

"Yes."

"Maybe they don't like having strangers around?"

Naya stood up. She looked down when Jenny leaned against her leg. "I noticed that things kinda got weird after Carol arrived."

"Has Carol said anything? Like she saw something or sensed something strange?"

"The house, according to her, is haunted. She mentioned that yesterday morning before the storm hit. Come to think of it, I saw that apparition that same morning. It was a man wearing some kind of overalls. He lit the fireplace." She pointed to the hearth. "He was kneeling right there. Even dipped his head in greeting when I came in, and then poof . . . he up and disappeared. Jenny was with me. She didn't even bark."

"You never mentioned that before."

Naya shrugged. "Out of sight, out of mind. I couldn't do anything about it. And I needed to get to town to grab last-minute purchases."

"I find your attitude about the whole thing confusing. But I saw that weird shadow movement on the second floor when we first came. I told you about that."

Naya wrapped her arms around her body. "To be honest, I have never once felt frightened. Not even when I saw that ghost. He didn't frighten me at all. I was more surprised because it was so unexpected but not frightening at all."

"How could you be so unaffected?"

Naya turned away from Michael's intense gaze and faced the fire. "I admit, it was weird and creepy, but I've faced death and defeated it. I lay in that ravine and saw things I don't even want to consider remembering."

She stared into the fire, watching the dancing flames dancing. "I remember lying there, listening to the voices telling me everything was going to be all right. All I needed to do was close my eyes, and it would be all over. But I didn't."

"You fought them back."

Naya nodded. "I told them I wasn't ready to go."

"What happened after?"

"It was peaceful. The pain was numbing, and I focused on breathing. The voices left me alone. The next thing I remember was a dog licking my face, and seeing the rescuers above me. Only then did I close my eyes and go to sleep."

"So this experience with the paranormal . . . it's not strange to you anymore."

"No. I think I already knew what to expect from buying such an old historic house. I just didn't pay attention. I fell in love with it, and it felt like the perfect place to escape the city."

"When did you start truly paying attention to what was going on? Anything you can recall?"

Naya frowned in thought. "I think it was only after I posted that picture of Jenny on *Instagram* that I truly started paying attention to what was going on. Then something happened during my live presentation that really had me wondering. That was yesterday."

"What presentation?"

Naya patted her body and looked around her. She found her phone on the floor next to the wingback chair. She picked it up and examined it, glad to see the fall hadn't damaged the expensive gadget.

"Let me pull it up." She tapped on the screen and let out a sigh of relief when it automatically responded. She opened the app, clicked on the recorded file of her IG Live, and held out the phone to Michael.

He grabbed the phone and glanced at the screen. "What am I looking at?"

Naya reached around Michael and tapped the clip to start playing her presentation "Well. I was doing my live vlog, showing how to make a charcuterie board. Remember? The one I served last night?

"Ah, the Ouija board."

"Yeah, that one. Anyway, during the live feed, I noticed the commentaries. A lot of the viewers said they saw something run past my back, but there was no one there. I was alone in the house. I told them they were kidding. But then . . . but then more comments came in. And they all said the same thing. That they saw something behind me."

Michael didn't say a word as he stared at the phone. She waited, watching Michael's expression change from one of speculation to confusion and finally to incredulity during the chaotic part of the film she remembered. She could tell the moment he was seeing for himself what her viewers had seen. A shaft of cold-bladed nervousness threatened to overwhelm her, and she had to walk away. She wanted him to reach his conclusions without influencing him in any way. Also, she felt Michael ought to watch the entire clip without her hovering beside him. She didn't want to make him feel self-conscious.

She took a step, only to hear a crunch. What remained of her mug lay shattered on the floor. Jenny walked over to her side.

"Sit," Naya commanded. Jenny sat and watched her pick up the pieces of broken ceramic. After making sure she hadn't missed any stray pieces, she stood up and went to the kitchen. Jenny followed on her heel.

"You okay there, girl?"

Jenny looked up at her and whined, but her ears were still on the alert.

Naya sighed and patted her head. "It's okay. Mama's okay now. You were such a good girl."

Jenny lay on her stomach, her head up, watching Naya's every move.

Not knowing what to do or how to comfort her dog, Naya did what she usually did when stressed out. She began to gather ingredients for a cake. She was in the middle of pouring batter into a baking pan when Michael appeared at the doorway.

He stood there silently, watching her, then coughed and came deeper into the kitchen. He put her phone on the counter, placing his palms on the stone on either side of it. He

opened and closed his mouth several times as though searching for the right words to say. After several attempts, he just
let out a huff and hung his head down.

"I watched that clip several times, and I must admit there
is no way to explain what I saw," he said. "The thing is, I don't
know what it was that was moving behind you, but it gave
me a sense of danger. Now I'm anxious, knowing you were
alone in this house when that happened." He took a deep
breath and looked at her. "At first, I thought maybe someone
was there with you, and you just didn't know they were behind you. But what I cannot explain is how that figure moved.
It just zipped past you faster than humanly possible. It was a
shadow. That's it. Just a shadow. How could there be one if
there's no one there?"

He shook his head and frowned. "With everything that's
been happening, I can't deny something is going on in this
house that cannot be explained. And I'm quite sure, from
what you've told me, that you know this, too. However, I believe there is no way you would have lived in this house without accounting for everything you encountered."

Naya patiently waited for Michael to continue for the longest time. Instead, she met with feverish silence and an increasing feeling that Michael was losing control of himself. She
shook her head, moved away from him, returned to the table,
and picked up the bowl to wash in the sink.

"What are you making?" he asked.

"Upside down cake."

Michael didn't move or say anything else. When she
glanced at him, his penetrating gaze made her look away. She
didn't know what prevented her from looking back at him, so
she made herself busy, taking the baking tray to the micro-
wave. Even then, she could feel his eyes on her.

Finally she sat at the table, took a deep breath, and met his
gaze. Only then did he move to pull a chair opposite hers and

sit down. She picked up the sweating pitcher of iced tea and began pouring it into two glasses. "The cake should be done in a few minutes. I made iced tea."

A sudden loud thud came behind her, making her heart pound. She jumped to her feet and turned toward where the sound came from.

"Naya, it's just Jenny," Michael said.

Naya panted as she stared down at Jenny. When Jenny's ears flattened over her head, Naya quickly went down on her knees and opened her arms. Jenny immediately lunged into her arms, whining. Naya gave her soothing, shushing noises.

She looked up at Michael. "She was fine earlier. Wherever she'd been, she's been spooked again."

"We're the only ones in this house, Naya. Whatever it was that alarmed her must've been that same thing that grabbed you earlier."

Comforting her dog made her feel better, but she felt tears filling her eyes. She tightened her arms around Jenny, running her hands up and down the dense coat. After a while, Jenny settled, backed away, and began sniffing around. Naya stayed crouched on the floor, not moving. She took in a stuttering breath when she felt Michael's arms wrap around her. Only then did her control slip, and the flood of tears began. She didn't know how long she sat there sobbing in his arms.

When her tears finally subsided, she stood and turned in Michael's arms to face him. "We need to do something."

"I agree," Michael said.

"Any idea what?

Michael let out a sigh. "Right at this moment, I have no clue. Why don't we clean up and then go upstairs to talk or make plans? If that doesn't work, we can just go to sleep. Maybe by tomorrow morning, we will have thought of something. Come up with some sort of solution."

Naya nodded and started to clear the island. "What I don't

understand is why this has suddenly escalated. I've been alone in this house for two months, and I have to admit that even before I moved in, there were already a lot of things that I couldn't explain. There were stories the workmen told me. The common thread was that they'd felt or experienced something strange, but none of it was in any way violent. I would sense something or someone behind me, but when I turned around, nothing was there. Sometimes, I would hear my name called out from somewhere in the woods, but no one would be there. But I've never felt any kind of trepidation. It was more like . . . How do I explain this?"

She rubbed her forehead and looked straight at Michael. "When I first walked onto this property and stepped inside the house, I felt welcomed, much like a warm hug. That's what drove me to go down to the town to find out about everything I needed to do to buy this property. I felt like I had come home. That here, I could stay and feel protected. That's why I don't understand what's going on now. I don't know why this sudden violence, especially what happened earlier. It's like I'm scared, but I don't feel like I'm in danger. That as long as I stay here, I will be safe."

Michael raised his arms, holding the back of his neck and letting out a harsh breath. "Naya, something grabbed at your hair. You cannot think to convince me I didn't see that."

Naya pursed her lips. "I'm not sure how to put this precisely, but have you heard of individuals being smacked back to reality after getting worked up or after someone panicked and lost all ability to reason?"

"What are you talking about?" Michael's eyes widened.

Naya knew she'd failed horribly at getting her point across. She knew she sounded absurd, yet she couldn't get rid of the notion that whatever presence inhabited her home had nothing to do with what was going on.

She tried again. "Like slapping someone out of a panic, and

just like that, they finally see the light." She rushed through the words, hoping they somehow made sense. Not that she sounded convincing. "That's what I'm feeling right now. It's like whatever is in this house that welcomed me so warmly and soothingly is telling me to snap out of it. Urging me to open my eyes, look around, and truly see what is going on. Because something *is* going on. Only I don't know what it *is* that's going on. I don't know what they're trying to warn me about. Somehow, being blind scares me more than something pulling on my hair."

"It was a ghost," Michael growled.

"Okay, I admit, it was a ghost. But the ghost had a message. The only way they could communicate was to pull my hair. To scare me just enough? But I need to know what they're trying to tell me."

"You never answered my question earlier when I asked you about when these things started happening."

"I told you. I felt and saw things almost immediately. As soon as I stepped on the property."

"No. I mean, when did it begin to feel wrong?"

"It never felt wrong. I just got apprehensive after Carol showed up."

"Why?"

"I don't know. I just felt that something was off."

"Again, the question. When did you start getting uncomfortable?"

"I've been trying to think about it, and the only time I could pinpoint was after I'd posted that picture of Jenny on *Instagram*.

"So it only started yesterday."

"Yes."

"How about before that?"

"Just the usual. Strange sounds, movements in my peripheries, Jenny staring at a spot on the staircase."

"But nothing concrete. Nothing scary."

Naya pursed her lips. "None."

"What changed?"

"Changed? Nothing."

Michael tilted his head to the side. "Are you sure nothing changed at all?"

"What are you asking?"

Michael shrugged. "Well, you said things escalated the moment Carol arrived."

"It did. But I'm not sure if it was just timing."

Michael's brows wrinkled deeply into his forehead. "Did you know she was coming over?"

Naya let out a nervous laugh. "No, she arrived unannounced. I didn't question it, I was just so happy to see her. Of course, it surprised me that she'd come, but I was feeling a little lonely. I knew Mom and Luke were coming, but it felt good to see a friend I hadn't heard from in a while come to visit."

"So you hadn't spoken to her for a while?

"No."

"How long since you'd last spoken to her?"

Naya opened her mouth and promptly closed it again. "You know what? I can't remember. I think it was before Andrew attacked me."

"Didn't she visit you at the hospital? At all?"

"Well, no, but remember, I got moved from that hospital because of that doctor you brought in. The former did not have the proper facilities to perform the surgery. Also, Carol works in a different state. She couldn't get out of work. That's why I was so happy to see her the other day."

"So she never called to warn you she was coming over?"

The question shouldn't have surprised her, but hearing her thoughts repeated aloud like that shook her.

"No, she did not."

"Just to clarify what you said." Michael lowered his arms and took her hands in his. "You hadn't spoken to Carol or seen her since before that attempt on your life. In the almost two years that it took for you to get through therapy, this is the first time you'd seen or talked to her."

CHAPTER EIGHTEEN

Naya stared at Michael, her thoughts roiling in chaos. Her doubts quickly solidified into reality. "It is strange that Carol would appear out of the blue."

"And all that time, there was no communication."

"That's the part I've been thinking about. I can't explain why Carol disappeared like that. I didn't question her suddenly showing up, not until that Ouija board incident. And you're right. The hauntings got scary the moment she stepped into this house. The timing of it . . . ."

Naya pulled away from Michael and backed away. She couldn't believe how stupid she'd been. How could she have missed all the signs? "Is this what they're trying to tell me? That I am in danger from Carol?"

"By any chance did you and Carol fight before that incident?"

Naya shook her head. "Not that I can recall, no. She'd always been there for me as a great and supportive friend."

"How did the two of you meet?"

"It was Andrew who introduced us."

Michael's brows rose high on his forehead. "He did? How did he know her? Did he say where from?"

"He told me she was a super fan and that he'd met her at one of my fan meets."

"Do you remember meeting her at that fan meet, or any fan meet?

"No. Andrew and I met for lunch, and he said he wanted to introduce me to Carol, who had been very supportive of my vlogs, my projects, etcetera. That she was an admin of one of my bigger fan sites."

"Was it normal practice for you to meet admins of a fan site or fan sites? Any fan sites?

"No, that was the first time."

"And you didn't think to question it?"

Naya frowned at how Michael phrased his words and nibbled on her lower lip. "I was just too happy to meet an admin, I guess. When she showed up at my lunch date with Andrew, I wanted to tell her to leave us alone during my private time. But then Andrew asked her to join us, and before I knew it, we were chatting like friends."

"Ah, so you got ambushed," Michael said, his voice gentle and understanding. Yet, somehow, that sympathy triggered her anxiety.

Naya took in a small, stuttering breath. Her stomach clenched almost immediately. "I feel so stupid now."

"No, you weren't stupid. You just trusted the wrong person. And you shouldn't blame yourself for trusting someone you thought you could and should rely on. You loved him, right?"

Naya blinked back the threatening tears.

"Many people, including myself, have made that same mistake to varying degrees," Michael continued. "In your case, it was a deadly situation. Carol's involvement is uncertain, but her possible motives are giving me pause. Call it a gut feeling, if you must."

"Yesterday, when you and Luke implied your suspicions about her, I didn't want to say anything. I know I should have said something." Naya shivered as the familiar icy cold realization of betrayal swept through her. She wrapped her arms tightly around her torso to hold back the shivers.

"It hurts me to realize Carol may be involved in this. It took me long, painful months to face the reality of what Andrew did to me. I have moved on with my life since then, or tried to. But now . . . I didn't want to suspect Carol's involvement in what's been happening here."

"Betrayal is always painful, Naya. We must deal with the reality that some of the living can be much more evil than . . . restless souls." Michael started pacing. After a long minute, he turned around to face her again. "Let's go back to last night when Rachel disappeared."

Michael was right. At that moment, the spirits in her home looked less and less evil compared to what Andrew and now possibly Carol did and continued to do to her. She still could not figure out how Carol was involved with Andrew.

"Well . . . We now know that Rachel did not disappear. God, I feel bad right now. She tried to tell her side of the story, but none of us really listened or even believed in her."

Michael crossed his arms over his chest. "I'm her brother, so I'll probably have to grovel and ask for forgiveness, but that's nothing new. Back to that night. Carol and Rachel were playing with the Ouija Board, right?"

"Yes. Rachel was the only one in the room with Carol. She's the only one willing to collaborate with the paranormal event."

Michael tapped the tip of his finger on his lower lip, remaining silent. Naya waited patiently, wondering what was going through his mind.

"You know what?" He pulled his phone out of his pocket. "I'm going to give Rachel a call right now. I'll put her on speaker and ask her about that night. You don't have to say anything, but I'll let her know you're listening, too. All right?

Naya put up her hands. "Good idea."

Michael unlocked his phone and tapped it twice. Naya heard the call connecting and suddenly felt nervous.

"What's up, big brother?"

Naya jumped at the sudden loud sound of Rachel's voice

on the speaker.

"Rachel, hey, Naya's is here with me. And, uhm, I'm going to ask you a question and I need you to answer me truthfully. Don't hesitate. Don't overthink your response. Can you do that?"

Rachel chuckled. "Oh, okay. I'll try my best. Go ahead. What's the question?"

"When you were in the living room with Carol, playing with that Ouija board, did you see the black inky thing?"

Naya tilted her head to the side when Rachel didn't respond immediately.

"Rachel, talk to me. I asked you not to overthink your answers. Yes or no. Did you or did you not see the inky black thing that Carol spoke about when you were playing?

Rachel let out an audible sigh. "No, I didn't. I didn't see it at all."

Naya's eyes widened and met Michael's startled ones.

Michael shook his head and raised a finger over his lips. When Naya nodded, he asked, "So why did you back up what she said? Can you tell us again about what happened?"

Rachel let out another heavy sigh. This time, it sounded like exasperation. "Ahh . . . I wish . . . okay. While we were playing with the board, we both had our fingers on, you know, on that shot glass, but nothing was happening, Carol asked if there was any wine left. I told her there was, and I turned to grab the bottle, only to see it was empty. So I told her I'd go get another and to wait for me. It was during the time I was in the kitchen, that I heard her scream. I rushed back, and I saw her lying on the floor. I thought she'd fainted, so I went to her, and I tried to wake her up, gently slapping her face like, you know, urging her to wake up. When she came to, I asked her what happened, and she told me about the shadow. That's when I ran to find you guys."

Michael met Naya's gaze. "I see."

Naya ran a hand over her face and wanted to speak up, but Rachel rushed on.

"Look, I'm sorry I wasn't clear that night, okay? That was the first time I had met Carol, and I was drunk and jealous. I found out that she was Naya's best friend. Like . . . where'd she come from? How come Naya never spoke to me about her? I know it's childish of me, and I have no excuse for what I felt, and I'm sorry."

She paused, taking an audibly shaky breath. "Naya, if you're listening, I know I can be childish, and I felt a little insecure. Um . . . I thought I knew all your friends, so I was a little surprised to find out you had a *best friend* who wasn't me, someone I'd never met or heard about. You never once even mentioned her. Even when you were at the hospital or after the surgery during the months of your recuperation, you never once mentioned her. It's been almost two years, and that night was the first time I'd met her."

Naya heard a sniffle and realized that Rachel was crying. Her heart went out to her childhood friend and again she attempted to speak, but Rachel wasn't done.

"Anyway, back to that night. While all of you were hovering over her, I thought that maybe Carol was making it all up. Later on, I planned to tell you about my suspicions, but I didn't. Again, I'm sorry. Blame it on my being drunk and childish. I was never a good drunk."

Rachel forced a chuckle before continuing. "It's just that everyone was shocked about the whole situation and fussing over Carol. My head was a little fuzzy because I was drunk, and that house is creepy, so, you know, my imagination went sideways for a little while. I decided I needed to save myself further embarrassment and went upstairs to sleep. But the next morning, I found out I supposedly disappeared. How could that be? I was in the bedroom the whole time. I confronted Carol earlier, but she said I was imagining things, especially as I was drunk the night before. I was just so over it. I didn't want to say anything anymore, especially after how all of you reacted. But yeah, I don't like Carol." She finished in a rush, breathing heavily.

It would take Naya a while to process what Rachel had confessed, but she needed to do something first. "Rachel, before anything else, I must apologize to you. I'm so sorry I didn't listen to you this morning. There's nothing I can say to defend my actions of not believing in you. I have to confess, Carol's story, your retelling of that supernatural incident, and the idea of Carol being assaulted by some paranormal entity—it truly frightens me. This house is admittedly . . . Well, some things are going on here that can't be explained rationally."

"Naya, it's okay. I understand. Really. I'm over it now. What I failed to mention is that I cannot fully deny something weird was going on last night."

"What do you mean?"

"Like whenever I used the bathroom, I swear I could feel something. At first, I dismissed it as, you know, my being drunk. But in hindsight, I'm telling you that it *did* feel like someone was in the bathroom with me. I refused to acknowledge them, but I'm telling you now. Also, I only had one glass of wine tonight, so I'm not drunk."

Naya let out a chuckle at the last bit of information. "I believe you. Going back to the reason Michael called you. We were trying to get the story of what happened that night straight. Nothing added up, and things have been happening here at the house. What you said about Carol is making things clearer. That maybe what happened last night had wasn't all paranormal."

Rachel let out an audible gasp. "Wait. You're scaring me. Did something happen?"

Naya winced, cleared her throat, and met Michael's gaze.

Michael gave her a thumbs-up and took over. "Yeah, sis, something did, but I don't want you to worry. Um, we'll tell you about it when you get back here, or how about we meet up in town tomorrow?"

"Michael!" Rachel's voice rose in pitch. "I won't be able to sleep until I find out what happened. Tell me what happened."

Naya rolled her eyes. "Go ahead. She's never going to let us go unless you tell her."

Michael made a face that Naya could only interpret as defeat. "Something grabbed at Naya—"

"What do you mean grabbed at her?"

"If you'll let me finish—"

"Fine."

"As I was saying, something grabbed her and pulled her up by her hair."

When Michael didn't continue, a sound of annoyance came from the phone. "Care to expand on that, brother?"

Exasperated, Naya took over when Michael still didn't say anything. "Rachel, Michael and I were talking when something grabbed my hair and lifted me. Jenny then attacked something behind the chair, but we didn't see anything there."

"Freak out."

Naya chuckled. "That's it? That's all you have to say?"

"Maybe, because I *am* freaking out. Guys, you know what? Why don't you come downtown? There's plenty of room in the hotel down there. Better yet, why don't you two just come here to Michael's house? Right now. Get out of that house. Things are getting scary up there."

"Well, that's the thing, Rachel. I don't feel scared."

"Michael. Can you check on Naya? I think that hair-pulling muddled her brain or something. What do you mean, you're not scared?"

Rachel's voice rose to a high enough pitch that Naya winced. To her amusement, Michael looked just as pained.

She cleared her throat. "Listen to me, Rachel. I feel that whatever these spirits are doing now is not because they wish to harm me, it's because they're warning me about something or someone. They've always welcomed me. I've always felt cared for and welcomed here. The realization that I was being cautioned only came to me during a conversation with Michael about the events of that night. Earlier, Michael asked me when the hauntings escalated, and I pinpointed it to the day Carol arrived."

"Let me get this straight. You're saying you've always known the house was haunted, but that things got weirder and scarier after Carol got there."

"Yeah, you got it."

The windows rattled, and Naya walked over to look outside and saw the perimeter lights flickering.

"It's getting worse out there," she said, looking over her shoulder to Michael.

Michael held out his hand. Naya hurried back and grabbed hold, huddling to his side.

He faced the phone. "Listen, Rachel, there's no way Naya and I can get down there tonight. The weather's turned, and it's already late. Don't worry, we'll be safe from human intruders. We have Jenny here with us." He laughed derisively. "If the weather's clear tomorrow morning, we'll meet up with you. If we get there early enough, we can have breakfast or at least brunch. What do you think?"

"I think that sounds great. I'll let the others know. Before you go, I need to tell you that Carol isn't with us. It's just Kelly, Luke, and me. Kelly said she'd lost track of Carol at the mall and hasn't seen her since. She thought she was with Luke or me, but we'd not seen her either. I don't know where she is. No one does. She's not answering her phone."

Naya met Michael's gaze. "Carol disappeared?"

Michael nodded, his expression grave. "She could be anywhere. Rachel, look. I need you to stay close to Luke and Kelly."

"I will. Wait, I just remembered something else. Carol mentioned in the car on our way down that she wanted to do some shopping before going back. I didn't pay much attention to what she was saying and forgot all about it until now."

Naya frowned. "Go back where?"

"I wasn't paying much attention, but I think she was talking about a flight. It just struck me strange she'd mention a flight when I knew she came up here in a car."

Naya's frown deepened. "A flight tomorrow? How is that even possible? There are no domestic flights scheduled for tomorrow, especially with the storm. I should know, I took them often enough. There are only three flights out of Amber Ville every week."

"I knew it. Look, now that we've talked about this, nothing about Carol makes sense. What if she's on her way up there right now? Or is already there? Do I need to call the sheriff to go up there and check on you two?"

"I don't think she can easily get up here, especially in this weather," Michael said. "Don't worry. We'll be careful. 'Bye, Rachel. We'll see you tomorrow."

CHAPTER NINETEEN

Michael's intense gaze pierced through Naya's thoughts. The faint, spicy cologne he'd probably splashed on earlier tingled her senses. But it was his physical proximity that sent shivers down her body. She was already on emotional overload, but the sensory one made her realize she was going over the edge.

She sat down, closed her eyes, and lowered her head. Whatever was going on in the house, and the almost certainty that Carol was involved in some nefarious plot to kill her, felt much like a weight dragging her back down into that ravine she'd escaped from.

Even after the conversation with Rachel and Michael's presence, Naya's thoughts ran circles in her mind, clouding her ability to think rationally. Beginning from the time they'd first met each other all those years ago, fast-forwarded to the present, never had she thought to question her future until that moment.

Did I ever love Andrew?

She thought she'd had.

Had I ever been in love with Andrew?

The answer, when it came, was a revelation that gave her strength.

No.

Have I ever been in love?

She drew in a stuttering breath.

Of course, she'd been in love before. Never even fallen out of love with that person. She looked up and met Michael's gaze.

No. She'd never fallen out of love with Michael.

Michael stepped in behind her, so close she could feel his warmth on her back. He wasn't touching her, and yet she could feel his heat. She spun in place, facing his chest.

She looked up, met Michael's gaze, and said, "I've always been independent."

He looked confused. "Where is this coming from? What are you talking about?"

"I've never been a follower."

Michael's brow rose higher on his forehead. "And?"

"I appreciate the support, but I do things on my own."

Michael placed his large hands on Naya's shoulders. Though she could feel the strength, his touch was gentle and reassuring. She felt her body respond, leaning into his touch.

He stared straight into her eyes. "You are who you are because of who and what you are. You're a strong, independent woman who's always known what she wanted in life. One who took risks after careful consideration. You have never been reckless. Now tell me why this sudden show of insecurity?"

"I have never been dependent on anyone. No one. I've always relied on myself."

Michael nodded. "I know that," he said, his voice gentle. "Now please, tell me what's going on?"

"I need you."

"You know you have me. You've always had me. There's no need to ask."

"You don't understand."

"Then make me understand."

"I've hidden from my feelings for the longest time, and made bad decisions because of it. I'm done hiding."

"And what do you want?"

"I want you."

"I already told you. You have me. But I also want you to know something."

"What's that?"

"You don't have to be afraid. You can be you around me, be the person you've always been. I expect you to remain true to yourself. I won't have it any other way."

"This person you see before you, she's a different person. After what Andrew did, I came to Amber Ville for a complete life change. I'm only just starting that change."

"And you're afraid I may not be able to catch up with that change?"

"Yes."

"I travel a lot. Where I choose to live is not going to affect my job. As it is, I can be in worldwide meetings from my bedroom if I want to and still succeed in running the company. Also, in case you've forgotten, I've got a place here. Doesn't that show you something?"

That made Naya smile. "You do realize I'm quite the eccentric?"

Michael's smile grew. "I wouldn't have you any other way. Now that I have you, I don't want to ever let you go again."

Her breathing quickened, and her pulse followed suit. Michael had always had that effect on her. He made her feel all the things she'd never felt with anyone else. Most definitely, Andrew never had that effect on her.

Michael stepped closer and cupped her chin. Lifted her head slightly so their gazes met. Heat flowed through her like a blazing fire, sending small explosions of desire into every crevice in her body.

"The recent chain of events seems strange, and there's no denying the paranormal aspect, but the rest seem contrived. Calculated. Andrew failed in his attempt to kill you, so you may find this funny, but this whole haunting thing seems like they want to frighten you to death instead."

"What's the goal?"

"Good question." Michael took in a deep breath. "Right now, I think we should go upstairs and go to bed."

Naya laid her hand on Michael's chest, her fingers splaying over the soft t-shirt he wore. Beneath her palm, she could feel the steady beat of his heart. "Let's go upstairs."

Naya splayed her fingers over Michael's back as he dragged her sweatpants down her hips. As soon as her pants and panties fell to the floor, her insides twisted in anticipation. She'd never thought she'd be where she was at that moment. For most of her life, she'd only ever fantasized about Michael standing before her and taking off his shirt, soon followed by his sweatpants. Now, here was in all his glory.

She couldn't stop looking at his body. They'd both changed so much through the years. Michael had always been the hulking, towering figure of a man who protected her and Luke when they'd been younger. Had been a faithful friend when she'd been older. But now, what had been pure muscle and brawn had changed into a lean physique—the result of a devastating virus. She had changed as well. Her face now held the scars of a brutal attack. But she and Michael had survived what would have defeated others and lived to tell the tale. The changes were welcome.

Michael seized her hips with his large hands, his foot moving between her legs to spread them. Looking down, she saw his bare feet.

She stood on her toes, arched her back, and opened her mouth to receive his kiss. A moan escaped her, a sound she couldn't hope to stifle. Michael picked her up by her bare buttocks and sat her on the edge of the bed. The moment didn't call for foreplay. She spread her legs wider, welcoming his larger body as he pressed closer. Michael dove deep inside her, her muscles clamping down around him as she rolled her head against the bedcovers.

"Open your eyes, Naya," Michael murmured against her lips.

Naya didn't hesitate. She opened her eyes and met his gaze. He swooped down and clamped his mouth over hers, staring into her eyes and thrusting deep into her, over and over, until all she could do was breathe through the rhythm and friction.

At the back of her mind, she knew this moment was more carnal desires than making love. It was pure and simple lust controlling them. Lust that had been held back and controlled for too many years. But this was no casual sex. Far from it. She felt it much deeper than that.

Later, they could take things more slowly, but at that moment, Michael's thrusts took on a rhythm she needed. In and out. She clasped his hips, pushing back against his thrusts, arching upward, taking every inch that he was giving her.

Her thoughts were consumed with the stretch and friction of his thrusts, filling her in ways she never experienced before. "Michael . . ."

He stopped moving and looked concerned. "Did I hurt you?"

She grasped her hands around the back of his neck. "You're mine now."

Michael froze, and his breathing stopped. "What?"

"Say it," Naya insisted. She needed to hear it from him. "Tell me."

His eyes gentled. "I am yours, Naya. I've always been yours. Only yours."

She loosened her grasp and pulled him down until her lips brushed his. "I love you, Michael." Her voice shook as emotions took over her.

Michael closed his arms around her torso, shifting them until his back was on the bed and she straddled him. The change in position made him plunge deeper into her, making her eyes roll to the back of her head. She flexed her hips, sinking lower over him, taking him deeper still until she could feel the pressure inside her.

Her thoughts began to sway. What would her family think of their sudden involvement? Even as the question entered her mind, she knew her family would be happy for her. Luke had always teased her about her unwavering crush on Michael. Did he know about Michael's feelings for her?

Michael's hands tugged on her breasts, tweaking her hard nipples, making her catch her breath. He leaned up, clamping his mouth over one breast, licking, nipping, kissing, sending her into sensory overload. Her body began to tremble, and she recognized the signs of her impending orgasm.

She leaned forward, touching her forehead against Michael's. Her knees weakened, and her legs trembled. She knew she wouldn't be able to stay straddled for much longer. As though sensing her loss of control, Michael lifted her, helping her lie on her stomach while moving behind her. He pulled her up by her waist until she was on all fours and thrust deep inside her again.

Naya bit on the covers to stifle her cries. The new position enabled her to take Michael even deeper if possible. His hands gripped her hips, pulling her against him, and she just knew she'd find bruises there when their mating was done. His hands moved to rub the small of her back, leaving warm trails in their wake. Now that she knew how it felt to have those hands roaming over her body, she knew she would be forever spoiled.

He lowered his face next to hers and whispered, "You're mine, too."

Naya's heart eased. She closed her eyes and focused on their bodies connecting. Behind her, Michael pumped his whole length into her, sparing her nothing as his balls slapped against her ass. It should have been funny, but it wasn't — far from it.

A moan escaped her. She snaked an arm to grab onto Michael's hip, digging her fingers into his firm flesh. He pounded into her harder, and she backed into him, accepting everything he was giving her.

Naya had sex before — at her age, of course she'd had, but what she was experiencing now was new. Primal. She wanted more.

As Michael's cock stretched her, she felt something else trying to enter her, the sensation something completely unexpected. An extraordinary sense of fullness penetrated her alongside Michael's cock, and through her lustful haze, she suddenly knew he had inserted a finger into her anus. Her eyes flew open, but she could only focus on the headboard. Overwhelming sensations washed over her whole body, making her want to scream. Her core tightened around Michael's cock and finger, making him grind into her. He sped up his pace as she stared at the wall with unseeing eyes, tears of overwhelming desire streaming down her face.

"Michael," she nearly yelled.

"Do you want me to stop?"

Her nails dug into the covers as she leaned her forehead into the bed. "Never."

Naya cracked her eyelids open and looked around. Disoriented and flushed, the first thing she noticed was the light shining through the window, as if a million diamonds fracturing it. It took a moment for her to realize what was so strange about the whole situation until it sank in that she hadn't woken to sunshine in a long time. That the sun itself was up made her sit up.

The sun was up. That meant the storm had passed.

She stood up on bare feet and walked over to the window.

Through the warped glass, she saw the front garden covered by a glittering white carpet of snow and the spruce trees in the distance dancing in the wind. The sight of the swaying trees disappointed her, for it meant the winds were still strong, which meant the wind-chill factor would be intolerable. Such was life in the mountains, she supposed. She turned away, taking in the surroundings of her room. There was no sign that Michael had been with her.

Memories of the night before made her bite her lower lip. She couldn't understand what had gotten into her, but she had ridden Michael like a mare in heat, and Michael had matched her passion all night long. She couldn't remember when they'd stopped or when she'd fallen asleep.

She looked down on her nakedness and grimaced. The night had been an eye-opener, but she needed a hot shower. Hopefully, there was enough left in the tanks.

She took her time in the bathroom. She had a hot shower to enjoy, and the silence told her the generators had ceased operating, which meant the power had been restored.

After her shower, she stood in front of the mirror and checked her reflection. She didn't look any different, but she did look flushed, and the expected purple smudges underneath her eyes were not there. A smile morphed over her lips as she raised a hand to touch them. Her lower lip looked fuller than usual, and she knew exactly why they looked like that. The kisses and other activities that flashed through her mind made her giggle. She wrapped a towel around her and walked out of the bathroom, then sat on the bed and started to towel her hair dry. Lost in thought, she didn't notice the door opening until she saw Michael walking in with a mug in each hand.

"Good morning," he said, smiling brightly. "I have coffee."

Naya assessed Michael with a newfound sense of possessiveness. Michael had always given her the impression that he was bigger than the average man, and in her mind, he was. His blue eyes, the same color as Rachel's, gleamed beneath a strong brow with dark brown hair. When he was younger, he'd had blond hair, but his hair grew darker as he aged. His shoulders were broad and tapered to a trim waist.

He walked toward her, his strides unhesitant, stopping a foot or so away from her. Surprisingly, his proximity didn't make her feel like he was hovering over her, not even when he bent to drop a kiss on her cheek before handing her the mug. Never taking her gaze off him, she took the mug and took a whiff of the fragrant brew. The aroma tantalized. Surprised, she dropped her gaze to examine the contents, and to her amazement, a beautiful tan-colored froth rested on the top.

Her gaze snapped up. "You made this?"

Michael shrugged. "Of course I did."

"How did you find the espresso machine?"

Michael shrugged again as he took a sip from his cup. "I spotted it in your office."

Naya laughed so hard that some of the coffee spilled on her hand. She quickly placed the coffee on the floor and wiped her hand on the towel she'd used to dry her hair. "You are an amazingly resourceful man, Michael Bradbury."

"I needed my coffee."

"How'd you find the beans?"

"I called Luke."

Naya chuckled, picked up the cup, and took a sip. "It is excellent coffee, Michael. Thank you."

Michael turned around and walked over to the chair by the window. "I also talked to Rachel. They're expecting us to go down for brunch."

Naya glanced at the clock. "It's ten. I didn't realize it was so late."

Michael sipped from his cup but didn't say anything.

Naya looked at him suspiciously. "You're amused."

"I didn't say anything." He smiled.

Naya picked up a pillow and threw it at him. The pillow fell short, landing by his feet. Michael picked it up and put it behind him but still didn't say a word.

"Ugh, you're laughing at me."

"I did no such thing."

Naya threw him a glare, to which he responded with a soft smile.

"What did Rachel say?" She picked up her cup, taking another sip.

"She said she and Luke made bets that we're now official."

Naya looked up and met his gaze. Slowly and carefully, she swallowed the coffee in her mouth before taking a breath. Heat spread over her body as memories of Michael's vigorous thrusting came to mind.

She swallowed again. "What did you tell her?"

"That it was none of her business. To which she started laughing. Luke got on the phone, expounding on how I should treat my younger brother-in-law kindly."

Naya humphed. "The brats."

"They've always known how I felt about you." The seriousness in Michael's voice sobered her amusement.

"Come here," Naya said.

When Michael didn't move, she reached out to him with a hand, gesturing for him to come closer. "Please come here."

Michael slowly stood up, walked over to her, and again stopped a foot or so away from her.

She patted on the bed beside her. "Sit with me."

She waited until Michael did as she requested before straddling him. He gripped her hips and held her in place.

She cupped his cheeks with her palms. "What's going on between us? It's not for laughs or a one-night stand."

"I know," he said.

"I am not about to publicize our relationship, nor am I going to indulge our families with details. We don't need to explain anything."

"I know."

"I may not go public, but I will never deny us. It will never be a secret."

"We'll keep it private."

"My fans will want to know who you are. They are a nosey lot. We can discuss what we want them to know, but I would prefer they not know anything."

Michael ran his hands up and down her sides. "Them not finding out about me may be an impossible dream. Nothing is private in this day and age. My work involves a lot of traveling, but I will always come home to you. Will that be a problem?"

"It doesn't bother me."

Michael pulled her closer to him until their lips met. He caressed her lips with the softest touch, a slow slide of his mouth against hers. He pressed tiny kisses over her lower lip, then the upper, as though questioning his right to touch her. She opened her mouth, an unspoken invitation that he was more than welcome. His mouth settled firmly over hers, hard enough that she could feel his teeth.

Naya sighed when the tip of Michael's tongue slid across her lips, as though taking a careful taste. She opened her mouth more, and he fully accepted her invitation. His warm tongue reached in and stroked hers, soft and slow. He tasted of coffee and man. It tickled something primitive in her. Her senses went into overdrive, threatening to overwhelm her, yet they didn't. She moaned. Michael responded with a moan of his own. He held her tighter in his arms while his tongue fondled hers with a greater force, becoming more demanding, like he couldn't get enough of her and was trying to assuage a ravenous hunger.

Everything suddenly became clear to Naya. This moment was no longer about sex. Not like the night before.

They were giving part of themselves to each other and getting more demanding.

Her back arched against him as a thrill of pure, unadulterated desire zipped up and down her spine, touching her skull, then back down again to her pussy. She could feel his cock against her moist opening, and she couldn't help rubbing herself against him.

Michael let her go, and she almost complained but held back when he took hold of the waist of his shorts, pulling them down. She rose on her knees to make it easier for him, and the instant he was free of his clothing, she sank back down, feeling his bare cock throbbing against her pussy. Sore or not, she wanted him inside her. She rose, prepared to sink on him, but he flipped her over, and she found herself on her back, lying flat on the bed with her knees hanging over the edge.

He drew back and looked down at her, the desire in his gaze focused fully on her. Her pussy throbbed with impatient need. She reached up, tracing her fingers over the defined muscles of his abdomen. Michael's eyes hooded as he watched her touch him. When her hand lowered, he leaned over and took her mouth, his tongue exploring with a thoroughness that left her wanting more. She'd never been kissed like that before, as though he were staking his claim on her. Her arousal rose to a desperate need. Another moan escaped her. This kiss was not just a touching of mouths, it was like he was making love to her.

Naya began to pant into his mouth even as she spread her legs wider, wanting him to satisfy her emptiness, get inside her . . . fill her.

"I need you so much," she gasped.

Michael stroked her skin, making her shiver in response.

She licked her lips when he planted his hands on either side of her head. Her mouth went dry in anticipation. Her heart began to beat frantically, making her feel all glowy. She'd been wet since she'd straddled him, but now she could feel herself dripping.

"Oh!"

Michael cupped her mound, gently rubbing along her slit, shutting off every thought like a switch. His assured touch made her arch hard, wanting only to get closer to that touch. Her gut felt heavy, her need rising to intolerable levels. Michael sliding his tongue over her lips only heightened her arousal. Conscious thought disappeared as the combined stimuli burned a fiery path from her skull down to her pussy.

She needed more of the pleasure that Michael was giving her. She braced her feet on the bed so she could push harder against Michael's hand. She grasped the sheets when his teeth scraped her chin and slid down her throat. Michael made a soft sound much like a purr and a growl as he gently nibbled down the column of her throat. A tiny part of her mind wondered if he was testing the limits of her control.

His tongue dove into the hollow of her throat while his hand never stopped delighting her lower parts. He traced her folds, making her choke out a moan as a shard of pure desire struggled to escape. His questing fingers investigated every crevice, smearing her juices and making her quiver. She let out a guttural, pleading sound when Michael sucked hard on a nipple. Against the entrance of her pussy, she felt his fingers press in. Her juices made for an easy entrance, causing her to arch against him. He continued to suckle on her breast as his fingers moved in and out of her, circling, stretching. When he continued to push deeper inside, his palm drew circles over her clit. Her hips jerked as she became overwhelmed with a need.

"Please," she breathed out. "I need more."

When Michael pulled his fingers free of her, she whimpered at the loss. She didn't have to wait long before he pressed his cock into her, slowly moving inside, sliding easily.

"Ouch," she muttered, moving her hips so she could take him in deeper.

"What's wrong?"

"Stings," she said. "Don't stop."

"Are you sure?"

Naya nodded, and Michael moved slowly, sliding in. She shuddered at the sensation of being widened and stretched. Erotic heat swept all over her, making her moan. Her arms came up to circle his neck. He pressed in deeper, stretching her some more. The slight twinge began to hurt more, but she welcomed the soreness. It wasn't detracting from the pleasure, it only added to it. She knew she would probably regret the pain afterward, but at that moment, she didn't care. Michael felt incredible.

"You like feeling me inside you, don't you?

Naya giggled. "Yes."

He pressed back inside, and she arched up to meet his thrusts. He moved deeper inside her, reaching that place where friction and heat melted something inside her. She couldn't contain the moans flying off her lips when he began to move faster. Sharp delight caught her unawares, making her quiver and cry out, thrusting higher and trying to make harder contact. Delightful sensations filled her senses from her core to her skull, and she could only think of seeking oblivion. Michael thrust once more, harder and stronger than before. Ecstasy exploded inside her, and all she could do was hold on.

When she opened her eyes again, Michael was tending to her, wiping her down with a damp towel.

He gave her a smile. "I think you've had enough, young lady."

"Yes." She moved her legs and inhaled sharply. "Oh my God, I think I'm done."

"You are more than done. I am done, too. I had to drag my ass into that shower." He threw the towel through the open bathroom door and plopped into bed beside her. "Wake me up when it's time to get up."

Naya braced her elbow on the bed and rested her head on her hand. "I think you've forgotten you promised Rachel we'd see them for brunch."

"God, do we have to?"

"Well, we could always call and make an excuse, but that would only lead to more teasing."

"I've never had this much sex in one day," he groused.

Naya's stomach grumbled. "And now I'm hungry."

Michael opened an eye and glared at her. "There's food downstairs."

Naya burst into laughter. She dropped a playful slap on Michael's stomach and then swung her legs off the side of the bed. "Come on, get up. Might as well go to town and meet the bunch. Also, I want to drop by the Sheriff's office."

CHAPTER TWENTY

M ichael focused on the menu in his hand, tuning out the conversation around him. Naya sat beside him, sipping a cup of coffee while going through the emails she'd pulled up on her phone. She didn't seem to mind that they were the center of a hot discussion between Luke and Rachel. Kelly didn't seem to be paying attention to anyone, rather appearing busy scanning whatever she was scrolling through on her phone.

As for him, he couldn't find the energy to open any emails. He felt like he'd been wrung through a spinner. His gaze drifted back to Naya. After all their physical intimacy of the night before and a little over an hour ago, he still couldn't wrap his head around the fact that he had been thoroughly claimed by Naya.

A soft smile formed over his lips as he remembered her words. *You're mine.*

He placed a hand on her knee and gave it a gentle squeeze. To his amusement, she moved her leg a little closer to his but didn't pause from typing out a message.

Naya stood up. "Excuse me, I have to take this call. Michael, I'll have whatever Rachel's having. Thanks."

"Where's she going?" Rachel said, turning in her seat. She turned back around, looking forlorn. "I thought we were going to eat together."

"I don't know, something must've happened," Kelly said, a sudden frown marring her forehead. "She was dealing with several emails."

"She looks a little frazzled," Luke said. He turned back to look at Kelly. "Mom, did you hear anything from the company?"

Kelly shook her head. "Nothing. It must be something only she can deal with."

"I wonder what happened. Did anything suspicious happen last night, Michael?"

"She woke up around eight but thought it was midnight. Her phone clock had glitched and showed the wrong time zone."

"How does that even work?" Luke asked. "That sounds like someone attempted to hack into her phone."

"If the clock is affected, someone did it manually from her phone. Not remote. Otherwise, it would show as a dubious activity," Rachel said.

"I had her change her passwords immediately," Michael said. He continued to observe Naya through the frosted glass as she spoke on the phone just outside the building.

"I'm sure it was enough," Rachel said. "Otherwise, she'd have to regain access."

"Can someone remotely access a phone?"

"It's been done, but only for those with low-security protocols in place," Luke said. "I wouldn't worry."

"Michael," Rachel said.

"Yeah?" Michael continued to watch Naya. She was frowning and speaking rapidly.

"Is everything all right between the two of you?"

"Why shouldn't it be?" His frown deepened when Naya began to pace the sidewalk as she listened to whoever was on the other line.

"You know Naya's not going anywhere. She's always had her eyes set on you. That Andrew was just a diversion."

"A deadly one," Kelly said.

"Naya and I are fine," Michael said as he watched Naya

grip the back of her neck and roll her head. She began to speak rapidly, and from how some of the people passing her were looking at her, she most likely sounded agitated.

"Excuse me. I'll be right back." Michael quickly slid off the bench, ignoring the protests coming from the others, and was reaching for the doors when Naya opened them.

She paused and then signaled for him to follow her outside.

"What's going on?" he said as soon as he joined her on the sidewalk. A gust of wind made him shiver, and he glared up at the blue sky.

Naya pursed her lips. "Remember last night when we found the wrong time on my phone?"

"Yes?"

"That was my finance manager. She said someone tried to access my accounts last night and said it was good that I had the foresight to have several security protocols in place."

"I see," he said, but he didn't see. "So everything's all right? Nothing has been hacked or worse?"

Naya shook her head. "Everything is fine, and you made me change the passwords last night, which helped. The bank security kicked in because of dubious activities."

"What did you tell your manager?"

"Told her to put a hold on all my accounts until I can fly to LA."

"You're flying back today?"

"I think I should. I had my assistant book a private flight back into Chicago in an hour. That just leaves me enough time to have breakfast and zip off to the airport."

"That's going to cost," he said, folding his arms over his chest. "Are the pilots even going to fly in this weather?"

"They are. As I said, I had them checked. The weather's still bad, and I'm sure it'll be a bumpy flight, but I have no choice. It's either stay here and allow whoever it is to gain access into my accounts and portfolios or fly out and settle everything once and for all. I should be back tonight."

"Do you want me to go with you?"

"No, it's okay. I'll be back tonight."

Michael let out a sigh and pulled her close. "Let's get back inside and tell the others."

"Okay," Naya said, nodding in his chest. "I'm so sorry, Michael. I have to go and deal with this."

"What to be sorry about? Come on, you barely have enough time to eat with us before you go. How about clothes?" He ran his hand through her thick, glossy hair and down her back.

"No need. I'll go as I am, and I have most of my documents with me and at the Chicago office."

Not wanting to let her go, he held her for a few more moments. Given how she held tightly to him, she didn't want to go either. They stood that way for a while, not minding the curious glances from the passersby. He didn't know how quickly she'd be able to deal with the attempted hijack on her accounts, but he would wait for her no matter how long it would take.

Michael stirred through the fog of sleep. He sensed that something felt odd, as though he was not alone in the room. He'd always been a light sleeper, but the medications he'd taken earlier were altering his perception. This time, it felt different. Fighting through the drug-induced sleep, he heard the door open and felt an unpleasant cold draft of air swoosh over him. When he could finally peel his eyes open, although he could barely see through the darkness, he could make out that the bedroom door was open. A few seconds later, while still trying to process what he was looking at, the blanket around his hips suddenly began pulling away. Startled, he found the energy to reach out for the lamp on the table beside him. The sudden brightness made him recoil, but it had served its purpose. There was no one in the room with him.

Since he'd been back at his place, there had been a few doubtful incidents that he could not dismiss as coincidence or blame on an overactive imagination. There was nothing concrete he could capture on camera, just an uneasy feeling he couldn't shake off. His home had never had weird vibes before, and it was too much of a coincidence that the strangeness had started after he left Naya's place. Could something have followed him to his house? Or as Carol would have it, attached to him? He had no clue what he was dealing with. All he knew was that the weird feeling he'd come to associate with Naya's house was now in his home.

He closed his eyes and tried to get back to sleep, but his senses were on hyperdrive, and his thoughts whirled with possibilities. He took in a deep breath and let it out slowly. Forcing himself to sleep would only give him a headache. The best thing he could do to prevent that was to get out of bed and probably watch television downstairs. He made his decision, got out of bed, swiped his phone from the bedside table, and made his way out of his bedroom, only to grimace and hurry to slip into fleece-lined slippers.

Having heated floorboards installed was the best decision he'd ever made, for it made it possible to walk around his house barefoot. Unfortunately, the long power outage must have affected the system, and now his floors were ice cold. Electrical jobs were lined up in a queue, so even if he requested someone to come out, he'd have to wait until he moved up the proverbial line. Once downstairs, he discovered the floorboards were heated, which meant it was a short of some kind. Which also meant he'd have to switch the system entirely.

"Just my luck," he muttered aloud. He brought up the message app on his phone, pressed the record icon, spoke a few instructions, and sent the text off to his PA. He knew it was early morning, but his assistant had been with him for almost five years and was used to his quirks.

Repair request taken care of, he went to the kitchen, opened a control panel from behind a woven wall rug, and switched off the floor heating. Now all he had to do was light a fire and hope the warmth and sound of wood burning would lull him to sleep. He'd taken three steps only to jump when his phone rang. Biting off a curse, he peered at his phone — Naya was calling.

"Naya? Where are you? Is anything wrong?"

"I just got back. Luke, Mom, and Rachel decided to stay in Chicago. They told me to tell you they're coming back next weekend and that they'll be staying at your house. I was looking forward to some alone time with you, so imagine my disappointment when I got here only to find out you had stayed in town. Now I can't sleep. You answered your phone fast. Were you awake?"

Michael rubbed his eye. "Something woke me up."

"Oh, good timing, then. I didn't want you to lose any sleep because of me."

"Nah. By the way. Did you hear from Carol?"

"Nope. Not a word. In the three days I was there, I had no luck contacting her."

"I don't like how she just up and disappeared like that."

"Same here. It only makes me more suspicious of her."

"Is Jenny with you?"

Naya chuckled. "She's right here next to me. Taking advantage of the pillow beside me."

"That's cute. Did you lock all the doors? Windows?"

"Yes, I did."

"Good. Well, the power outages did wonders for my heating system. The floor is cold. I just sent a message off to my assistant to get my heating fixed."

"Shorted?"

"Most likely. I've already switched off the system."

"I was just going to say that. So, what's going on with you?"

Michael smiled to himself as he pushed on the video call request.

"You know, I hate talking to you without seeing your face. Put on your video."

"Ugh, I knew you would do that." Shortly, Naya's face came on the screen, her hair in disarray and spread over a pillow. She moved her phone to show Jenny sleeping on the pillow next to her. "Look at her. Isn't she a sweetie?"

"That should be me in your bed," Michael said as he knelt in front of the fireplace and moved the screen. "Continue talking. I'm putting down the phone so I can light a fire."

He inspected the firewood, placed the crumpled newspaper between the pieces to make it burn quickly, and then added some kindling.

"Okay, I'll watch. Better than nothing. Other than YouTube, I can't connect to any of the services," Naya said. "Add firewood on top, but make sure to leave enough room for air to circulate."

"Naya."

"Yes, Michael?"

"You do realize I was the one who taught you how to build a fire?"

Naya giggled. "Oh, that's right. You did."

"They'll get the signals sorted one way or another. We can't rush those things now, can we?" Michael said as he pushed the pilot knob and then the igniter button. The fire bloomed instantly. He picked up the phone and showed Naya the flames.

"Oh, that's a lovely fire you have going there. Quickly, too."

"I just turned it on."

"Of course, you have to have a gas fireplace. Why didn't I know that?" Naya laughed through her mild sarcasm.

Michael chuckled as he stood up. "You know I can light fires well enough, but why go through the hassle of using matches when I can just turn on the gas?"

Naya raised a lone brow. "You already know what I'm going to say about that."

Michael sat on the sofa in front of the fireplace and put his legs on the footstool in front of it. He grinned broadly at Naya's image. "Yes. I know what you're going to say. And you're right. It's just that I didn't think about it when they asked me if I wanted gas or electric. I remember thinking, what if there was a blackout, and so I said gas."

Naya's smile froze, and a sudden frown marred her forehead. She tapped on the screen. "Michael?"

"Yeah? What is it?"

"Is there someone in there with you?"

Michael knew he was alone in the house, yet couldn't help throwing a look over his shoulder before turning back at Naya. "No. I'm alone. Why?"

"Because I just saw someone walk into the other room behind you." Naya's mouth twisted. The screen jostled as she moved to a sitting position.

Michael's blood ran cold as he slowly lowered his feet and stood. He took several steps backward in the direction of his landline phone. "Did you see a shadow, or did you see a real someone?"

"I saw someone, but I can't tell if it's a man or a woman. They wore all black with a cap over their head." Naya's frown deepened. "I'm going to call the police." From the way the phone jostled, she was already heading downstairs to her office.

"Yes, same here." Michael picked up the landline phone.

"Shit, it's dead."

"Damn it, Michael. Can you lock yourself in there?" The rising panic in Naya's voice came through loud and clear.

Michael moved toward the double doors. "Yes, I can, but these are glass doors. Whoever is out there can still see me or break it."

"Can you hide somewhere?"

He glanced around the room. "I'm sure I can find some-place to hide."

"Thank God you're not one of those macho men characters."

"I'm not stupid, Naya," Michael scoffed. He spotted the door beside the fireplace. "I've got a powder room I can get in, and it's got a window I can escape through."

"Get in there as quickly and as quietly as you can. Hold on, the police are online. Hello? This is Naya Rollins. I'd like to report a home intruder in Michael Bradbury's house."

Michael stepped inside the powder room and locked the door as quietly as possible. He looked up and carefully examined the ventilation window, which appeared large enough for him to get through. Slowly, cautiously, while Naya spoke to the police, he lifted the latch and carefully pushed it out. "Shit."

"What's wrong? Michael? Talk to me."

"The opening's too small. The window opens outward, but only about six inches. There's no way I can get out of here." Michael checked on the frame. "Okay, hold on. I can unscrew this thing. That is if I can find something to unscrew it with."

A rattling sound from the other room made him look up. "There's most definitely someone inside my house, Naya. They're trying to open the doors. When I woke up earlier, it was because I felt I wasn't alone. When I didn't find anyone I dismissed it."

"They went inside your room? Oh, my God." Naya began

to speak rapidly, presumably relaying everything to the police.

A loud crash made Michael grit his teeth. "Naya, I think they just trashed my glass doors. Remind me never to use glass doors again. I'm getting all my glass doors replaced with wood. Interior decorators be damned."

"The police said someone's on their way. They should be there in about five minutes."

Michael poked at the screw with the tip of his too-short thumbnail. "I don't think I have that much time."

"Have you found anything you can unscrew the window with?"

"I'm looking." Michael rifled through the drawers and almost yelled out in relief when he found a nail clipper, which he raised high to show Naya.

"Oh, thank God. Use the file."

"Yes, on it." Michael placed the hooked end of the small file into the screws and started to turn while pressing simultaneously. When the head turned, he worked furiously, trying to ignore the worrying sounds of things being thrown about in the other room.

He gritted his teeth at a particularly loud crash. That had to be his widescreen monitor. "God damn it. I just bought that."

"Focus, Michael."

"I am. I am," he said through tight lips. After successfully removing one screw, he started working faster. "Seven more to go."

The door to the powder room rattled, making him pause. He could hear the sound of sirens approaching from a distance, and the rattling stopped. Whoever it was on the other side of the door must have heard the sirens, too.

"I think the police are almost here," he said.

"Oh, thank God. Michael, I'm driving over."

"You don't need to—"

"Shut up. I'm already down the drive and will be there in half an hour. Why do you have to live so far away?"

"I was here first. How was I supposed to know you'd settle here?" Michael straightened at the increasing sound of police sirens. Not long after, he saw the flashing lights illuminating his front garden. "The police are here."

"Don't get out until you are certain it's safe."

"Thank you, Naya."

"If anything happened to you—"

"Hey. I'm all right."

"Mr. Bradbury? This is the police. Are you in there?"

Michael leaned forward so he could see through the window opening. "I'm over here!"

"Are you safe, Mr. Bradbury?"

"Yes."

"Stay where you are until we clear the area."

"All right. Thank you." Michael sighed in relief. "An officer just told me to stay put until they give me the all-clear."

"I heard. Michael?"

"Yes?"

"You're coming home with me. You can't stay there."

"I can always go to a hotel."

"I won't accept a no from you."

"You're so controlling."

"I am most definitely not! Seriously, Michael. You scared me to death."

"*I* scared you? You have ghosts in your house."

"Well, at least they're harmless. They keep me company."

"I can't believe I'm believing you." Michael sat on the toilet lid. It sank under his weight, and he knew he would have to change it to something sturdier.

"This intrusion into your house. The attempt on my life and my accounts. Carol's disappearance. Why do I get this feeling it's all connected."

"He's dead, Naya."

"Yes. I know."

"But?"

"I have thoughts."

Someone knocked on the door. "Mr. Bradbury? Are you in there?"

"Yes. I'm still here," Michael said, standing up. "Naya, the deputy's back."

"Sir, my name is Deputy Anderson. The area's been cleared. It's safe to come out now."

"Naya. The deputy says it's safe for me to come out."

"I heard. I'm halfway there."

"All right. I'll see you in a few. And again. Thank you, Naya."

"I love you."

"I love you, too."

Michael looked around as the deputy wrote on his pad. His TV room was a disaster. Glass fragments on the wood floor sparkled in the light. His brand-new fifty-seven-inch curved monitor lay face down on the floor, surrounded by shattered glass and dark debris, most likely broken pieces of the monitor.

"I've got everything, Mr. Bradbury," the deputy said. "Thank you for your time."

"I should thank you. You got here quickly." Michael couldn't remember the man's name. When he came out of the bathroom, he'd walked into chaos. There were cops everywhere. He didn't even know which one was Deputy Anderson.

"It was a quiet night, and we were already in the area. We came as fast as we could," the officer said. "You're an important man, Mr. Bradbury. Luckily, you were on the phone with your girlfriend."

"Yes, I was lucky."

"I'll finish up here. Will you be staying here for the rest of the night? I suggest you check into a hotel until we catch the intruder. Goodnight, Mr. Bradbury." The man tipped his cap and started to walk away but paused. "You need to know we received a call from one of your neighbors. They saw someone suspicious running across their lawn, and when they saw the lights across the street, they figured a connection."

"He's coming home with me."

Michael looked up to the sound of Naya's voice. She walked purposefully toward him, her long, loose curls haloing her determined expression. She wore a pink fleecy robe and fur-lined boots like armor. The sight should have made him laugh, but it didn't. The sound of crunching snow under her every step and the frozen puffs of breath hovering around her head captivated Michael. He'd never seen her as strong or as beautiful as that moment, and he felt himself falling in love with her all over again.

"Naya." The name came out like a prayer.

"Is that Ms. Rollins? She's your girlfriend?"

Michael didn't answer as he walked to meet Naya halfway. Her gaze flicked over him from head to toe and back, but the dark glitter in her eyes told him a different story.

She stopped a foot from him, gazing up at him in silence before reaching up and cupping his face in her chilly hands. "I was scared to death. Don't ever do that to me again."

Michael couldn't think of how to respond to the demand. To compensate, he took her in his arms and pressed his face into her cold neck. The woman had not even bothered to change into something warmer, probably just slipped into her boots straight out of bed. He didn't know how long they stood there, wrapped in each other's arms, but the sound of the people around them finally broke the spell. Naya leaned back, but not far enough to take a step back. Michael dropped one arm but kept his right one around her waist.

"Did I hear the deputy say they may have a suspect?" she asked.

"A neighbor reported seeing someone, and they're checking it out."

Naya wrapped her arms around her torso and looked around them. "It looks like they're going to be kept busy for a while. Is that the woman who owns the local paper?"

"The officer advised me to check into a hotel, and I wouldn't be surprised if the local media were here. This is probably the most exciting thing to happen after the storm."

"I thought I heard the officer say something about a hotel. Either way, you're coming home with me. It's safer there."

"Thanks to who or what? A dog and several . . . visitors?"

"It's better than in a hotel. Also, we'd be together."

"I never thought I'd be grateful for something I cannot see. To a dog, yes, but not, uh, visitors. Never those."

"None of them are evil."

"I know. They just like to loiter."

Naya shivered. "I guess we'll just have to get used to them, but they still scare the shit out of me when I stumble into them."

"You're shivering. Let's get back into the house. I'll go talk to the officer in charge and grab some things."

An hour later, Michael was back at Naya's house, in the bedroom he and Luke had shared. They'd left the police still going through his house. The police informed him that the investigation wouldn't be completed in a day. With the mess left there, Michael knew it would take at least another two or three days to get his house straightened out.

He dropped his backpack on the bench at the foot of the bed and took in his surroundings. The hair on his arms stood.

A quick look behind him showed him what he already knew, no one was there. He had a feeling the resident ghosts had come in to check on him. Funny how twenty-four hours in Naya's house already had him rethinking the concept of the paranormal. Not for a moment had he thought he'd get to the point of shrugging off their presence and even thinking of them as sentient residents. Brushing the thought aside, he went to the bathroom and took a quick hot shower.

Slipping into his clothes, he buttoned his shirt and exited the bedroom. He was turning up his sleeves as he made his way to the bottom of the stairs. The aroma of soap, fire, and cinnamon blended to create a welcoming scent that made him feel at home. Naya was nowhere to be seen, but he thought he knew her well enough to know she would be in the kitchen.

Naya's green-eyed stare scanned him as he walked into the kitchen, made him self-conscious and yet reassured at the same time. Naya was a strong woman, and he knew many who would shy away from such a personality, but he wouldn't have her any other way. That inner strength had given her the will to survive the worst situation and recently given her the logic to call the police as she talked him out of his fear. He wasn't ashamed to admit it. The intrusion had scared him, but it also made him rethink his lifestyle choices, one of which was the security of his home. Naya had the right to it, and her penchant for what he had initially thought of as overkill now made sense.

With each passing second, he became more self-conscious of Naya's regard, yet he felt reassured. He'd known her for over half his life, and he'd wanted to keep her from the first moment he'd seen her. Naya was his now, and he was hers. There was no way he was ever going to let her go again.

Over the years, he'd learned to rein in his all-consuming desire for her. At first, it was because they'd both been too young, then because he knew he had to let her live her life freely and make her own decisions. He'd refocused all his needs away from everything connected to Naya.

This mountain home was Naya's retreat, her place away from the chaos of urban life. Just like Amber Ville had become his sanctuary where he could safely spend time to examine and overcome the capitalistic world he had to step into more often than he was now comfortable with.

Once, Naya had said she'd felt welcomed the first time she'd stepped foot on the property. At first, he'd thought the claim bordered on the ludicrous. He glanced at the ceiling, and a feeling not unlike a welcoming warmth, almost like a physical embrace, washed over him. The sensation seemed to come from the house itself, which was a little disconcerting. He'd never felt anything like it.

Naya's lips connected with his, startling him back to the present. Feeling her body against his, he fisted his fingers into her hair, pulling slightly to tip her head back. A moan escaped her as he deepened their kiss. His tongue sought entrance, and she opened her mouth wider. He lost track of time until Naya pulled away. A smile tugged on his lips when her cheeks blushed a glowy soft rose.

He gently cupped both sides of her face. "You are so beautiful."

"Don't."

"Why not?"

"Because I'm getting shy."

Michael sucked in a breath. "I want to see you come under me."

Naya began to tremble as he ran the tip of his finger down her cheek to her neck. When he paused over her carotid pulse, her breath hitched, and the hollow at the base of her neck deepened.

"Take off your clothes, Naya."

His gaze never left hers as she undid each button of her

blouse and parted the edges, exposing her bare breasts. His gaze dropped to her nipples. Both irresistibly reddened and beaded. Unable to help himself, he bent and took first the right and then the left into his mouth, giving each a hard suck and a little nip. Naya whimpered, her hands dropping on either side of his head and trying to pull him off, which only made him suckle harder on the plump flesh. He pushed her shorts and underwear over her hips and down her legs. She quickly stepped away, dropped her blouse, and kicked the pile off to the side.

"Turn around," Michael said, his voice husky. Instead of waiting for her to turn, he gently maneuvered her to face the island.

He quickly slipped his shirt over his head as she moved to the island, placed her palms on the surface, and glanced at him over her shoulder. His gaze slowly swept over the arch of her back, her full, hard buttocks, and her long, muscular legs. He closed the distance in three quick strides and planted his lips on the soft skin between her shoulders. Her hands curled behind her to lie on his thigh as he encouraged her to bend forward, placing her chest on the island. He imagined the granite surface was cold on her skin from how she gasped and shivered.

His hands gently caressed her arms and sides as he rained kisses down her slender back, enjoying every inch of her bared flesh. Each dip and curve was licked, sucked, and nipped. Goose bumps rose over her flesh, accompanied by multiple shivers. He placed a hand between her shoulder blades and reached down to finger her core. One touch, and he knew how ready she was. Her back arched when he inserted a second finger inside her pussy, pushing to the hilt.

When Naya moaned and spread her legs further apart, Michael inserted a third finger, easily slipping inside her warm, wet, welcoming heat. He moved his fingers, creating a rhythm, and she rocked in time to his ministrations. From how the walls of her pussy tightened around him, he knew she was close to coming. Without pausing, he curled his fingers and pressed down.

"Michael." She yelled his name as her body twisted under his caresses.

The kitchen filled with her moans and other wordless sounds as she came undone under his hold. When her shivers subsided, she looked over her shoulders and met his gaze. Seeing her flushed cheeks and satisfied smile was all he needed to feel accomplished. He'd pleased his woman, and that was all that mattered.

"I've never come that hard before," she murmured between panting breaths.

Whoever she had been with in the past, Andrew included, had been dicks.

"Come here." He pulled her up into his arms. "Let's go upstairs. I don't want to continue dealing with an audience."

"Audience?"

Michael gestured with his head over to where Jenny lay on her belly. He had to admit she had been a good girl in her silent observation of their activities, but he would prefer privacy.

"Oh goodness," Naya whispered. "Has she been watching us this whole time?"

Michael chuckled. "Let's go upstairs. Maybe she'll stay in her bed?"

In the bedroom, Michael stripped out of his remaining clothes and crawled into bed, where Naya lay naked and inviting. His gaze fell on her inner thighs, glistening wetly from her juices. She raised her arms over her head and gripped the headboard, spreading her legs wider and planting her feet firmly on the bed. Her bold invitation sent his blood surging down to his cock, leaving him dazed for a moment. He threw a glance in Jenny's direction, happy to see the dog curled in her bed with her eyes closed her eyes. Returning his attention to Naya, he braced his hands on either side of her and lowered his head until their lips met. His tongue danced with hers in foreplay as her hands slid up his shoulders and wrapped around his neck.

He lifted his head, staring down at her as he carefully guided his cock into her. She arched her neck and closed her eyes.

"Open your eyes, Naya."

Immediately, her eyes snapped open and met his gaze.

"That's right. Don't look away. I want to watch you when you come."

Inch by inch, he slid into her welcoming heat until his hunger grew beyond his control. Unable to help himself, he slammed deep inside her, her squeal of surprise making him press deeper, not stopping until he was fully embedded inside her. Her walls contracted around him, the strength of her muscles too delicious to withstand, making him bite on his lip to regain a modicum of control.

Naya leaned up until her lips met his. "Don't stop. I need you to move."

He was not about to reject her invitation. He began to move, easing in and out, filling her with each thrust. Her nails digging into his back were all the encouragement he needed. Naya's eyelids fluttered as she held on, their noses touching, their breaths mingling. He couldn't help but mimic the sensual noises she made as he continued to piston his hips, plunging to the hilt with each thrust.

He could feel his balls grow tighter as he thrust faster, and knew he was not going to last as long as he'd hoped. When Naya's body stiffened under him, he saw the ecstasy on her face. That was all he needed. Determination warred with his need to seek a swift oblivion as he lifted her bent legs to his shoulders. The sight of his glistening cock inside her gave him pause, the contractions around him making him groan out in painful bliss. Lifting her torso high into his arms, he thrust up and almost yelled out when her muscles tightened around him. The pleasure-pain was reaching almost unbearable levels.

"Michael." Naya's yell almost did him in.

He groaned deep in his throat, the new position burying him deeper into Naya than ever before. With her athletic body allowing her the most exquisite flexibility, she folded herself into his arms, making his cock align at the perfect angle. His thrusting into her became easier, and he abandoned himself to the primal dance without thought.

The world disappeared as he thrust harder and harder, faster and faster. His only claim to reality was the insatiable desire to pleasure the woman he loved beyond thought. Beyond definition . . .

Naya held tighter to his neck, staking her claim on him as he laid his claim on her. His orgasm built, and he surrendered himself to the inevitable. Her body began to tremble, signaling her impending release. He'd waited so long to have Naya in his life as a lover that he remembered, too late again, his number one rule for safety and precaution. Reason flew from his normally logical mind, and before he could stop it, his seed pulsated out of him, filling her. Something primal within him took over, and he thrust deeper, not wanting any of his seed to spill from her. As though to answer his unspoken question, Naya opened her eyes, dug her fingers into the back of his neck, and wrapped her legs around his hips. When he moved to pull out, she pushed her pelvis up and clamped down tighter.

She let out a cute little growl. "Don't you dare."

At that moment, Michael knew he would be in danger of

Naya's wrath if he pulled out. The primal part of him was sure of only one thing, and that was to never let Naya go. From the way her whole body gripped him, he knew she was experiencing the same feeling.

When he no longer had anything left inside him, he collapsed into her arms. He buried his face in the side of his neck, breathing in her scent. To his surprise, Naya flipped him over, and he found himself staring in wonder at the woman now straddling him with hair cascading over her face, her cheeks flushed from exertion, her lips plump from his kisses.

She flexed her hips, and much to his surprise, though he was spent, he was far from limp. He watched as she rotated her hips, pressing down on him and whimpering. Recognizing her need, he reached down and pressed on her clit, feeling her tremble once more.

"Come for me, baby," he encouraged.

He slid a finger beside his cock, causing her to gasp with a look of surprise. He continued to stretch her out and rubbed his palm against her clit. The dual stimulation made her scream, and her hips moved faster until her whole body stiffened and she fell into his waiting arms.

Pleased he'd pleasured his woman, he closed his eyes and wrapped his arms around her.

Before sleep claimed him, he would swear he heard the house exhale and settle.

CHAPTER TWENTY-ONE

Naya stretched and couldn't keep back a moan from escaping her lips when muscles she hadn't known existed—especially those between her thighs—twinged in protest. Normally after working out, she would shrug off the resulting stretch and burn, but this time, she wouldn't. Her sexual marathon overindulgence was to blame, and she loved the reminder.

She rolled her head on the pillow and ran her gaze down Michael's naked back. He was slipping on a pair of shorts she couldn't remember him wearing. She'd once read that men generally sexually peaked at eighteen. After what Michael had been like earlier, she couldn't even imagine how he was as a teen. Their sex marathon should've exhausted her, but strangely enough, she was wide awake. A glance at the digital clock on the table by her bedside told her it was half past two in the morning.

"I can't believe the time," she said, stretching her arms over her head and pointing her toes.

Michael turned on his heels, looking around for something. "Do you happen to remember where I dropped my shirt?"

"I think you took it off in the kitchen," she said. "Where are you going?"

"I was thinking of getting a snack and something to drink downstairs. Care for something?"

"Water would be good."

Michael knelt on the edge of the bed and dropped a kiss on her mouth.

She clung to the kiss, caressing his bristly cheek before letting him go. "A snack would be good, too. I think I'm getting hungry."

"I'll be right back."

Giggling softly, she gave his cheek another caress. "You are a gentleman, Mr. Bradbury."

His green eyes twinkled with mirth. "You're a temptress, Ms. Rollins, that's what *you* are." He gave her another quick peck on the lips and walked out.

Alone, Naya stretched her sore muscles again and grimaced. She got out of bed, standing on wobbly legs and contemplating changing the sheets. Seeing the wet spot quickly made up her mind. She pulled off the ruined sheets and dumped them on the floor. After replacing those with fresh ones, she looked at the pillows and comforter that had fallen to the floor and decided to replace them as well. It didn't take her long to finish remaking the bed.

A glance at the time told her Michael had been gone for ten minutes, and she wondered what was taking him so long. She looked down at herself and grimaced. She gathered the discarded bedding, walked out of the bedroom, and shoved it through the laundry shoot.

She leaned over the banister and yelled, "Michael? I'm going to take a shower." She waited, but when Michael didn't answer, she returned to her bedroom and entered the bathroom.

Naya was in the middle of washing off the soap from her body when a cold draft made her shiver under the heat of the water. Squinting through the suds and steam, she barely made out a shadow standing at the doorway. It moved toward her when another from further back came into view.

"Michael? Is that you?"

When she didn't receive a reply, she took a step back. Heart racing, she looked around her, wishing she wasn't naked and standing on wet tile or she'd bolt out of the cubicle. The shadow moved closer. Only then did she realize it wasn't a man. The other shadow was gone, but before she could process it, she felt a presence beside her. Slowly, she turned her head to the side but saw nothing. She turned back to the door and took another step back, bumping against the cold tiled wall.

Danger. Naya was certain she heard the word inside her head.

She drew in a stuttering breath and clenched her fist. There was nothing in the cubicle could be used as a weapon, unless she considered the bar of soap or the fresh bottle of shampoo.

She vaguely noticed the shampoo bottle wobble on the shelf.

The door to the cubicle slid to the side, revealing Carol standing with one arm on the slider and the other behind her back. The smile on her lips chilled Naya to the bone. She hardly recognized this evil psychotic she'd once considered a friend.

"He forgot this," Carol said, pulling Michael's shirt from behind her.

Heart pounding in her chest, Naya stared at the shirt Michael had been looking for. "Where did you get that?"

"Michael dropped it in the kitchen." Carol shrugged. "I thought I should bring it up here."

"What did you do to him?"

"He's downstairs. Jenny's with him." Carol smirked. "They're okay, but they shouldn't bother us for a while."

"Why are you doing this?"

Carol rocked on her heels. Back and forth. Back and forth. For a moment, Naya thought she looked overwhelmed, but then she burst into maniacal laughter. She continued that for a while, and Naya could do nothing but stand still under the rapidly cooling water.

A thin white mist wafted behind Carol, quickly vanishing into the wall.

Carol's laughter cut off as suddenly as it started, and she stepped forward, stopping short of stepping into the shower. "She's actually asking why?" Her jaw clenched, her fist clenching and unclenching on Michael's shirt. "You're like a lightning rod attracting everything around you. Everything you touch turns to gold. Everyone who meets or sees you falls in love with you. Everything you do is a success."

Naya shivered as something cold touched her shoulder. She tried trying to process what she should fear the most— the odd sensation or the insanity that was standing in front of her.

Then Carol's words sank in.

Naya frowned. "Wait. Are you saying all of this is because you're jealous of me?"

"Jealous? I'm not jealous of you. Why should I be?" Carol scoffed. "I'm a nurse, and that makes me special. I take care of people. But you? You're just a money-making machine. If that makes you special in the eyes of the sheep who worship the ground you walk on, then maybe you are special. But not in my eyes. To me, you're evil."

"Are you saying it's my fault? It was Andrew who tried to kill *me*."

"Shut up!" Carol shook from the force of her scream. "When Andrew first saw you, it was one of your ridiculous viral posts. He said you were the perfect tool. We made plans. It was just supposed to be a quick deal. But then the idiot fell in love with you. And you acted as if you were also in love with him, so he got fooled into thinking that maybe he had a better chance with you. With *you*, not *me*. You stole him from me. Did he ever tell you we'd been together since we were kids? We lost our virginity to each other, did you know that? Thirteen. From the first day we met, we did everything together. Until you came along. You ruined everything."

"He never told me—"

"Of course he didn't. If he'd had, I would have killed you myself. That was our secret. I told Andrew to get rid of you, but the stupid idiot managed to fail even that one simple task. So where did that leave me? He left me with nothing. You left me with nothing. He had to die."

Naya shook her head. Carol wasn't making sense. "I was left for dead at the bottom of that ravine. From the official reports, Andrew jumped off that cliff on his own."

"Yeah, he jumped. I remember it all too well. I was there." Her irrational grin reappeared.

"What do you mean you were there?" Naya's fear peaked, but she had to keep Carol engaged. She needed time to think of a plan. Like how to quickly get out of the cubicle and take Carol down.

The shampoo bottle wobbled more vigorously than it had before. The movement brought it to the edge of the niche.

"You still don't get it, do you? Figures. You've always been a little slow." Carol rolled her eyes. "I was there when he jumped off the cliff because I told him to jump. Off. The. Cliff. Is that clear enough for you?"

"You told him to jump?"

"Well, yeah." Another eye roll. "You see, I told him to make sure he got access to your money before he got rid of you. Instead, he went ahead and tried to kill you before he gained access to it. Of course I got mad at him. He was so sorry, saying he got overly excited. I lost my temper and told him he should jump off the cliff. Just because he was such an idiot. God . . . Andrew would do everything I told him to, but I must admit, him actually jumping off the cliff surprised me." She leaned against the shower enclosure and giggled.

"You're sick."

Carol straightened and placed a hand on her chest. "Me?

Well, I guess I am, but then you're way worse. You're a capitalist whore."

"Why did you come here?"

"I thought it was time to finish what Andrew and I had started. And you know what?" Carol placed a foot inside the cubicle. "It's going to be so easy."

When the shampoo bottle rattled loudly, Naya didn't look at it, but she finally understood, and a plan began to form. All she needed to do was be patient a little longer.

"Easily fooled, yes," Naya said. "I admit to that."

"Yeah. All done talking. I guess it's time to get rid of you."

"I think you forgot one important detail there, Carol."

"Yeah? What's that?"

"You'll never gain access to my money."

"No biggie. That's no longer my goal. I found myself someone better."

When Carol placed her other foot in the cubicle, coming closer, Naya noticed something dark begin to take shape behind Carol.

Just one more step.

The shadow hovered over Carol.

"You mean Luke."

"I am not saying anything, but you're really hot with your assumption." Carol smirked.

"You don't fool my brother."

"Oh, it will be so easy to get to him, you know, once you're out of the picture. Yes . . . so easy." Carol took a step, but something caught her mid-step. She let out a gasp and wobbled. Her arms flailed as she tried to regain her balance.

That was all Naya needed to swipe the shampoo off the niche and smash it against Carol's cheek. Carol dropped to her knees on the wet floor. Naya's wrist throbbed from the impact, but she didn't stop to think. She slammed the shampoo bottle over Carol's head with all the force she could muster. The bottle exploded, its contents splattering everywhere. Carol dropped facedown, but Naya was beyond angry. Bracing her hands on either side of the cubicle, she kicked Carol in the face once, twice, and then a third time.

Naya breathed heavily as she stared down at Carol, counting the seconds. Carol's head flopped to one side but lay still. If she saw so much as an eyelid flutter, God help her, she was going to kick the bitch in the head again. The water fell around her, but the chill didn't register.

After spending more seconds than she cared to count staring down at Carol, she turned off the water and stepped over the prone body. Once outside the cubicle, she grabbed the robe hanging from the hook on the door and shut the door behind her. She quickly scanned the bedroom to find something to brace against the door. Suddenly, the chair by the window flew across the room, stopping with a scraping halt in front of her.

"Thank you," Naya said to no one in particular, hurriedly bracing the top of the chair against the door handle.

She sprinted out of the room and down the stairs while screaming *Michael* at the top of her lungs. A grunt to her left made her slide to a halt. On the floor, Michael lay on his back. Next to him, Jenny lay still.

"Oh, God. Oh, God. Please be alive." Naya kneeled by Michael's side and checked him, letting out a whimper when she felt his pulse.

He had a burgeoning lump on his head. She spotted the heavy glass pitcher a short distance away and winced. Michael groaned, and his eyes began to flutter open.

"Michael, Michael. Wake up. Come on, sweetheart. I need you to get up. Now. We have to get out of here."

Michael nodded, a groan escaping his lips as he did so. "That bitch got me."

"I know. Now, I need you to stand up. I have to pick up

Jenny. I'm not sure how bad she is, but she's breathing."

"I can get her," Michael said, getting to his feet. He wobbled for a second before he crouched and lifted Jenny's hefty body into his arms. "Let's get out of here."

Naya didn't wait a second longer. She hurried over to a freestanding cabinet and pulled a drawer. She took out one of the burner phones she kept there. There was no telling how long Carol would be out or how fast she could get out of the bathroom.

She ran to the front door, swiping the spare keys hanging on a hook on the way out. They were in the car, Naya in the driver's seat, and were heading down the driveway in under a minute. Jenny was still out cold, but from what Naya could see, she was breathing easily.

"I'm calling the sheriff," Michael said. He grabbed the spare phone, tapped in the number, and rapidly told whoever answered what had happened.

Naya looked up at the rear mirror. The house looked hauntingly beautiful. She turned her focus back on the road, or lack of it, before her. Thankfully, the snow had stopped falling while she and Michael were busy, and visibility was better than she'd expected.

"The Sheriff is sending men over," Michael said. "We'll probably meet them down the road."

"Where are we going from here?" Naya said, glancing at Michael.

"The sheriff said to get to the hospital. They're expecting us there."

Naya nodded but stayed silent. She took another look in the rearview mirror, but the house was no longer visible.

"I don't think I killed her, but if I did, I'm not sorry," Naya said.

"What are you talking about?"

"I hit her pretty hard, and when she was down, I kicked

her three times in the head."

"Self-defense."

"If you say so." Her hands tightened on the steering wheel.

"I say so. And besides, she was trespassing."

"She was a guest."

"Not today she wasn't. She was trespassing. Did she say anything that would incriminate her?"

"It would be my word against hers, but she admitted she and Andrew planned to kill me once they had access to my money."

"Damn. Sounds like an Agatha Christie novel."

"Yep. Cliché."

"What else did she say?"

She frowned. "This is the strange part. She said she was there when Andrew attacked me and told him to jump off the cliff for preempting my death."

"He jumped because she told him to do it?"

"That's what she told me."

Michael shook his head. "What did you use to hit her?"

"I bought a liter of shampoo the other day." She threw him a quick glance.

Michael's eyes widened. "You used a shampoo bottle? Ouch."

"There's still shampoo on my hands from when the bottle exploded." She held out a hand to show him. The shampoo had barely dried, but it didn't feel as slippery as it had earlier.

"Whatever made you think of using it?"

"A friendly ghost."

"Thank you, Casper."

"It was a she. I think. I'll name her Candy."

"Why Candy?"

Naya shrugged. "Casper for male. Candy for female."

Michael chuckled. "Guess that works."

"Yeah?"

"Yeah." Michael reached out and rubbed her bare knee, his expression serious. "You all right?"

"I should be asking you that."

"I'll be okay. Jenny, too." Michael chuckled. "She's snoring."

"We should take her to the vet."

"I spoke to the sheriff about that. He told me he'd have a vet waiting at the hospital for us."

Naya nodded. Her hands gripped harder on the steering wheel, her eyes focused on the road ahead. She didn't know how long she drove, but she soon saw several headlights in the distance.

"That's probably the sheriff," Michael said. "Pull over to the curb. We should stop and wait for them."

Shifting her foot, she pressed on the brake and gently steered the car to the side of the road. Two patrol cars passed her, but one stopped in front of them. A uniformed man stepped out of the driver's side. She recognized Sheriff Ferise when he stopped by the driver's side and braced a hand over the door.

"Ms. Rollins, Mr. Bradbury," he said, tipping his cap.

"Good evening, sheriff," Michael said. "Thank you for coming by so quickly."

"We had help. We got a positive hit on a CCTV across the street from your house, Mr. Bradbury. We couldn't reach you, so I called Dr. Rollins, who identified the woman who broke into your house."

"It's Michael, please. You called Naya's mom?"

"Yes, sir. She identified the woman as one Carol Sweetman. After cross-referencing, we got two hits on her. One for assault and battery when she was eighteen or so, and the second was a police report for an incident at a hospital down in Miami."

"Carol's a nurse," Michael said. "What were the charges?"

"Wrongful death. It was the best they could do since they didn't have evidence for murder, but then she up and disappeared."

"When was this?" Naya asked.

"Two months ago," Sheriff Ferise said.

"Carol said she and my ex-fiancé planned the attack on me two years ago. She also said she told Andrew to jump off the cliff." Naya looked down at Jenny, who had begun to stir. "Can we take Jenny to a vet?"

"I'll have one of my deputies take you and Mr. Bradbury to the hospital. I'll tell dispatch to ask my daughter to meet you there. She's the local vet."

"Thank you, sheriff," Naya said. "I think Carol hit Michael over the head with a heavy glass pitcher. I'm not sure what she did to Jenny."

"Don't worry about that right now, Ms. Rollins," the sheriff said. "The doctors will check out Mr. Bradbury, and my daughter's great with animals. I told her your dog is to get all the special care she needs."

"Thank you." The words caught in her throat, and to her horror, tears began to fall. She tried wiping them with her hand, but they just kept falling. Her eyes began to sting, making her belatedly realize that her hands had dried shampoo on them.

"It's all right, come here," Michael said, leaning over and wrapping his arms around her.

"I was so scared." Naya sobbed into Michael's shoulder. "I thought she'd killed you. Is Jenny going to die?"

"Hush," Michael said. "Sheriff, if you don't mind, we need to get Naya to the hospital. I think she's in shock."

"Defending your life and loved ones can do that," the sheriff said. "Don't worry. I'll make sure she doesn't get charged. Self-defense in a home invasion is not something anyone should be found guilty of."

"Michael?"

"What is it, sweetheart?"

"Is Jenny really okay?"

"She's wagging her tail, and her eyes are open," Michael assured.

"I want X-rays and MRIs and CT scans and everything done. I want . . ." Another sob broke through and racked her body.

"Yes, we'll do everything for Jenny, Naya. Don't worry about it." Michael said.

"I thought you were dead," Naya sobbed out. She needed to talk about what had happened, but the tears wouldn't stop. A pinch on her arm made her turn her head. She didn't recognize the woman with a syringe in her hand.

"She'll sleep now," the woman said, her voice sounding so far away.

Naya suddenly felt like she was floating on water and couldn't seem to keep her eyes open, exhaustion driving all sounds to the lowest volume. Try as she might, she couldn't fight against the blanket wrapping around her and the warmth spreading through her limbs. She surrendered to the darkness quickly descending over her. The arms holding her gave her comfort, as did the paw that she held onto tightly until she knew no more.

CHAPTER TWENTY-TWO

Two months had passed since that fateful day of Carol's attack, and Naya sat facing her family at her dining table. She'd hoped Michael's parents could have joined them, but they were off on another cruise and wouldn't be back for another five weeks. At least her father, mother, Luke, and Rachel had found the time to escape work to celebrate the holidays with her.

Michael sat quietly beside her, smiling and nodding his encouragement. They'd both agreed she would take the lead on this conversation with her family. They'd already spoken with his parents, who had given their blessing.

She tapped her glass with a spoon to gain everyone's attention. "I love you. All of you. Thanks to all of you, I survived the worst." She glanced at her hand intertwined with Michael's. "Michael has been a part of my life for a long time, but I have been too afraid, too embarrassed, to admit how I felt for a lifelong friend. He's shown me in a short time that I had no reason to feel insecure, that I had a lot to live for. I've always been a fighter, and this time, I want to fight for me and Michael. I hope you understand that?"

Edward chuckled. "Honey. There's nothing to explain. We've all been well aware of Michael's feelings for you." He winked at her. "And yours for him."

"Yes," Kelly said. "We've all wondered when you'd finally admit your feelings."

"What?" She looked from one parent to the other. "You did?"

"Naya, you were the only one who was hiding from yourself. We all saw it. I don't know if Michael knew, though." Luke turned to Michael. "Did you?"

Michael shrugged. "I thought she didn't want to be associated with an older guy she'd known for most of her life and probably thought of as a brother. I figured I didn't have a chance."

"Well, you both suck at seeing the obvious, that's for sure," Rachel stated in a frustrated voice. "I'm the youngest, yet I saw how things were between you two. It seemed so normal, and I thought it strange that no one acknowledged or talked about it. I lost count of how many times Michael would come home looking dazed and couldn't stop talking about the sassy girl next door."

"I never did that." Michael shifted one leg over the other. He turned to Naya, who raised a brow at him. "I was never dazed."

"Oh, you were dazed, all right." Luke turned to Rachel, and they slapped their palms in a high-five.

"Well, it was complicated," Naya said, heat rushing to her cheeks. She glanced at Michael and saw him clench his jaw, but his cheeks were just as flushed as hers.

"Nah, it wasn't. You two were just blind. Ya know, all this could've been avoided," Luke said, waving his hand in their general direction. "This coming out meeting is so unnecessary."

"We wanted to let you know that we're serious with each other now," Michael said.

"Michael, you don't have a single comedic bone in your body." Rachel rolled her eyes.

"We also wanted to let you know we plan on getting married and settling here. In Amber Ville."

From the abrupt silence, startled faces, and gaping mouths, Michael's words must have shocked their families.

Rachel suddenly stood up and glared at her brother. "But this place is haunted! You know I can't have another ghost peaking at me from the closet incident. I'll die of fright."

"Come on, Rach, that never happened," Luke said.

"It did, too." Rachel glared at Luke.

"A ghost peeked in on her?" Edward turned to Kelly. "Should I be worried?"

"It was just Jenny," Kelly said, patting Edward's hand.

"Ah, Jenny," Edward said. He looked down to his side and made tutting noises. "Where's that girl?"

"She's sleeping by your feet," Kelly said. "Now pay attention. I think we're about to get to the good part."

"You should have heard her scream, Dad," Luke raised an arm to fend off the slap Rachel aimed at him.

"You can stay at my house, Rach?" Michael suggested.

"How about giving me your house so you can have an excuse to stay in Naya's house?" Rachel countered.

"Okay." Michael tilted his head. "I'm sure it'll be easy enough to transfer the deed to my house to your name."

Rachel's eyes widened. "Are you crazy? You're willing to live in a haunted house for love?"

"Aw, but home is where Naya is?" Luke's amusement earned him a glare from Michael.

"Look, I don't care for that house anymore," Michael said. "It was a place to stay while here. But to be frank, I lost interest after Carol broke in. I've since made it more secure, but it's no longer the same."

"Well, if you put it that way?" Rachel settled in her chair, a satisfied smirk on her face. "You've gone soft, Michael. Being in love suits you."

"Thank you." Michael raised Naya's left hand and kissed it.

"You're engaged." Kelly gave Naya an expectant look.

Naya raised her hand and showed off her ring. "Yep."

251

"Finally! Thank you, thank you!" Kelly threw up her hands to the ceiling.

"Mom!"

"Don't get me wrong, but having Michael around to help me worry over you is a huge welcome."

"I don't need anybody worrying over me, most especially you or Michael, but thank you, Mom."

"It's a mother thing." Kelly shrugged. "You'll understand once you have children of your own. Oh, and I love you, too, sweetheart." She smiled. "Now, can we have dinner? I'm starving."

"I think I'll have some of those appetizers," Edward said, reaching for the charcuterie board in the middle of the table. "Impressive piece of Ouija board you have here, Naya. Good choice to serve meatballs on."

Rachel gasped loudly. "Naya! Why do you still have that thing here? After everything that happened? Why don't you get rid of it?"

"It's part of the house, Rach," Naya said. "Besides, you don't have to worry about it any longer. I took it to the church in town and asked the priest to do whatever was necessary."

"What did they do to it?"

"I'm not sure, and I really didn't ask. All I know is that they said it was finally safe and just a regular board. They did caution me not to let anyone play with it."

"Not me. No." Rachel glared at the charcuterie board as if it offended her. "It's a beautiful piece, but it's dangerous."

"It never was dangerous to begin with," Kelly said. "It's how it's being used that can make it dangerous."

"No, it never was dangerous," Naya said. "It served its purpose."

Rachel frowned. "Which was what?"

"It warned Naya she was in danger," Michael interjected. "And for that, I have to agree with Naya that we shouldn't get rid of it or destroy it."

"Not you, too, Michael?" Rachel's eyes were large with surprise. "Of all people, I never thought you'd be one to believe in the supernatural."

"I thought you said there were no ghosts here," Edward said. "Why this talk of the supernatural all of a sudden."

"Because the house is haunted!" Rachel crossed her arms over her chest and sat back in her chair.

"Let's just say the house came with existing characters and give it a rest. Okay?" Kelly raised her glass to a toast. "To Naya and Michael. May this be the beginning of a new life for both of you."

"Can we eat now?" Edward grumbled. "Naya prepared such a feast, and it's getting cold."

Everyone laughed at Edward's plea.

Naya grinned broadly. She never thought she'd find herself as happy as she was at that moment.

"Yes, Dad. Let's dig in."

A movie played on the LED monitor in Naya's bedroom, but neither she nor Michael were watching. She sat perched on the edge of the bed with her knees bent, both feet planted on the bed at her sides, and Michael looming over her between her legs. She wasn't looking at him, though. Her gaze had locked on the mesmerizing view of where their bodies were joined. Michael's cock, thick and long, slid in and out of her, stretching her in the most delightful way when his glistening cock disappeared inside her.

She almost giggled. The sight reminded her of when she'd been younger and had curiously opened a porn sight. It was one of those things she'd felt guilty about. But now that she was on the receiving end, seeing and feeling the friction Michael created inside her, she finally realized the difference between fantasy and reality. Watching their personal connection, hearing herself and Michael making the noises as he filled her with his girth, the smell of his skin and sweat mingling with hers, and tasting his kisses drove her love for him to new heights. She couldn't look away. Not when tremors shook her body, not when sensations bordered between pain and pleasure snapped inside her, not even when she yelled out when her orgasm hit. Michael's yell soon followed, his neck muscles prominent as he pumped harder and deeper and emptied himself into her. Only then did her eyes roll back with the most exquisite feeling. No way, shape, or form was she ever going to give this up.

Long minutes passed before Naya's muscles stopped trembling. She didn't think much of it until Michael moved, and the friction between her legs made her clench her pussy. Michael groaned loudly and eased off her, leaving Naya lying there, breathing hard, legs wide open, and staring up at the ceiling. In the background, she heard Michael washing up in the bathroom. She didn't move, not even when Michael came out and tended to her, wiping between her legs with a warm, moist towel.

Suddenly, the towel was replaced by a warm, wet tongue clamping over her clit. Then she did move. She clasped her hands on his head, his hair cool and damp between her fingers. She dug her fingernails in when he moved lower, nipping, licking, lapping her core. It didn't take long before Michael brought her to another explosive orgasm. Her back arched, and her knees squeezed around his head, which only made Michael work his tongue deeper inside her. As she worked to catch her breath, she felt the cool towel pressed against her overly sensitized skin. When he was done, he picked her up in his arms and deposited her on the bed. He leaned over to his left and came back up, handing her the bowl of popcorn.

"You're killing me," she groaned as she dug her hands into

the bowl and popped a few kernels into her mouth.

"Thank you, sweetheart," Michael drawled. "All I want to do is pleasure you, watch you break apart as you climax."

"Why?"

"Because that is when you're the most beautiful."

"Liar." She grabbed another handful and scooted up to a sitting position.

"Not when it comes to you, gorgeous."

Naya gestured to the TV. "We missed the first fifteen minutes."

"Fifteen only? You're easy."

"Shut up." She settled against Michael's side and watched the movie play out. "Do you think Mom and Dad heard us?"

"I don't want to know."

"But what if they did?"

Michael pointed to the TV. "Let's watch, shall we?"

Naya giggled. "Can we rewind at least?"

"Nope."

"Okay."

The movie went on for another hour until the poor heiress was found dead on her bed. Naya felt goosebumps rise over her skin at how similar the plot was to what had happened to her. The main difference was that she survived.

"I can't believe I was stuck in an Agatha Christie-style mystery," she muttered.

"With a paranormal twist." Michael turned to look at her. "You ought to write a book."

"This is not the time to make a joke, Michael." Naya chewed on more popcorn.

"I'm not joking. People truly want to know your story, Naya. Your followers, the whole world, want to know your story."

Naya grimaced. "People will criticize me and say I'm cashing in on my misadventure."

"Misadventure?" Michael took the bowl and placed it on the nightstand beside the bed before facing her. "What you went through was not a misadventure. You were a victim of unscrupulous psychos who wanted to kill you for your money. That is not something you asked to have happen to you. You would have died if it were not for your loyal followers who recognized that something was wrong with your posts. They even brought in the dogs on their own accord to look for you. You're lucky you have such loyal fans."

"But the antis will say a lot of nasty things."

"And you always listen to critics who want to dictate your life and how you earn or spend your money?"

She lowered her gaze from Michael's challenge. "No."

"Exactly. Look at it this way. You were literally stuck in a mystery novel and even pulled me in. Some might say I'm a bonus."

"Again, not a joke, Michael."

"No, what happened to you is no joking matter. Carol will most likely plead insanity and will be placed in a high-security psychiatric ward. She will never see the outside world again. She won't even make parole because she's already connected to several murders, thanks to the DNA evidence that Sheriff Ferise's search turned up. I would have been a statistic if not for you." Michael raised a challenging brow.

"I know."

Michael dropped a kiss on her mouth. "Going back to the Christie novel concept. The way it usually went with her stories is that two lovers would plot to kill someone innocent or not so innocent so they could gain access to their money. Just like those fictional characters, Andrew brought Carol to that lunch date, and you got pulled into her charm. You never questioned her relationship with Andrew, and that's not your fault."

"No, just my naivety."

"Maybe, but there was no reason to suspect. You were happy and comfortable in your relationship with Andrew. When you began to suspect and ask questions about Andrew's odd behavior, that's when he and Carol thought to step things up. They wanted to control you, and for a while, they thought they did. They didn't factor in your independence or intelligence."

Naya played with the unpopped kernels in the palm of her hand. "I remember talking to Carol about my troubles with Andrew. She was a good listener and even told me to go with my feelings. I never told her about my plans, though. Or that I was going to break up with him. Come to think about it, I remember breaking up with Andrew after I talked to her."

"Andrew must have told her, and they both panicked about losing the money."

"But killing me just defeats the purpose, doesn't it? With me dead, how were they going to access my money?"

"I never claimed they were brilliant criminals."

"I worked hard to get where I'm at and even harder for my businesses to be self-sufficient. I guess they never thought about how businesses work."

"Well, she'll soon be behind the looney bars with no hope of getting out."

Naya heaved a sigh. "I never thought I'd come face to face with pure evil."

"For some people, like Carol and Andrew, it doesn't matter how they gain access to money. They simply latch on, like the greedy parasites they are."

Naya wrapped her arms around Michael's torso, closed her eyes, and laid her cheek on his chest. "I've missed you so much."

"What's this? What are you talking about?" Michael wrapped his arms around her.

"Talking to you. Being with you. I've made so many

mistakes in my life. Andrew and Carol being the worst. Those mistakes were made when you weren't around, times that I distanced myself from you because of my fears of getting rejected."

"Ah, sweetheart. There is a reason for everything. I was scared to love you or get rejected by you, too. I also make a lot of mistakes, you know. Andrew and Carol, they were evil. They made us question ourselves without us realizing it. That's how they worked. They manipulated to control. I guess that's why so many mystery novels are out there, hiding some truths within their stories. People wouldn't think of those stories if there wasn't anything valid to base it on."

"Except for the paranormal twist." Naya's gaze drifted to the antique chair by the window. "They helped me, you know."

"They?"

"The ghosts."

"I thought you said only one did, the female."

"No. I saw the door open and noticed the male shadow standing behind Carol when she walked into the bathroom. The female was beside me in the shower."

"You can tell which is which? They showed themselves to you?"

"I've never seen her, but the man, yes. He looked to be in his forties and wore those safety overalls. He was respectful, too."

"Damn." Michael fell silent.

Naya's gaze remained locked on the chair by the window. She would never forget how the chair had slid toward her, over the carpet and then the floorboards. Like it had been pulled by invisible ropes. The chair was a Quince made of mahogany. It appeared delicate with traditional hand carvings but was much heavier than modern reproductions.

"The female showed you the shampoo bottle to use as a

weapon."

"She did, yes, but he pushed Carol. Made her lose balance. It gave me the opening I needed to grab the bottle and hit her with it."

"They're good then?"

"They're good. Jenny has learned to tolerate them, too."

"I've watched her play with someone outside," Michael said, chuckling.

Naya lifted her leg and placed it over Michael's. "It's been two months since that night, and they haven't shown themselves or made their presence known."

"I think they've gone back to lurking in the shadows now that their perceived danger, Carol, is no longer in their territory."

Naya stifled a yawn and closed her eyes. "They didn't like her."

"I think they like me. After their initial suspicion, they left me alone." Michael let out a heavy yawn of his own.

"That's nice." Another yawn had her saying, "I don't think I can continue watching TV."

"Sleep." Michael dropped a kiss on the top of her head.

"I love you, Michael."

"I love you, too, sweetheart."

Naya smiled as she took a deep breath. After the initial stutter, her life map was finally right on track. She'd never thought to have to share that life with ghosts, but as they turned out to be friendly, she didn't mind.

The background noise of the movie still playing lulled her toward sleep, and just as the world slipped away, she clearly heard the house heave a sigh of relief.

ALSO FROM JO TANNAH

Tell Him
Compelled
Winter Roses
Grass Stains and Flip Flops
Around The Block
His Christmas Valentine
The Knockers
A Calling Bird
Calling Birds
Unchained
STIGMA

Tales from the Archipelago:
   Kilig
   The Secrets He Keeps

Taboo Series:
   Taboo
   A Taboo Christmas
   Taboo Pleasures
   Christmas Unwrapped
   The Summer Knows

Hidden Series:
   Hidden Evils
   Hidden Dimensions
   Hidden Fates

Rise of the Symbionts:
Royal Guardian
Royal Consort
Royal Symbionts
Tarragon
The Crown and the Sword

CyNapse Security, Inc.:
Objectified
Kaleidoscope

The Adventures of Marcus Kildud:
The Hunt

Chronicles of the Serai:
Heart Held Hostage

The Phantom Hunters:
Waylaid

With Ann Mickan:
Lemonade Stand
A Lemon Flavoured Christmas

ABOUT THE AUTHOR

I am a wife, mother and blogger by day, a writer by night. It can be difficult, to say the least, but it is a challenge that keeps me on my toes.

I grew up listening to folk tales my father and nannies told either to entertain us children or to send home a message. These narratives I kept with me, and finally, I wrote them down in a journal way back when I kept one. Going through junk led to a long-forgotten box, and in it was the journal. Reading the stories of romance, science fiction, and horror I had taken the time to put to paper brought to light that these were tales I had never met in my readings.

The tales I write are fictional, but all of them are based on what I grew up with and still dream about. That some of them have an M/M twist is simply for my pleasure, and I hope, yours as well.

Twitter: @JoTannah
Instagram: https://www.instagram.com/jo_tannah/
Facebook: https://www.facebook.com/pro-file.php?id=100012354600386
Website: http://jotannah.com
Email: jotannah1@gmail.com